The Iron Room

Acknowledgments

I'd like to thank my entire family, who has been nothing short of amazing. The support, and love that I have received is overwhelming. These books simply wouldn't be possible without you.

To my Parents,
Thank you to you guys for sculpting and culturing my creativity.

To Alexis and Lauren, my best friends,
Your support is amazing. Thank you for proofreading this book chapter by chapter.

To Andrew,
I love you. The way you build me up has me feeling as if I can accomplish anything.

To my Grandparents,
To feel that you are proud, is all I ever need.

1

I heard voices surrounding me but couldn't find the strength to open my eyes. I felt weak, and exhausted. My head began to throb until it became almost unbearable, but still, I could not open my eyes. I drifted into a black nothingness.

Katie

It was the first week of school, and to say I was excited would be pushing it. Normally, I looked forward to this day- fresh pencils, new binders, new books and especially new clothes. All of those remained, but there was a somber mood hanging in the air today at Prairie High School.

The disappearance of a few high schoolers lately, had everyone in this small-town buzzing. There were fingers being pointed in all directions, from the creepy pharmacist to even Old Man Jennings. None of these leads panned out, but the rumors didn't stop circling.

About a month ago, a girl named Anna Lewis went missing. The local police assumed that she had run away from home, or maybe left with an older boyfriend. Her parents were persistent in that none of that could possibly be true. However, everyone else started to fall into that very same assumption. Anna was popular, and also a huge party girl. It didn't seem that far-fetched to most of the town, that she had ran away from home. Her parents were conservative, and constantly chastised Anna for her less than proper behavior.

Then, another girl went missing- Tara Brooks. Tara went missing two weeks after Anna. She was the same age as Anna- eighteen. The two girls couldn't have been more different. While Anna spent her nights getting drunk and having fun- Tara had her nose in a textbook. She was at the top of her class, and in all the Honors and AP classes. She unlike Anna, didn't seem very likely to run from home.

People started to worry. Two missing girls? The cops were scratching their heads, and the townspeople had begun to suspect anyone and everyone. And then the "sightings" came in. Everyone had claimed they had seen either girl at some point out and about. There were even as many as two formal sightings being documented every day. None of those turned out to be true. I don't think people were trying to lead police in the wrong direction, but rather saw it as their own personal way of helping out.

My name is Katie- short for Kathleen. I'm seventeen- like Tara and Anna. My dad is Sheriff Johnson and has spent a few too many nights confiding in me about the case. It has this whole town stumped, as there were no clues of value left behind.

Both girls had disappeared in the middle of the night. Anna was last reported being seen leaving a party, drunk. Tara's mother claims she was in her room studying, and when she went to check on her later, she was gone.

I had tried to do some digging of my own, but my dad is vehemently against it. The people who did this knew what they were doing. There were no witnesses and no evidence left behind. It makes sense why he wouldn't allow me anywhere near it. The similarities we all share worry him too. Not only are both girls my age, but we all look alike- brunette with light blue eyes. Other than that, we had nothing in common.

I was nothing like Tara, who excelled at everything or Anna, who was wildly popular. I fit somewhere in the middle- like a happy medium. I didn't have straight A's but was a solid B student. I went to parties every so often, but I certainly wasn't the one throwing them.

I did have a best friend named Amy, who was my twin, except having different mothers and different fathers. Her mom was best friends with mine, and they had both been right by my side when my mom died. It was three months ago. It was a car accident, and a drunk driver had side swiped her car.

Her death was especially hard for me, because it wasn't gradual, as if she had been sick or anything. I wasn't able to prepare for saying goodbye. She was just gone, in the blink of an eye. She had died on the way back from the store to pick up some medicine for me, and a part of me always felt guilty- like it was my fault.

Amy had tried to rid me of that guilt and was always there to remind me that the only person to be at fault, was the drunk driver.

Easier said than done.

Our families had remained close since the accident, and I felt practically like family. Amy had a brother named Mark, and he was the closest thing I have ever had to a brother. He was always there when I needed a shoulder to cry on and gave me some masculine advice from time to time.

Nevertheless, I had a great support system, and a big team of people looking out for me. Having the sheriff as my father guaranteed that no one in this town ever messed with me. That made high school, and mean girls, a little bit easier.

I was starting my junior year, and was excited to finally graduate, and leave this little town forever. Many people loved the idea of a small town, as it felt like a tight-knit family, and I had to agree. It was like a family. The problem with living in a small town your whole life is that it can begin to feel a bit suffocating. Everyone knows what you're doing, at all times in the day. Nothing goes unnoticed in Prairie.

Amy and I were nervous about our new creative writing class. We both shared a mutual love of reading, writing, and literature. That was one of the things that truly cemented our friendship. I was reading in the library one afternoon, and she was over to my right reading the same book. Who knew that Dickinson could bring people together?

Mr. Grander, the teacher for the creative writing class, is new. He moved to Prairie a few months ago, and new people are usually accepted with open arms, and usually a tuna casserole or two.

Given the timing of his arrival, and then the soon following disappearance of two high school students set off "alarms" and raised a lot of suspicion towards our new teacher.

My dad looked into him, and even got enough for a warrant, but Mr. Grander was as clean and cookie cutter as they came. He checked out.

And so, it went, townspeople were slowly but surely being checked off the list. There were no suspects at the moment, so the townspeople were creating their own suspects. Fingers were being pointed in all kinds of directions, and it created a rift in Prairie.

My alarm to get up rang and rang, and I decided to finally bite the bullet and get up. I couldn't hide in my room anymore. Summer was over, and it was time to start living my life. I wouldn't let my mom's sudden death, or the disappearing teenagers scare or intimidate me any longer.

I picked out a new outfit I had just bought-
navy jeans and a delicate floral blouse covered with
orange and pink blossoms. I paired it with a cream-
colored converse and pulled my hair into a loose
ponytail. I was going to do my makeup, but my mood
only allowed for me to attempt mascara. Once that
was done, I grabbed my bag, phone, keys, and headed
downstairs for some breakfast.
"Hey Katie! Are you ready for the first day of
school?"
"I guess. No more special than any other day- besides
the fact that it'll be my first public sighting since
summer," I joked.
"You were dealing with a lot. Plus, you know I rather
have you at home these days anyways. It's just not
safe." He said shaking his head.

I sat down just as he scooped eggs onto a plate
and dropped a slice of buttered toast onto my waiting
plate. I hated to cook and would probably eat one
meal a day if he didn't cook breakfast and dinner.

We had become co-dependent since the
passing of my mother. We relied on each other to
help us through the day and turned to one another
when we needed to talk.

With the help of my dad, Amy and her family,
I was ready to face anything.

My dad poured himself a cup of coffee and
headed into his room to get ready for work. I had to
leave soon, as I started school an hour before he had
to go into work. Why he didn't wait until later to get
up blew my mind. I would sleep until the very last
minute if I had the option to do so. He claimed that it
was, "wasting the day", and that he would rather do
something productive- like cooking me breakfast.

I knew my dad wanted me to embrace this year with open arms and make the best of it. I wanted to allow him to see me at least try, so that's exactly what I planned to do. He didn't ask much of me, even less so since her death, and if this was the one thing that I could do to make him happy- I would do it.

Today was a new day. It was the first day of school, and even thought it was September I planned to encompass a "glass half full" attitude this year.

I finished up my breakfast and reflected on the summer. Losing my mom was the hardest thing I have ever gone through, and there were times where I didn't know if I would survive it. It nearly broke me in half and did a number on my dad. It was a miracle he was still able to get up and go to work every single day. In a way, I feel like the missing girls and all the attention surrounding it have given him an outlet for all of his energy. He is able to keep his mind busy and focused throughout the day, and when he gets home at night- he deals with his feelings. It seems to work for him, and maybe it would work for me too.

This year, I would aim to become a straight A student. I didn't necessarily care about grades, but getting straight A's is no easy feat. It would take all of my focus, time, and energy. It was exactly what I needed. I texted Amy and let her know I was coming to pick her up.

Amy: Sounds good, what are you wearing?

Katie: The outfit I showed you last week! Got to dress the part, lol.

Amy: I love that one! See you soon. Xoxo

I yelled out to let my dad know I was leaving, and before I reached the door, he jogged over to me, and gave me a big hug.

"Be careful, Katie. It's not safe."

"I know dad, I will be- I promise."

He kissed my forehead, and I was out the door. I understood how he felt, especially since the girls that disappeared looked similar to me. Maybe they did run off, or maybe they were taken.

If that's true, then you should be careful.

I will admit that the three of us looked similar. But that doesn't mean anything. We don't have anything in common.

Neither do Anna and Tara...

I brushed the negative thoughts to the back of my mind- where they rightfully belonged. I wasn't going to let myself have a bad first day worrying about this alleged kidnapper, who at this point we had no proof that he or she even exists. Until we did, I wasn't going to worry.

Once my car was warmed up, I started off to Amy's house. She only lived five minutes away, so the drive was a breeze. Or, it would be, if the traffic wasn't so bad. Honestly, I didn't know what I expected, especially with her house being right next to an elementary school.

Parents there didn't like to slow the car down and let the child out. No, an elementary school was a full stop, wait until they get inside deal. It took forever and made any drive past it horrendous. Better safe than sorry, I guess.

I arrived at Amy's house within ten minutes. She was standing on her big white wrap around porch patiently waiting for my arrival, like always.

Naturally, she was dressed to the nines in a navy blazer, complete with a white blouse, and a pair of white skinny jeans accented with sky high wedges. She had incredible taste, and a very large bank account to back it up.

Her dad owned the only bank in town, and also did loans. He was probably the wealthiest man living in this town, but he was also incredibly humble. That was something I always admired about Amy, and her family. They were never boastful or looked down on others due to their financial status. Amy climbed into my Jeep.

"Are you excited? It's our first day of junior year!"

"You know what? I actually am! Fresh start, here I come."

She squealed and reached out to give me a hug. I put my foot back on the gas, and we started over to Prairie High.

I could do this.

It was about ten minutes until first bell when we arrived. I swiftly parked and we started up the steps. I felt my nerves racked but decided to take it all in stride. Deep breaths.

I'm ready.

2

Amy

I was so glad that Katie seemed to finally be getting out of the rut she was stuck in all summer. Not that I consider losing a parent to be a rut, but still. Jenna's death took a toll on all of us. We all knew and loved her, and when she unexpectedly passed, it broke our hearts.

Katie took the loss the hardest, but Sheriff Johnson was a close second. Katie worried that her dad may be overdoing the extra hours as work and using them as an excuse to not have to deal with his feelings.

Knowing Katie, she would soon follow suit. She would do absolutely anything to stop feeling as bad as she does. Poor girl even blames herself for the accident, as if it was her fault in the slightest. That has been one thing I have desperately tried to break-her guilt. It will eat away at her, until it destroys her.

Katie is my best friend, and I love her. However, one of her downfalls is that she is empathetic to the point of self-destruction. She feels everyone around her and takes the world on her shoulders. One day, it will crush her.

This morning seemed to be different. She seemed lighter, happier. I hadn't seen my best friend in this state in months, and I genuinely hoped that it was because she was finally beginning to heal properly and not just glossing over old wounds, pretending they didn't exist. She was known to do that too.

"Meet you at first break? I have math first, and it's on the other side of the building." Katie said voice full of optimism and cheer.

"Of course. See you then… and good luck!"

We gave a quick hug and started in our separate directions. We had creative writing third period, so that was a bonus. The class was being taught by a new teacher this year, Mr. Grander. Katie and I bonded over a love of books, and writing. When the class became available this year, it was a no brainer. I was excited to see that Katie had seemed interested in it. I wanted her to focus her energy on something positive, and I have always felt that writing gives you a sense of control in your life. That's something I think she truly needs right now.

I walked into Chemistry, and my brain immediately shut down. I never did good with any type of science class as it just didn't interest me. I always did well enough to pass the class, but my interest was instantly diverted the second they started talking about plant cells.

The class was your usual run around of introductions. Of course, the teacher didn't give us a day to dip our feet in the water but decided to throw us right in the deep end- but with a smile of course.

We had already been given our first assignment. It was a five-hundred-word essay on chemical bonding, and what we knew so far.

How much could I know about chemical bonding? It's the first day of school!

The bell rang to move to the next class, and I just about died of happiness on the spot. The thought of sitting through another minute of Mr. Aryn's lecture, would have been inexplicably painful. Mr. Aryn was a young pinched face man who always looked incredibly pissed off. I heard he wasn't the fairest teacher either.

I headed over to my next class, and nearly ran over my brother in the process. His sandy blonde hair looked like he just got out of bed, and his green eyes looked panicky.

" Mark, where's the fire? Slow down!" I scolded, but did a terrible job at doing so, because Mark broke into laughter.

"Really Amy? Where's the fire? You bumped into me! I need to go," he said, and with that he was off and out of sight.

My family was so weird.

I wanted to check how Katie's first class went, so I sent her a text.

Amy: Was your class as boring as mine? I nearly fell asleep!

Katie: My head is spinning. What are numbers again? And when did they start adding letters?!

Amy: I have no clue. Good luck with Chemistry, my teacher sucks. See you in Creative Writing! :)

I entered the Calculus classroom and found a seat close to the back. Math wasn't exactly my strong suit either, so I wanted to be able to hide myself as much as possible. The teacher, Mrs. Callun opened her mouth to speak, but was interrupted by the loudspeaker.

"Hello everyone. This is an administrative announcement, from Principal Kern. Hi everyone, it's Principal Kern here. I know it is the first day of school, and it is a Friday. I encourage you all to have a safe weekend, and to be on the lookout for your surroundings. Students Anna Lewis, and Tara Brooks are still missing, and we don't want any others to go missing. So please, be careful, and have a great first day and an even better weekend!"

We don't any other people to go missing? What an idiot. How about you actually do something besides sit behind a desk and bark orders? The people in this obnoxiously small town were beginning to hold grievances towards Katie's dad, Sheriff Johnson.

I don't really understand how that makes any sense, as he is the one leading the investigation and working tirelessly day and night, but that was how small minded these people's minds were.

They felt that the kidnapper, if there was one, should have been caught by now, and that the girls should have been found. Apparently, the lack of findings indicate not that we have a smart suspect, but rather that Sheriff Johnson was incompetent. Unbelievable.

"Amy Puntzer? Did you hear me?"

I looked up. Oh crap, she was doing roll call. "Here! Sorry, Mrs. Callun."

The roll call continued, and Mrs. Callun began breaking down our next few weeks and what we would be learning. She was a red-haired older woman with kind brown eyes, a lot nicer than Mr. Aryn, and a hell of a lot more interesting. She seemed to genuinely care about our learning experiences, and that she wanted us to take more from this course than just new math skills. Maybe Calculus wouldn't be all that bad.

She talked for another thirty minutes, and then decided to do an ice breaker. We had to turn to the person to the left of us and give them two facts about us. I turned to the left and was bummed out. It was Johnny Antin. Johnny was all looks, and no ambition. With dark brown hair that practically hung in front of his eyes like dog and sparkling blue eyes. Unfortunately for me, he was the school loser, who walked around high as a kite every day and who seemed to truly have no interest in school, learning, or pretty much anything.

This would be fun.

"Let me guess, you hate school and you hate everything else, right?"

"Wrong. You all think you know me, but you don't."

"So, I'm thinking of a different Johnny Antin, one who also hates literally everything."

"You're Amy Puntzer, right? Sheriff Johnson's daughter's best friend."

"Uh, yeah…"

"Well here's two facts about me for you. I believe that Sheriff Johnson is incompetent, and I believe that his daughter knows full well where Anna and Tara are."

What the hell?

Why would Johnny even think something like that? Sheriff Johnson has been working so incredibly hard to solve this case and find those girls. Katie told me herself how he has retraced their last known steps about a hundred times and spoke to everyone in the surrounding areas. Nobody saw anything, so they're no help. How is he supposed to crack this case with no evidence and no clues? Johnny, like everyone else, had no clue.

"Seems to me like you're the one who thinks you know everything. You're like everyone else in this brainwashed town. Here's an idea- why don't you find Tara and Anna yourself since it's so easy?"

"I'm trying to," Johnny said and turned away.

This was going to be an exciting year. I got the seat partner from hell.

I guess icebreaker time was over. Thankfully, the bell rang soon then after, and I beelined for Mr. Grander's creative writing class. The best part of my day. I slid into the classroom, and Katie was already waiting at the back with a seat for me.

My savior.

I mentally went back and forth over what Johnny said, and was unsure if I should mention it to Katie. She hated hearing negative things about her dad, but Johnny said something about her too. This is what best friends do right? Going against my better judgement, I decided to fill her in.

"What?! Why would I have any idea of where the girls were? That's insane."

"I know Katie. I'm sorry, but I thought you should know. Don't worry, I shut him down."

"I'm not worried what they say about me. People in this town thrive off gossip. But, my dad? He's doing all he can…" she said sadly.

I know he is.

I was undecided of what to do, so I did the only thing I could, and gave my friends hand a comforting squeeze. People would always talk, especially in a town like this. We couldn't let it affect us.

"Hello class, my name is Mr. Grander. I will be teaching Creative Writing. So, first order of business is…"

I didn't hear what he said because Katie had mumbled something.

"What did you say Katie?

"I'm tired of this. I am going to do my own investigating. I'm going to find Anna and Tara, once and for all."

3

Katie

Growing up with the sheriff as your dad definitely had its perks. I had a pretty easy school experience, where the other students were concerned. I also reaped the benefit of getting to hear information that wasn't released to the public. My dad had a habit of coming home every night and unloading the day's findings onto me. I never knew what to say, but I remembered every bit- especially in this case.

Now all that information would prove useful. I was going to find these girls myself.
I had to.

It was no surprise that people were trashing my dad's name. But when Amy told me that her seat partner said that *I* knew where the girls were- I was extremely confused. Is that what the people in this town had resorted to? Not only did they think that my father was an idiot, they thought that I had something to do with it.

I couldn't wait to leave for college. I desperately wanted to get away and create a new life for myself. I wanted to start over. But first, I needed to find Anna and Tara.

I knew the basics of this case. Anna was walking home drunk from a party. That one was difficult, because anyone could have taken her, and all the other kids were too busy chugging beer to notice. Tara's story never sat right with me. She was in her room, and then gone later? Either the kidnapper forced her out of the house, or she willingly went somewhere.

Now I knew how my dad had felt. My head was spinning trying to piece it together. While my dad vented a lot about the case, he never told me certain details. I needed to get to the station and read his files on the case. I couldn't properly solve it or find the girls until I knew all the pieces to this warped puzzle.

"Katie! You can't look for the girls yourself. I don't want you to get hurt," Amy scolded.

Too late. I need to do this.

"My dad is the sheriff, so I am probably the safest person to investigate. Obviously, the person lives here in this town. It doesn't make sense for an out of towner to come here and kidnap not one, but two of our girl's weeks apart."

"Maybe so, but that isn't your problem. It is horrible what happened to them, but please, let it go."

"I can't, and if you can't accept that, then it's your problem," I said just as the bell rang.

I was too busy mentally piecing this together, that I didn't hear a word Mr. Grander said.

I grabbed my books and headed out of the classroom. I didn't want to deal with Amy's negativity right now. I needed something to focus on this year- and this was it. I would funnel all my time and energy into solving this case.

"Katie, wait!" Amy yelled for me, but I was already turning the corner of the hallway.

I found my locker, and began to put my books in, and take out the books for my next class, World History.

Oh, joy.

"Hey stranger, how's your first day going?"

Mark.

"Surprisingly, not too bad. How is yours?"

"Oh, you know how it is Katie. I feel like I have been rushing from class to class all day!"

"Me too. I just don't understand this warped schedule. One class is on the other side of the school from the next. I might have to start sprinting soon. But, if I don't leave now, I most definitely will have to. See you later!"

I jogged, not sprinted to the next class. I slid into the seat right as the bell rang.

Thank you, God.

"Hello class, my name is...."

And so, the rest of the day went as follows: Introductions, a bunch of babbling, and then a healthy variant of either homework or icebreakers. They were predictable, I would give them that.

When the last bell of the day rang, I felt myself relax. School days seemed to pass by like snails in a race. Each class more boring than the next and followed with disgusting lunches and constant looks. That's what everyone had been doing all day-staring. No one had dared to actually say anything, but they didn't need to. I knew full well what they were all thinking.

Be positive, Katie.

Right, positivity. That was my new approach. I just had to keep that in mind, and I would be good to go. Thankfully, I didn't have much homework especially compared to Amy. I decided to pick up some food and bring it to the station to "surprise" my dad. I needed access to those files. Amy would be fine, as she rode home after school with Mark.

I knew Amy would come around eventually. She always boiled over at first, but slowly simmered out once she stewed on it a little bit. Truth is, she was probably scared. This whole situation was incredibly frightening. In all our years, we had never had a scandal bigger than "petty theft" in this town.

I tried to tell myself that fear was the big motivator when it came to everyone in town pushing rumors and spreading mindless gossip, but that could probably be attributed to the lack of things to do around here.

They loved to spread their rumors, especially baseless ones. I remember once in ninth grade, this boy walked me home from school. Mrs. Gellar saw, and less than an hour later the whole town was buzzing about my new boyfriend. When news got to him, he had to break it to me "gently". Imagine my surprise.

I started up my car and headed through the local drive thru. I got my dad's favorite- bacon cheeseburger with curly fries and a chicken sandwich for myself. Once I paid, I began the quick drive over to the station. A perk of living in a small town like Prairie is that everything is much closer than you would think. It doesn't take more than fifteen to twenty minutes to get anywhere.

Soon enough the station came into view. I spotted my dad's car and snagged a spot right next to him. Once I had exited the car, I was greeted by every officer in sight. I grabbed the bag of food and headed inside.

I beelined for my dad's office, much too exhausted from my first day at school to extend an overzealous number of niceties. I saw him hunched over his desk, with his head in his hands.

Maybe it was a bad day to visit.

"Hey Dad, how is it going?" I asked while pushing open his office door.

He looked up abruptly, obviously shocked that I was here, and quickly recovered.

"Oh, hi Katie. It has been a rough day, let me tell you. How was your day at school though?"

"As well as can be expected. I'm doing what you suggested. I'm looking on the bright side of things."

"That's good hon. I'm very proud of you. Lord knows it's not easy, especially when you live in a judgmental town like this," my dad said, sighing heavily.

"What happened now?" I inquired.

"Oh, it is nothing for you to worry about. You brought food, huh? I'm starving coincidentally. Let me go brief one of the officers, and I'll come eat right now. Make yourself comfortable."

He swiftly exited the office and left me alone in my thoughts. This was perfect. I closed the blinds, and the door. I moved over to his desk and the files for the case were right there. I took all the documents, and quickly faxed them over to my home printer. I heard him retreating to the office.

Now I just needed to get home before he does.

"Alright hon. I'm starving- let's eat!" he said, while rubbing his hands together.

"Uh, rain check Dad? I'm so swamped with homework. The teachers really loaded it up this year. Meet you at home later?"

"Sure thing, I know how heavy the course work can be. I should be off within the hour and will meet you home. I love you."

"Love you too, dad."

"Hey hon? Do me a favor and drive safe."

"Always do," I said with a wink. I grabbed my sandwich and headed out of the station.

When did I become a liar?

I scrambled into the car and peeled out of the station. Another perk of being the sheriff's daughter? I didn't ever get speeding tickets.

I think I made it home in record time and was walking through my front door when I received a text from Amy.

Amy: I'm sorry about today. This whole thing is really scary, and I don't want you to get mixed up in it. I don't think you should do this yourself. Please reconsider.

I put my phone down on the couch. I didn't have time to deal with Amy right this moment. There were more important things to focus on. I headed straight for the printer and sure enough, my papers were waiting for me.

I grabbed the entirety of them and headed into my room. I sat cross legged on the bed, and one by one read each document. Just as I deduced earlier, I knew a lot of the information already in these files. It was just a simple overview of what both girls were doing the night they went missing, and witness accounts from who saw them last. I don't know what I was looking for, but I had really hoped to find some answers.

I knew there was something here.

I continue to mindlessly flip through the pages, until my eyes landed on a word: *eyewitness.*

Eyewitness? My dad said there was no eyewitnesses to either girls going missing. I began to read the testimony. The eyewitness was a woman named Andrea Towner, and she lived right next door to the Brooks residence. She claimed that on the night that Tara went missing, she saw her climb out of her window, and get into a man's car- willingly.

What the hell? Why was this information never released? Why didn't he tell me?

She saw all that, but didn't get a license plate number or even a partial? I kept reading. She claimed that she didn't call the police at the time, because she just figured Tara was having a little fun or blowing off steam. After all, Tara did get into the car willingly.

Maybe Tara had a secret boyfriend, and they are together right now. But that doesn't explain Anna's disappearance. In a town like this, two missing people within weeks of each other seems unlikely to just be a coincidence.

I wondered if this Andrea Towner had seen the man's face. In a town this size, surely, she would recognize whoever it is, but with it being late at night, I highly doubt it. Everyone in Prairie knew that Andrea loved her wine, so who knew if her testimony was even plausible.

Perhaps that's why my dad never released this information. Upon further investigation, he probably deemed it useless or not reputable.

One thing that is for sure, is that I need to find out for myself is Andrea Towner's eyewitness that night is baseless or actually reputable.

I needed to talk to Andrea and see what else she saw that night.

4

Amy

"You don't understand, Mark. She is conducting this witch hunt all on her own!"

"That's not a good idea. Did you advise against it?"

"Of course, I did, but you know Katie. She's stubborn and set in her ways," I let out a long sigh.

I didn't know what to do. If Katie continued down this wormhole, she would end up getting hurt. I didn't want her to experience any more pain. She had to be stopped, before it was too late.

"If you want to put a stop to Katie's sleuthing, there is one option..." Mark said, with a sly grin plastered on his face.

"And that brilliant plan is?"

"Tell Sheriff Johnson what Katie is doing. There is no way on Earth he would allow that."

I don't want to get her in trouble.

If I told Sheriff Johnson, then Katie was surely be on the hook. From what I understand, he takes great measures to ensure that Katie never got too wrapped up in police business. He had a job, but always wanted her as far away from his world as possible. He saw firsthand how dangerous the job could be. Katie didn't have the badge like her dad, but she had the investigative nature at heart.

Someone who enjoys investigating as much as her, without the years of training, badge, and gun to back it up- created a disaster.

I didn't want to get Katie in trouble with her dad, especially since the two of them had been really getting on these past few weeks. I think the situation ended up bringing the two of them closer than they ever were. Katie would never forgive me if I threw a wrench in her plans and got her in trouble all at the same time.

I decided what to do.

I would offer her my help and steer her in the other direction. If Katie got too close, she would get hurt.

I decided to text her.

    Amy: Hey Kates. I'm sorry about yesterday. I wanted to lend a hand, if you will have me.

        Katie: I'm so glad to hear that. You'll never believe what I found. Meet me at 564 Auburn Rd.

    Amy: Auburn Road? Tara's street?

        Katie: I'll explain later.

"Hey Mark, can you drive me to meet Katie?"

"Sure thing, but what's going on?" my brother seemed suspicious, but I didn't want to worry him.

"We're going to hang out, and talk."

Mark agreed, and he headed out to his car. I really needed to get my license. Then, that sweet Mercedes in the garage collecting dust would become mine.

We got into his car and turned towards me.

"Where are we heading?"

Don't let him know you're going to Tara's. Lie.

"Carrington Park. We're meeting there."

"You got it," and he turned the car onto the road.

Carrington Park was few-minute walk from Tara's street. I would wait until he dropped me off, and turned the corner, before I would start heading over there. I know what it seems like. But Mark never enjoyed sneaky or secretive behavior. He always felt strongly that being upfront and honest with someone was the best way.

Delusional.

We arrived at the park in no time, and he let me out of the car.

"Where is Katie?"

"Oh, I just got a text. She's in the bathroom."

I ran off, before he could ask any more questions. I made it halfway into the park and turned to see his car going around the corner. Thank god.

I started back towards the entrance of the park, and practically began sprinting over to Tara's street. I made it there within three minutes, but nearly died from my asthma. Worth it.

I pulled my inhaler out of my bag, and took a few puffs, and spotted Katie. She was sitting in her idled car across the street from Tara's house. She looked up, saw me, and motioned me over to sit in her car with her.

I took my time walking over, simply because I didn't think that my lungs would allow me another run.

I opened the door and was met with a friendly face- as always. That was simply who Katie was. She was so full of light, optimism, and warmth. I was glad I was beginning to see a tiny bit of who she was finally come back to her.

You're a horrible friend.

No, I was just trying to keep her safe. At least that was what I kept telling myself.

"So, I know I owe you an explanation…" Katie started, and gave me a small smile.

"Yesterday, I visit my dad at the station and made a fax of all the papers he kept in the file on both girls."

"What? Katie you can't do that!"

"Well, I did," Katie said ignoring my outburst, and continued.

"So, I was looking through the files. Most of what was in there, we knew about. But there was something that my dad never told the public about-there was a witness."

A witness?

How could there be a witness? And more importantly, why would Sheriff Johnson lie? He was always proud of the fact that he was very transparent with the townspeople, and they prided him on that. If the fact that he was withholding a chunk of evidence from the public got out, they would begin to lose trust in him- not that they hadn't already.

This could never get out.

"Who's the witness?" I questioned, genuinely curious.

"Andrea Towner."

"The lady who likes to booze it up 24/7? I doubt she is a reliable source."

"It doesn't hurt to ask, does it?" Katie said, and climbed out of the car.

I scrambled out after her and tried to keep up with her fast pace. I knew she was dead set on cracking this case, but why? Obviously, it was a horrible situation, but I was wondering what made her feel she was the one that needed to do so.

"Wait up, Katie!" I tried to yell, but she kept walking. Then, she turned around.

"Wait out here, I will only be ten minutes, if that."

I stood frozen in my tracks. She wanted me to wait outside. I wanted to help her, well help her away from the case, but both of those proved nearly impossible especially with Katie being stubborn about my help.

I sat down on the curb and waited for her to finish up her conversation with Alcoholic Annie.

5

Katie

I felt slightly bad about leaving Amy behind. In fact, I had full intent to bring her along with me this morning, but the way she reacted in the car didn't sit right with me. I knew full well that Andrea Towner liked to drink, but I wanted to be able to get her statement and talk to her without a cloud of doubt and judgement surrounding us. Even if Amy thought she was helping, she wasn't. She was making this whole situation harder for me.

I struggled over what I would say to my dad. Surely, he had some excuse lined up already. Knowing him, I knew that it would more than likely be a good one. I didn't care about what he had to say, he had a job to do and he failed at doing so. I thought he was a great Sheriff, but you simply cannot withhold evidence and witness statements regardless of how baseless you feel they might me.

You really jumped on the "I hate Sheriff Johnson" bandwagon, huh?

No, that was not what I was doing. I loved my dad. I just wanted to see for myself what Miss. Towner had to say, and there was only one way to do so.

I knocked and waited. Silence. I knocked a few more times, and once again was met with silence. I would have thought she was out, but I saw her old beater car parked in the driveway. I decided to ring the doorbell, and this time I heard banging and stomping coming from behind the door. I went to turn and leave, but the door swung open.

There standing was a very disheveled, obviously intoxicated, and smelly Andrea Towner. Maybe she didn't just like her wine, but all alcohol. *She smells like something died in her clothing.*

"Now why the hell are you banging on my door?

"I'm sorry to bug you, Miss. Towner. I had a few questions," I stammered an apology.

"Questions about what? I don't know anything about anything."

"Uh… it's about the night that Tara was taken."
Please know what I'm talking about.

"She was not taken. I told the Sheriff. She got into the car with that Puntzer boy- by herself."
Puntzer? Mark?

"I'm sure you're mistaken. It was dark…"

"And I know what you're going to say. Yes, I was probably drunk, but I know what I saw. Especially with Mr. Carlton's big ass security light across the street. I saw that boy's face clear as day. I also saw Tara get into the car *willingly*. Now if you will excuse me…"

I opened my mouth to speak, but had the door slammed in my face. I turned to walk away, and just stared at Amy. Why would Mark pick Tara up that night? I didn't even know they were friends. Well, Mark was friends with everyone, but Tara? She was so closed off to everyone...including boys, because she was so focused on studies. Why would she go somewhere with him that late? And why did she never return home?

Was Mark the last person to see her alive?

My head was filled with questions, and I knew I couldn't turn to Amy- or Mark for answers. I also couldn't lie to my best friend, so I would just bend the truth a little. I would make Amy feel like I thought Miss. Towner was ridiculous. I had to. If I ever put any suspicion on her brother that would sever our relationship- I just knew it.

If it was Mark, then what is his connection to Anna? I knew Mark was friendly with everyone, but Mark certainly wasn't a party guy, and that is where Anna spent most of her free time.

So, what was the connection? How did this all fit into place? Maybe Mark wasn't the last person to see Tara that night.

Maybe he dropped Tara off somewhere as favor, and whoever she was really with took her.

Did the same person that took Tara take Anna too? Get real.

I needed to find a connection between Anna and Mark, before I pointed any fingers. My thoughts were interrupted.

"Did she say anything?" Amy wondered, seemingly nervous.

"Yeah actually. She said she saw Tara get into Mark's car," I said half-laughing.

Real convincing, Katie.

"Mark's car? Is that a joke? That lady is so hopped up on alcohol, and God knows what else. She is accusing my brother now?" Amy was pissed off.

"I don't think she's accusing him, but I do think she was far too drunk to recall anything she saw. Mark? She's crazy, Amy. This is obviously a dead end."

My words seemed to calm Amy down enough, to change her mind about marching up there and yelling at poor Andrea Towner. I know Andrea was heavy on the drink, but she recalled those details very easily, and wasn't slurring her words. Still, it isn't enough to go on.

Did Miss. Towner tell my dad the same thing? Did he investigate only to deduce that she wasn't reliable? Did he talk to Mark? Were Miss. Towner's claims baseless?

There was only one way to find out.

Amy and I got into my car, and she invited me to come inside when we arrived at her house. I passed and made up an excuse about needing to catch up on all the first day homework. Thankfully, she had received a lot too, so it didn't seem like a lie. I hope.

She ran inside, and I took a glance at their driveway. Mark's car was parked there, and I wondered if he really did have something to do with the disappearance of the girls. He always seemed like such a nice guy, but ever since I talked to Miss. Towner, I have had a horrible knot in my stomach. Something definitely wasn't right.

As I drive home, I mulled over whether or not to bring it up to my dad. I concocted a plan of how to bring it up, without implicating my indiscretions in the process. I got home, parked in the driveway, and was pleased to see that my dad was home.

"Hey Dad! How was work?" I said walking through the door.

"It was good, come in here and tell me about your day," he yelled from his study.

I walked into his office, and he had paperwork scattered all around. He must be deep in a case. Maybe the case about the two girls?

"It was a little weird. I was at the grocery store, and I ran into Andrea Towner. Do you know who that is?"

"I might. Isn't she the town drunk?"

"I guess you can say so. She talked to me about something."

"What was that?" my dad asked suspiciously.

"Well, she was wondering if there had been any progress after she gave you her eyewitness statement, on the night of Tara's disappearance."

He took a deep sigh and put his head in his hands.

"Look, I know we said we don't lie to each other, and I'm sorry. I took her statement, and yes, the alcohol plays a huge role in how reliable she is. She made some strong claims against someone in this town, and I don't want to pursue it if it's untrue."

"Mark Puntzer?"

"Yes. Don't worry, I think she plucked a name out of a hat."

I didn't want my dad to think that I was looking into Mark. Well technically, I wasn't looking into anybody- yet. I was just collecting facts. But he didn't need to know that.

"Look Katie, I am so sorry I lied to you. I don't know why I did. I promise, from here on out- no lies between us."

Okay, well now I feel bad.

We hugged, and I retreated into the kitchen to fix something to eat. I mindlessly flipped through the fridge until I settled on a classic- peanut butter and jelly sandwich. I grabbed the peanut butter from the pantry and started on my sandwich. When it was done, I loaded everything back into its place, took a seat in front of the television, and took a big bite.

I always forgot how good these were. Mmm.

Peanut butter and jelly sandwiches are incredibly underrated. I sat there for a minute, devouring my sandwich, and felt my mind shift to Mark. I had no clue what I would do. Did I think Mark was capable of orchestrating two kidnappings? Absolutely not. Did I think something weird was going on? Without a doubt.

What to do... what to do.

Where the hell would I start to look? In the file, there was no witnesses about the kidnapping of Anna. There were a few people who said they saw her leave around 12 in the morning. No one decided to walk with her or give her a ride home. Although, most of the people at that party were completely drunk so maybe that is a good idea.

I knew that Mia Anders said that she saw her stumble out. Maybe, Mia remembered more than she thought- or more than she said. I needed to talk to her.

Surprisingly, I had her number back from middle school. Let's hope it's still the same one. I took a chance.

Katie: Hi Mia, it's Katie. I wanted to talk to you about something. Are you free tomorrow?

Mia: Omg, Katie Johnson! It has been forever. Of course, what time?

Katie: 10 a.m.?

Mia: That is so early, girl. Okay coffee is on you!

Whew. I hoped Mia would be forthcoming, but I wished more that she would remember something. I needed to know what she saw or didn't see the night that Anna went missing.

I sat in front of the television for the rest of the night, finding Desperate Housewives reruns a welcome distraction for my restless night.

I hadn't realized how late it had gotten until my dad popped his head in the living room to let me know he was turning in for the night.

I opted to go to bed as well, even though I truly did have lots of homework. Another problem for another day, I guess. Plus, I had to meet Mia at 10. I was out within the minute.

6

Amy

I had no idea what was going on with Katie these days. It was nice to see her finally start to come out of the shell and break down the walls she had built all summer. I would call her endlessly, always met with voicemails. Her dad reached out to let me know that she was going through a rough time, and to not take it personally.

That I could understand. But this, this endless pursuit to find Anna and Tara- I didn't understand it.

Sure, they were nice girls. Well, Tara was. Anna was always kind of a bitch. Needless to say, she was still pretty popular and very well liked.

When Anna went missing, and Tara followed soon after, it sent the town into a frenzy... that was still going on. Fingers have been pointed in so many different directions. One that didn't even make sense. For a while, the townspeople were convinced that my dad was in on it. My dad, the kindest man in this town who was always helping everyone out- sure. It was so fruitless and baseless, and so it made sense that accusation blew over in no time.

Still, in a small town like Prairie, things like this didn't happen.

Until now.

Katie has an investigative streak in her, she gets it from her dad. Any type of curious bone she inherited from her father is only further enhanced when he comes home and babbles on and on about cases. It's not good for a young girl to have to hear stories like that, stories like this. I have no clue where those girls are. I would like to believe that they made it out of here. That they left this god forsaken town on their own accord.

I don't want to believe they've been taken... I can't.

Ever since this afternoon, Katie has been really cold towards me. She doesn't seem willing or wanting to share any information with me, and her interaction with the drunk only seemed to further that. That woman accused my brother of being the last to see Tara. I knew that Tara and Mark were friends, and she had helped him study a few times here and there.

But they were *only* friends. Tara didn't have boyfriends, and Mark was always slightly awkward around pretty girls- especially Katie. He's had a crush on her for as long as I can remember.

I know for sure Mark didn't even know Anna- well personally that is. Truth is, everyone knew Anna- they knew of her bubbly laugh, charismatic personality, and iron first she used to rule the social hierarchy at our school. Other than that, she wasn't too bad.

Ever since Katie dropped me off yesterday, I had felt like my head was spinning. Not only did I question my friendship with her as of late, but I was worried about her. I mulled over all the possibilities and the consequences if I were to go to her dad about what she was doing.

Sheriff Johnson wouldn't like it. I knew he was all for discussing cases with her, but I knew he would never want her to actually throw herself into the investigation. Especially with his wife's death, he had been extra protective of Katie recently.

She was so hard-headed, and strong willed. Usually, she would listen to reason when it came to me. However, after the past few days I had no clue if she would listen to anything I had to say. She was elbow deep in all of this detective work.

There was only one person she would listen to usually- Mark. I only hoped that he could get through to her, and that she wasn't suspicious after those stupid claims Miss. Towner made yesterday. *Fingers crossed.*

I decided to talk to Mark first and see if he thought it would be a good idea. Mark was always really good at being able to bring me clarity, especially when it comes to Katie. I pulled myself out of my warm bed and walked across the hall to his huge bedroom.

I knocked and waited for him to answer. Mark was always someone who enjoyed sleeping in late but was also a very light sleeper. I knocked louder, and the door swung open.

"Amy, do you know what time it is?" Mark looked disheveled like he just woke up.

"I do, Mark. Most people wake up before noon. We need to talk."

He moved aside and motioned with his arm for me to come in. Mark's room was huge. He made mom and dad get him the California king sized bed, and seventy-five-inch flat screen tv. The room was complete with a royal blue paint on the walls, and a small white couch accented with a mini fridge by the bed. Jesus.

I made my way over to the sofa and laid down. My head was hurting with all this passive aggressive drama from Katie. Mark closed the door and took a seat on the bed across from me.

"What's up baby sis? You seem upset." Mark asked, face looking both concerned and nervous.

"Katie picked me up yesterday, and she went to talk to Andrea Towner," I explained.

"Miss. Towner? The drunk? Why would she go and see that alcoholic?"

"Okay, you have to swear to keep this a secret. I don't want it to come back and hurt Sheriff Johnson." I looked at Mark, waiting for his confirmation to keep quiet.

"I swear. What is it?"

I continued, "So I guess Sheriff Johnson kept a secret eyewitness account private. The night that Tara went missing, Andrea had told him that she saw Tara getting into a man's car... your car."

I expected my brother to be outraged and irritated with these false claims. Instead, he was silent.

"Mark... what's going on?"

"It was me." Mark said and looked at me somberly.

"What do you mean?" I could feel my heart beating out of my chest.

Was my brother admitting to kidnapping?

"I saw Tara that night. But I didn't hurt her, and I definitely didn't kidnap her."

"Tell me everything, Mark."

"Tara was smart, we all knew that. She studied all the time, but it wasn't enough. Her mom had her in so many extracurricular activities, that she was starting to crack under all the pressure. Even though it was summer, she knew that senior year was a big year. She wanted me to go in the school system and change her grade in math before the grades got sent out."

What the hell?

"Wait, what? Grades got sent out in June."

"They did, but she hid hers. She was waiting until the teachers had turned in for the summer and figured that would be the safest bet. She needed a perfect score for college. Once this year started, the teachers would never notice. They would have new classes, new students."

"Why would you agree to something like that? You could be expelled. You don't need the money."

"I don't, but I always thought Tara was cute. I thought that maybe... but she wouldn't go for it. It doesn't mean I *kidnapped* her! Please tell me Katie doesn't think I did."

I don't know Mark. She played it off really well yesterday. I can see right through her after all these years. That means she probably believes it at least partially and is still investigating."

"Well, we can't have that. She will get hurt. You need to stop her. And please get the idea of me being a kidnapper out of her head, please. I would hate for Katie to think of me like that."

"You got it."

I turned and left Mark's room. I knew he would bring me to see what I had to do. I loved Katie, and she was my best friend. I was glad to see that I wasn't the only one who saw that she could get really hurt especially if these girls were really kidnapped. I can't let anything happen to her, especially after her mom. The decision was made. I had to tell Sheriff Johnson what Katie was up to.

7

Katie

I woke up that morning, feeling really nervous about meeting up with Mia. My stomach was churning over my interaction with Amy yesterday as well. She was my best friend and shutting her out of all this was only making me feel worse and worse about the whole thing.

I decided I would have this coffee with Mia, and then tell Amy everything. Keeping everything bottled up was going to make me explode. I hated secrets. I still couldn't tell my dad, mostly because he wouldn't allow it.

But that wasn't necessarily a lie, but rather a lie of omission.

Yeah, I know. It's no better.

I knew Mia would be dressed to the nines, and even though it was just coffee, I opted to do the same.

Yellow dress, beige wedges.

Yeah, that screamed, "I'm not trying hard," but oh well. I threw on my outfit, combed my hair, and threw on a little mascara. I didn't wear too much makeup but relished in my long eyelashes and decided to make them pop today as an added confidence booster.

Once I finished getting ready, I checked my phone. 9:48. I had to leave soon but knew the coffee shop was no more than five minutes away. I headed downstairs and was surprised to find my dad sitting at the kitchen table, coffee in hand, looking pissed off. "What's wrong? Did something happen at the station?" I inquired, attempt to gauge my dad's mood. "I just got off the phone with Amy. She told me everything."

Fucking snitch.

I felt my heart slam against my chest. Damn it! Why would she tell him anything? So much for being a good friend. I knew she was against me investigating what happened to Anna and Tara, but I was tired of everyone trying to shelter me all the time.

If I decided to do something, I didn't want anyone trying to tell me I couldn't. It's infuriating that Amy is doing this, and now thanks to her, my dad is about to as well.

"You cannot be investigating this case alone, Katie. It is too dangerous!" my father seethed and slammed down his coffee cup.

My dad was never much of a hothead, but my safety was no laughing matter where he was concerned. For him to scold me right now felt a tad bit ridiculous, especially when he was the one lying! "Too dangerous? Is it because you didn't want me, or anyone for that matter, finding out about your eyewitness? You lied. We don't do that."

"Did you go through my police files Katie? What gives you the right? You could have asked, and I would have answered anything, but to go behind my back is unfair and sneaky." My dad looked disappointed, and I felt a pang of guilt. I didn't want to upset him.

I guess Amy didn't tell him everything.

"You're right. It was wrong, and I'm sorry. I need something to focus my energy on, besides mom. It's the only way I will be able to move on."

I wasn't trying to play the dead mom card, but I said it because it was true. Of course, I wanted the girls found, but completely immersing myself in this investigation would help keep her off my mind, just for a little. It was too painful to think of her all day, and it nearly destroyed me this summer. I wanted my life back. My mom would have wanted me to have my life back.

Don't think about it.

"Promise me you will stop investigating. If my suspicions are right, these girls were kidnapped, and by someone in Prairie. I don't want you to get hurt. And I miss her too, Katie. Believe me when I say this isn't the way to move on. Don't you think I would be all healed up by now?" My dad attempted a smile, and I knew his words were sincere. It pulled at my heart strings. Not enough to make me stop searching though.

"I will. I love you. I have to go because I am going to be late. I'm meeting Mia for coffee in… now. Sorry, I have to go!" I ran out the door and headed into my car.

I decided to send a quick text to Mia letting her know I was a few minutes away, as well as an apology for being late. As I was turning the corner onto the street where the shop was, she sent a quick message saying it was okay.

I spotted the coffee shop and snagged a good parking spot directly in front of the bookstore next door. Perfect, I could pick out a few new books after.

Mia was easily seen. Like I figured, she was wearing all white skinny jeans, with gold bootie heels, a gold blouse, and long dangly earrings which perfectly accented her elegantly messy updo. Suddenly my dress and wedges felt inadequate. She turned and her eyes locked with mine.

"Katieeeee! Oh my god, how long has it been?!" She shrieked, which earned us a few side eyes from neighboring tables.

"Like a few days, Mia. I saw you at school remember?" I said with a light-hearted laugh.

"Oh, duh. I would have ordered your coffee, but I don't know how you like it."

"That's okay, let me order really quick."

I turned and headed over to the counter and gave the menu a once over. I decided coffee would make me too jittery, and I was already anxious.

"One herbal tea please, a medium."

I paid the barista and took my steaming cup of orange and spice tea. I nearly dropped it on the way back to the table, because someone came up behind me and whispered,

"Hey stranger."

I turned slowly, recognizing the voice immediately.

"Hey Mark."

"I wanted to talk to you Katie, is now a good time?"
"It actually isn't. I'm here with someone," and I
gestured over to Mia who was watching intently. She
gave Mark a smile, and he looked absolutely pale.
"Okay Katie, Well give me a call when you're free.
Enjoy." Mark turned and headed out of the café.
Without a drink.
Did he come here for me? Did he follow me?
        C'mon Katie. This was Mark we were talking
about. He was always Amy's sweet brother. He
wasn't like most brothers in that he didn't pick on or
mess with Amy. There was no way he was capable of
stalking, or even kidnapping someone. I couldn't
understand why Miss. Towner saw him with Tara that
night. My head started spinning all over again.
"Hello… earth to Katie." Mia joked, and started
laughing at my obvious zone out.
"Sorry," I stammered an apology and bolted to the
table.
"So, what is it you wanted to talk about Kates?"
        I cringed. She knew I hated being called
Kates.
"I know that you saw Anna stumble down the street at
the party that day. Did you see anyone with her?"
"Jesus, Katie. Kind of morbid. But no, like I told your
dad I didn't see anyone. She did pull out her phone,
and it looked like she was trying to call someone. But
I went back inside."

So, like I thought, the information was useless. Damn it. I was now falling deeper and deeper into this case with all these pieces, and I had no idea how any of them fit together. Mostly because none of it actually made any sense. Mark. Miss. Towner. Mia. My head couldn't properly piece this together, and it was frustrating.

"Okay, yeah, thanks. My dad just wanted me to verify for his records. So, how do you like school so far..." We continued talking for the next hour mindlessly. I only did so on the account of I didn't want to seem rude, and like I was only there to press her for information.

Which you were.

I politely excused myself and promised we would hang out again soon. Once I was out of the coffee shop, I downed the last sip of my tea, and slipped into the bookstore. I was immediately welcomed with the smell of old books. I don't really know how to explain the smell, but it was good.

"Hi dear. Here for some more?" Mrs. Yao asked me, smiling, as she organized the nonfictions.

"You know it. Anything good?"

"I do have a few over here..." and she led me into the newer book section.

I thanked her and began what would be an hour-long book flipping session. In all my indecisiveness, I finally decided on two- a murder mystery and a romance.

I figured the romance would at light slightly lighten my dark mood, and that maybe the murder mystery would give me some clarity on this mind fuck case.

"That'll be five dollars even."

"No Mrs. Yao, that's too cheap! I don't want to take advantage of you."

"Take advantage of me… please. You're my favorite customer. Consider it a discount." Mrs. Yao said and winked at me as she took my five and pushed my two new books toward me. She turned and walked away, probably to avoid any argument from me.

Such a sweet woman.

I turned to head out of the bookstore, and as I pushed the door open, my phone chimed with a text.

Dad: Hey Katie, picked up lunch for us. Be home soon?

Katie: Yeah, just grabbed some books. On my way.

Dad: Rad.

Who taught my dad the word rad? And why was he using it? I shook my head and stifled a laugh. My dad was always trying to be hip, but I don't think anyone my age even says "rad" anymore.

I started my engine, and my phone beeper again. Please don't let it be my dad again…

No such luck.

Amy: I'm sorry.

I shook my head. I know she meant well but going behind my back to tell my dad what was going on was stepping way over the line. We were best friends, but it didn't give her any reason to meddle. I sighed. Amy was stubborn, and hard-headed. I knew that. I couldn't really be mad at her, could I?

Katie: It's okay. I know why you did it.

Amy: I am just worried about you.

Katie: Don't be. I have got this
handled.

Amy: Do you? Mark said he ran into
you.

Katie: Yeah and took one look
at Mia and bolted. Lol. What is with your brother and
girls?

Amy: He's chicken shit. Hey, see you
at school?

Katie: I'll pick you up. See you
tomorrow.

I put my phone back in my bag before
reversing out of the spot and heading home. The last
thing I needed in this gossip town was rumor
spreading that I like to text and drive. Oh yeah, my
dad would love that one.

All in all, I did like living in a town like
Prairie. It had its downfalls don't get me wrong, but it
also had its perks. I liked being able to get somewhere
within ten minutes and going into a restaurant where
they knew your order by memory. Growing up in
Prairie meant there was always a helping hand when
you needed one.

As of late, no one has been feeling super
generous lately. To anyone who didn't live here, it
would seem normal. But to those who are born and
raised, the tension is palpable. Everyone is on edge,
and after what I have discovered- rightfully so.

Although I don't even know exactly what I
have discovered. A bunch of dead ends, apparently. I
drove past the hardware store, and spotted Mark
leaving with two huge bundles of rope.
Why does he need rope?

Stop. Don't think horrible things about Mark. He was a saint.

Isn't he?

8

Mark

I just saw Katie's car drive by, and her eyes nearly bugged out of her head at the sight of my carrying rope to my car. Jesus. She really thought I was some crazy killer. I need to talk to her, and fast. The last thing I need is Sheriff Johnson asking questions and sending these annoying gossipers into a frenzy.

Honestly this whole dang town has been in a frenzy. All over those girls Anna and Tara. Tara is cool. I like her. Anna just seems like kind of a bitch. She was never nice to me. I remember especially that one time in the hallway when she spilled her coffee all over me and had the audacity to yell at me! Me!

Maybe it is a good thing she's gone.

I know it is horrible to think, but she wasn't a nice or good person despite what the town is making her out to be. They're trying to build Anna up as some kind of saint. She was nothing of the sorts, and the coffee incident was just one of many. She always treated those below her like dirt.

Tara was always full of light and kindness. She kind of got a bad rap on the account of she never hung out with anyone outside of school, and always had her head buried behind a book. I didn't know her too well, but when she hired me to change her grades, I did get to see a different side to her, I saw a human side.

On the outside looking in, she seems like this robot. But Tara doesn't just study because she has to, she wants to. I have never seen someone who has such a genuine love for knowledge, learning, and especially books.

I remember on one rare occasion, she told me that she always dreamed of having a library like the one in Beauty and the Beast, complete with a ladder with wheels.

I really liked her.

No one knew that I developed feelings for Tara, especially Tara herself. If anything, I wouldn't even call it feelings. It was more a small crush.

This whole thing really sucked. I, like everyone else, was extremely confused when Tara when missing a few weeks after Anna. The police were trying to make a pattern, but it was obvious that there wasn't one. Those two couldn't have been more different.

I have felt like crap since Tara went missing. Timeline wise, I think I was the last to see her that night. I have felt so racked with guilt, and sometimes I can't sleep because I think of all the what-ifs. What if I didn't leave so soon that night? What if I dropped her off later than I did? What if we didn't meet up at all, and she was safe in her home?

I finally came clean to my sister about the grade change exchange. I hated keeping secrets, and while it wasn't that big a deal, it felt wrong.

Like true Amy fashion, my sister took the news well. I knew she would.

My sister always had my back.

Amy also told me that Katie had been looking into this case, and now her sights are set on me. I would be a little confused, but after Amy let me know that the town drunk played a role in my demise, it all made sense.

I have no doubt that Miss. Towner saw me that night. I was there. I didn't take or hurt Tara. I could never.

That alcoholic should never be taken at her word though. Once she starts on the wine, and then switches to the hard stuff, she couldn't tell her ass from her foot.

A little harsh, no?

It was true though. Now, I faced a worse problem. Katie seemed to think I was guilty of something, but I didn't know what yet. I don't even think she knows what either. She has gotten deep in this case and is now realizing what everyone else did a while ago- none of it makes sense.

It only seems natural that in a case like this one, hearing a familiar name like mine would spark some suspicion. It certainly sparked curiosity in Sheriff Johnson when he first interviewed Miss. Towner and spoke to me that day. Obviously, I was cleared of all guilt on the fact that I didn't do it.

Mr. Johnson was easily able to see I wasn't capable of this, nor was there any evidence that proved otherwise. Now, I just needed Katie to see that.

If she though low of me in any way, I don't know if I could handle it.

Her opinion meant everything to me.

I decided to text her and ask if she was free or could at least talk on the phone. I wanted to explain. I know it may come off desperate since I saw her this morning, and already asked her the same thing. But the quicker I could get this solved then the sooner I could relax.

Mark: Hey Katie. Sorry about scaring you this morning. I feel like we need to talk. Can we meet later? I want to explain everything.

Katie: Sure. Park at 11?

Mark: Sounds good, meet you there.

Now I just needed to convince Katie of my innocence, before it was too late.

9

Katie

I can't believe I agreed to meet Mark in a park. At eleven. But I needed to figure this case out, and I think talking to him in person may help.

I didn't want to let him know that I was suspicious of him, but then again, I didn't even know if I was really suspicious. Truth is, I knew I was grasping at straws. I know this case is all over the place, but it is only because I am missing certain pieces of the puzzle. Maybe, Mark could fill some of those in for me. I considered texting Amy and asking if it was okay.

Part of me wanted to really know if she was okay with me questioning Mark, but another part of me deep down just wanted someone to know where I was in case, he did try something.

Give the guy a chance to explain before you brand him a psycho!

Right. I needed a clear head going into this, and I needed to figure out what type of questions I wanted to ask. Did I want to go in full guns blazing? Or did I want to play it off as some rumor that was bugging me? Dead mom card?

Pull yourself together, Katie. It's just Mark.

Okay, now I needed an excuse for leaving the house. My dad would definitely hear me if I decided to try my luck at sneaking out. I wanted to make an excuse for leaving that would make sense to my dad. Sleepover at Amy's. He would be happy to see that I was finally getting out of the house, but the issue of school tomorrow presented a problem.

Fingers crossed.

"Hey Dad?" I called into the living room, praying that he would be awake and agreeable.

"Yes?" He said, sounding alert, and then laughed at his show. Okay, good mood.

"I promised Amy I would sleep over tonight, and we were going to watch some movies, and finish up homework for tomorrow. Is that okay?"

"No problem. But leave now, it's starting to get dark."

I checked my phone. It was 10:05. Okay. It was late, but too early to meet Mark at the park yet. I decided to pack clothes to truly solidify the lie. I hated lying, but my dad would never agree to it. He always felt Mark had a crush on me and was adamant about a no dating policy. Not that it ever stopped me before, but still.

I had tried to explain to him time and time again that Mark is only a friend, and never someone I could see myself being with. Plus, his sister is Amy! Anyways, I grabbed my navy duffle bag and packed shorts, a shirt, slippers, a toothbrush, hairbrush, and an outfit for school tomorrow. I decided that I may as well stay over there, since school is tomorrow, and it would be weird to come back into my house late tonight. My dad would be ready with questions. I opted to text Amy but wanted to leave the part out about me meeting Mark.

> *Katie: Hey, is it okay if I sleepover tonight?*
> *Amy: Sure, what time are you coming?*
> *Katie: Probably around 11:30 or 12.*
> *Amy: Late! But okay, text me when you're on your way.*

By the time I finished packing, it was 10:25. Okay, that meant I only needed to sit in my car for a little bit. I walked down the stairs and my dad was fast asleep in his favorite armchair. It was Sunday, but I knew he had been at the office all week. As acting sheriff in Prairie, he never truly got a day off and he was always extremely wiped out. I didn't want to wake him, so I left a sticky note on his forehead that I had left.

I took a bag of Cheetos from the kitchen, as a nice little snack while I sat and waited. I figured I would just wait alongside the curb at the park. The nice thing is that it was always nicely lit, even in the evenings. I would hate to be at a pitch-black park. I only lived about a five to seven-minute drive from the park, so I started up the car and allowed it to warm up for a few minutes.

I started my drive and noticed not a single car on the road. That wasn't atypical, especially in Prairie. Considering it was now 10:40, it made sense that everyone decided to turn in for the night.

I arrived at the park and checked the time- 10:45. Fifteen minutes. I decided to open my bag of chips as a means of distraction because my nerves felt fried.

What would I say to Mark?

Just ask him if he did it. Or, demand an explanation for why he was at Tara's.

I didn't want to demand anything on the account of it would ruin my friendship with Amy if I accused Mark of something like this, or if he did do it- I was terrified of what he would do. I was stuck between a rock and a hard place, with no way to get myself out.

Trying to plan out what I would say was bringing me no sense of security or comfort at all. In fact, it was stressing me out more! I grabbed at the bottom of the bag and found that I had eaten all the chips. So much for a distraction. My phone lit up with a text from Amy.

Amy: Mark just left the house… weird. You on your way?

Katie: Not yet but will in the next thirty minutes. Sorry, homework is killing me!

Amy: Sounds good, and I know. The course load is insane this year. I have romance movies stocked up, so don't plan on sleeping tonight! See you soon. XO

Okay. That was taken care of, and I saw a car coming in the distance. I instantly recognized Mark's car, because it was always the nicest on the block-secondary only to his parent's BMW's.

I felt as if I was shaking, and that my heart was beating a hundred miles a minute.
Breathe, Katie.

He parked behind me and came into the passenger side of my car. I unlocked the door, and he climbed in, smile plastered all over his goofy face.

How could I think he would be capable of something like this? Mark was always the sweet guy, the one you could depend on. He wasn't the type of guy to go around kidnapping innocent girls.
Okay, well now I feel guilty.

"Hey Katie. Thanks for meeting me. I talked to my sister, and she filled me in and what happened with Miss. Towner..." he said, and I could tell he wanted to explain more.

"Yeah. I'm sorry Mark, but I must admit it doesn't make sense, and then to hear your name... well you must know what I think."

"I do, and I want to change that. I want to explain. The night that she saw me with Tara is right. I was there. I was only meeting her so she could pay me."

"Pay you for what, Mark?"

"I had done something for her that I don't feel comfortable discussing, and it was payment for that. Look, I liked Tara and she didn't deserve what happened to her."
Neither did Anna.

"And Anna did? What are you trying to say Mark?"

"Look, we all know she was kind of a bitch. Yeah, it sucks. But Tara was kind to everyone, and she really didn't deserve it- not that Anna did, but Tara deserved it less."

I couldn't believe what I was hearing. Neither of those girls deserved whatever happened or may still be happening to them. Who cares if Anna was slightly rude to some people? That doesn't give anyone the right to go ahead with kidnapping her, and it certainly doesn't make it okay for people with grudges to talk poorly about her. She was still a person.

So much for the sweet Mark, who was kind to everyone.

"I can't believe you Mark. She was a nice girl, in her own way," I said and looked at Mark as his face turned from contrite to angry.

"Yeah right! Anna was a cold-hearted bitch. Forget about her though. You need to stop looking into this, it's only going to get you hurt, and I don't want that."

"What is that even supposed to mean Mark? I know that you and Amy are just trying to look out for me, but you don't need to. I will be okay. My dad is the sheriff after all," I said with a smile half-joking.

Everyone knew my dad was overwhelmingly overprotective when it came to me. Maybe that didn't matter to the person who took these girls, but that was fine. There were more perks to having a sheriff for a dad then most people realized. It means that I took tons of martial arts lessons as well as basic self-defense. I also knew how to fire a gun. I wasn't scared of anyone, especially in this little town.

"We are trying to look out for you. The people in this town are genuinely scared, Katie. And for good reason! Everyone can easily see that these girls were kidnapped, including your dad. I'm sure he told you to stay away too, right?"

"How did you know about that? Did Amy tell you she told on me?" I wondered if Amy had been open about her snitching activity to her brother, or if that was something that she wanted to keep private.

"No. I was the one who told her to say something. It is not okay Katie. I didn't want you to get hurt."

"Jesus Mark, you guys cannot micromanage every small aspect of my life. I don't like the feeling of everyone breathing down my neck. It's not cool. I would appreciate it if you backed off. Your sister's interference, I can understand. But you? No."

"You don't get it do you Katie?" Mark's face took on a somber mood.

"Get what?"

"I'm in *love* with you! How can you not see that?"

What? Mark? I knew my dad always felt he had a little crush on me, but to be in love with someone was on an entirely different level, one that I don't even think my dad knew about. I certainly had no clue.

Did Amy know?

My head was starting to spin. How long was this going on? Did I feel the same way? *Could* I feel the same way? I had too many questions floating around, and meanwhile, Mark was staring at me, clearly waiting for me to respond.

I didn't know what to say.

"Are you sure, Mark?"

"Yes, I'm sure Katie. I know it's not what you had expected to hear, but it's true. I have been in love with you for a while now. Don't worry, I know the feelings aren't reciprocated, but I just thought you should know."

"I'm sorry, Mark. I always thought we were friends. I don't want things to be weird between us now."

"It's okay. They won't be. Like I said, I knew the feelings weren't reciprocated. I just wish you would stop this investigating nonsense. None of us want to see you hurt."

"I'm sorry, but you know I can't do that. If it is any consolation, I don't think it's you anymore. That doesn't mean I can stop looking though. These girls were taken, and I firmly believe that. Someone needs to help them Mark, and I won't stop until they are found."

"You leave me no choice then," Mark said, and I felt a poke in the side of my neck and suddenly ice slid through my veins.

10

Mark

Fuck. Katie was lying unconscious in my arms. I didn't want it to be this way, but she left me with no other choice. Fuck! Amy was going to be pissed off. I needed to get Katie home, and fast.

I pulled her into the back seat of her car, so she was lying flat and low. I couldn't risk anyone seeing her. The gossipers would have a field day with that. My house was five minutes away, and with my driving, I could make it in two. I needed to take her car and hide it. I would come back for mine later.

I didn't want this for Katie. I always envisioned us being together, not her being one of them. She was too good for that, too pure. Why was she so damn stubborn? Now I had a situation on my hands, and not one that would go over well with my sister.

What did you do Mark?

I kept telling myself that Katie left me no other choice. Of course, this wouldn't be what I planned, but her persistent amateur detective work kind of put me under a microscope. I started up Katie's car and headed over to my house. Oh god, Amy was going to flip out.

I pulled into the long driveway a few minutes later and waved to my gate attendant as he let me in the gates. He smiled and waved back. Nothing more. I wasn't surprised, as lately my dad had ramped up the NDA's and made it mandatory for every employee to sign. That was a godsend in a time like this.

Amy was already suspicious when I left home earlier today, and I had been very coy about where I was going. She tended to be kind of nosy, and I didn't want her to interfere in my talk with Katie. I was successful in getting her to believe I wasn't responsible for Anna and Tara's kidnappings, but she was dead set on continuing to dig for the truth.

The truth was much worse than any false reality she could have constructed.

Right on cue, my sister came barreling out of the house. She looked happy, and then concerned when she noticed I was in the driver's seat of Katie's car, with Katie nowhere to be seen.

"Mark, what the hell is going on?"

She came around to the driver's side and glanced at the back seat. Her eyes went wide, and her hand flew to cover her mouth.

"You didn't. Mark, are you stupid? Why would you take Katie?" She practically screamed at me; I was nervous she would wake Katie. Although the tranquilizer I gave her was sure to keep her out for a few more hours.

"Will you be quiet? I had no choice Amy. She wanted to keep looking!"

"I could have stopped her!" Amy screamed at me and shoved me hard against the driver's door. I knew how much she loved Katie- but so did I! This was for her own protection.

How did she not see that I was doing this for everyone's sake?

The whole family could be implicated if Katie were to find out the truth. I couldn't allow my dad's business to suffer, or to put my mom in the way of unnecessary gossip. This had nothing to do with them.

Amy sighed, and looked frustrated. I understood where she was coming from, but she had to know this wasn't easy for me either. I needed her to see the truth and help me get Katie in the house before George the gate attendant saw the scene and decided to tear up the NDA.

"I know you're mad Ames but please help me get her to the room."

"God Mark, you're making a mistake." Amy scolded me but opened the back-seat door and went around the other side of the car to try and pull Katie out by her arms. I ran over to help her. Katie was a thin set girl, but dead weight was really hard to carry.

We pulled her around the back so mom and dad wouldn't see. We opened the back-basement door, and both took Katie down the stairs to the locked iron door. I pulled the large key out of my back pocket and unlocked the familiar iron wrought chain. Mom and Dad had this place-built years ago, and it was used as a bomb shelter in a way. Why, I don't know.

Once I unlocked the door, the familiar muffled screams greeted me. Tara and Anna were chained up to their respective posts, with tape over their mouths. Honestly, the tape felt a bit much, but they wouldn't shut up!

Thankfully there was a nice corner for Katie to stay in. It had a mat and was close by the heater, even though it was never used because it could make this place quite warm with all the iron in it.

Amy grabbed a chain from the closet, and unlike Anna and Tara, she fastened it around Katie's ankle rather than her arm. We wanted her comfortable, after all.

Amy had tears in her eyes, and I felt myself get angry. Why was she exhibiting any form of weakness in front of these girls? If we showed weakness, they would prey on that. We weren't merciful, and we weren't kind.

It's because it's Katie.

Yes, I know. But Katie is asleep, so the tears are doing nothing but pissing me off. When I get pissed off, I lose control. Amy needed to get her head in the game. We couldn't start getting weak or making stupid mistakes. It could cost us.

I gave a final once over to ensure all my girls were locked tight and grabbed my sisters hand and left the room. I locked the chains and gave it a second shake to make sure.

"Amy, I need you to come with me to get my car. We can't leave it sitting at the park."

"Mark…" my sister looked at me and started crying. Jesus. What the hell was going on with her?

"Amy, stop!" I screamed, and she immediately stopped crying and looked at me with fear in her eyes. Fear… as if I would ever hurt my sister.

"We need to go and get this done Ames. Think of the family."

She immediately dried her eyes, straightened her posture, and grabbed the keys out of my hand.

"Let's go."

We headed up the stairs, and I tripled locked the basement door. The nice thing about the room was that it was soundproof. Not only that, but our property was so big that no one could even make it close enough to hear the girls scream if they wanted to.

So why did I do it? That is a loaded question... best saved for another time. Right now, I had to get rid of a car.

I climbed into the driver's seat, and we rushed over to the park. No surprise, it only took us a matter of minutes. I guess I could consider myself lucky that Katie picked such a late time to go meet up with me. It wasn't really late, but it was to anyone in this crummy town who goes to bed at 8 p.m. sharp.

Still, I kept my eyes peeled for any cars, as Amy climbed out and headed over to my car. She didn't have her license, but kind of knew how to drive.

She better not wreck my damn car.

I let her get behind me, and we headed back home. I made it home at least a few minutes before her so I had a chance to stow Katie's car in one of our many garages. Once I spotted Amy pulling in the gate, I motioned for her to park outside the garage that Katie's car rested in.

She pulled herself out of my car, and I was pleased to see that she had composed herself finally. We simply could not allow any spot for weakness or vulnerability. Certainly not with something like this at stake.

"There is a duffle bag in Katie's car. Where was she going?" I figured my sister would know better than anyone.

"She was going to stay the night here."
Perfect.

Okay, so that was great. At least we had… two outfits. I didn't want for my Katie to have to use the same outfit for too long- she was much too good for that. Besides, I had planned to get her some new clothes anyways. I took care of my girls.

While I must admit this wasn't what I envisioned my life with Katie every turning out to be, it was what had happened, and I would accept it gratefully.

I grabbed Katie's clothes, and the rest of her duffle bag to bring inside. I would keep it in my room for now and use it when needed.

"Amy, if Sheriff Johnson starts looking for Katie, you need to say she never made it here last night. Got it?"

"Got it Mark." She seemed pretty okay with the plan. I needed her full cooperation. That's when I had a brilliant idea.

"Better yet Ames, call him early tomorrow and ask if Katie had left yet to pick you up. That way he realizes she never made it. Also, call her phone first a few times so it looks legit. We have to do this all by the book- he is a cop."

"Okay…" Amy seemed unsure and looked as if she had something more to say.

"What is it?"

"Where *is* her phone Mark?"

I reached in my back pocket, and waved Katie's blackberry back and forth. I swiped it out of her car earlier, and I knew it would come in handy. I also remember Sheriff Johnson mentioning something about a tracking app on her phone, so I would need to delete that immediately. I clicked on the home screen. Shit. Password protected.

Try Jenna. Katie's mom.

I typed in the name "Jenna" and sure enough I was in. So predictable. I loved my parents too, but parental attachment in some kids was insane. I easily found the app hidden amongst some other ones in a separate folder. Delete.

I wanted to give Katie a few days to reacclimate to her new environment. I know it would take a while- and Tara and Anna were still struggling. Unfortunately, they would need to get used to it. This was their new home. I would keep them safe and protected, at least from the world. Or keep the world save from them. There was nothing to worry about.

Amy on the other hand, had a wicked taste for torture. She tormented both of those girls, but especially took a liking to Tara. Sometimes I would have to excuse myself. I knew my soft spot for Tara was a problem, but it didn't make me weak. I wasn't weak.

Tomorrow I would go to school with Amy and pretend like nothing happened. Katie was out sick, that's all. Then her dad would realize she was actually missing, and just like the past two times, all hell would break loose in Prairie.

This time would be different. This time, it was Sheriff Johnson's own daughter that went missing, and there would be a manhunt without a doubt.

I wasn't worried. I knew how to cover my tracks. I headed up to my room and pushed Katie's duffle bag under my bed. I laid down, and once my head hit the pillow, I felt sleepy.

I was so exhausted, but overwhelmingly excited for tomorrow... well today. How is it one a.m. already?

I started the day off with only two girls, but now I had three.

11

Katie

I heard voices surrounding me but couldn't find the strength to open my eyes. I felt weak, and exhausted. My head began to throb until it became almost unbearable, but still, I could not open my eyes. I drifted into a black nothingness.

Open your eyes Katie. Open your eyes. I could feel my head pounding with a splitting migraine. I slowly peeled my eyes open, and they felt as if they weighed a million pounds. It took a second to adjust my vision.
What the hell?

I saw Tara, and then Anna. Both girls were asleep but chained to posts by their arms. Tara was sporting a black eye, and Anna had a blood-stained shirt. Jesus Christ. What was this place? I had no recollection of last night. One minute I was talking to Mark, and the next it was an empty blackness.
Mark.

Mark kidnapped me. What the hell was this place? Oh god, Amy. She had to be looking for me right now. Did she know? Was my dad looking for me? Oh god, was Mark going to kill me? The questions were giving me a migraine. I wanted to wake the girls and shoot questions at them but felt guilty at the same time.

Anna was taken first so she had to be here for at least a month, right? Oh my god, I can't believe I was right about Mark all along. How could he do something like this? I needed to get out of here. I would be damned if I died down here.

Against my better judgement, I shouted at the girls. Slowly but surely, they both opened their eyes, and looked at me somberly. I felt so bad for them, being trapped in here.

You're trapped in here too now.

I looked around the room and took everything in. There was a big iron door, covered with chains. The floor was a hard, and cold metal. There was a huge heater on the wall that looked like it had never been used. The walls looked as if they were made of iron as well, and it was dimly lit down here. There were no windows, but small mats and blankets laid on the floor for us. Each girl got their own color blanket. Tara was laid atop a royal blue blanket, and Anna a lime green. Mine was red.

I can't believe this happened.

"Why are we here?" I asked the girls, hoping with everything in me that they would have an answer for me.

Instead of answering, I was met with two blank stares. I surveyed both girls. They looked drained, and as if they had lost all fight in them. What happened to the spunky Anna who was the life of the party? Surely, she had a little fire left in her. What did he do to these girls to break them down so badly? Would he do it to me?

Why couldn't I have agreed to stop looking?

Don't think like that. You needed to save them. You still can.

I knew Mark better than either of these two girls. If any of us had a shot of getting through to Mark, it would be me.

"Can you guys please tell me what's going on?"

"Isn't it obvious? We're trapped, and there's nothing you can do." Anna spit it out, her tone dripping with spite.

Why was she angry with me?

"How did he take you?"

"He got me into his car, because we had an agreement where I would pay him to change my grade. We were meeting up so I could pay him. When I tried to give him the money, he pushed it away and leaned in to kiss me instead." Tara explained, as she nervously played with her hands.

"Did you?"

"Of course not. I didn't feel that way about him. That's when he pulled out a syringe and stuck me in my neck. I woke up here." Tara motioned to the iron room we found ourselves in.

The Iron Room. Would this be the place I died?

You're not dying here.

"What about you?" I turned towards Anna, obviously the angrier of the two.

"I was walking home from a party, and he asked if I needed a ride. I got in, and honestly, I was so drunk, I thought he was someone else. He started going on and on about how I treated him like shit. I think he wanted an apology, but I didn't give him one. Instead, he stuck a needle in my neck." Anna started crying.

Was that his signature? I never saw him pull out a needle last night, but I did feel a poke in my neck, and I woke up here. He had to of drugged me.

"What does Mark do to you guys?"

"Mark? He's not even the worst one." Tara laughed a humorless laugh,

"What do you mean?"

"It's his sister Amy that has the worst temper, and she loves to take it out on us." Tara pointed to her blackened eye.

Amy hurt these girls too? What the hell was going on here?

I couldn't believe what I was hearing. I never thought Mark to be capable of something this malicious and evil. But Amy? My best friend had the most compassionate and giving heart. Why would she hurt Tara and Anna? What did she gain from it?

She knew where they were all along. They both did. I felt sick to my stomach.

"I never thought Amy was the worst. I always thought it was the parents that were the most brutal."

I looked at Anna, and my eyes nearly bulged out of my head. The parents? Sharon and Paul?

"I know what you're thinking, but yeah. This whole thing is a family affair. Every day they each take turns coming down here. Sometimes one of them hurts both of us, and sometimes they only do one. The mom and the sister are the most violent. The dad just likes to make us strip."

I'm going to throw up.

The whole family was in on this? I couldn't mentally process everything that I had been told right now. My brain felt like it was going to explode. The same family who supported me endlessly and cooked a massive amount of dinners and lunches when my mom passed were the same family that was responsible for kidnapping and torturing girls.

"What about Mark?" I wondered if he was just the pawn in all this.

"Oh, Mark likes to just look. Sometimes touch. But he is all about watching." Tara said, and I saw a single tear roll down her cheek."

"Have you guys tried to escape?"

They both laughed, lacking humor, and turned to me.

"Once... but with these chains on? They don't even unhook us to get to the bathroom. We get buckets."

I wondered who would come down here tonight. Did Sharon and Paul know I was here? Did Amy? Would it change anything if they knew it was me? I hoped so. I would help these girls, but first I needed a plan. A good one.

12

Amy

I would be lying if I said that Katie wasn't in my thoughts today. I wanted to go down to see if she was awake and offer an explanation before school, but Mark forbade it.

I had already started phase one of his plan when I called Katie's phone a few times this morning. Once he realized she was missing, Sheriff Johnson would use some sort of locating device to track her phone- which was already disposed of. Mark handled everything when it came to covering up our tracks. If we missed one thing, made one mistake… it would ruin us. Tara was one of those mistakes. Another mistake of Mark's was being seen by that idiot drunk. She needed to stop talking, or she would become a problem- one that needed fixing.

I always told Mark that this could never turn emotional. It had to be strategic. Anna was planned. We didn't like the way she disrespected Mark, and something had to be done. An example needed to be set.

Tara was an accident. Mark's accident. He developed feelings for her, and that was an act of convenience. Thankfully, it seems she acclimated well. But she did have a little mouth on her- and I was keen on keeping it quiet.

Phase Two of Mark's plan required a little emotion on my part. I needed to make this call to Katie's dad the most convincing piece of acting I had ever done. He had to believe that his sweet little girl never made it here last night.

Mark has been up early this morning, dismantling Katie's car. He would take all the pieces apart and burn what he could and hide the rest. After today, Katie Johnson wouldn't exist.

Since Mark's original screw up of taking Tara, he had been working slightly overtime to ensure that the looky loos in this town never turned their sights this way. But why would they?

We were the most respectable family in Prairie.

I thought we were finally out of the clear. Yeah, everyone claimed to be looking for the girls, but no one knew about the missing eyewitness. The thing is, when she originally came forward, Sheriff Johnson came to my dad personally. He knew how things in this town could easily spin out of control and wanted to give our family the benefit of the doubt.

He liked us. So, we never thought that Mark's name would be brought up again. Why would it? Sheriff Johnson had no plans to mention anything about Mark being the last person to see Tara, and who in their right mind would take the local drunk at her word?

Oh right, Katie.

The fact that Mark took Katie was tearing me up inside. We truly were best friends, but at the end of the day- family comes first. If I have to choose between Katie and the preservation of my family, it's a clear choice. I just wish it didn't have to be this way. My heart went out to Sheriff Johnson, because I knew that him losing his wife had nearly crushed him half to death. Katie would tear him to pieces. We had to start being really careful and laying low.

Playing the grieving best friend would be an easy front to fake, because I wouldn't really be faking it. I wish I could help Katie, but it is out of my hand's now. She should have listened to me earlier, and this never would have happened.

I need to call Katie's dad.

"Hey Amy. How was your girls' sleepover?" Sheriff Johnson sounded particularly chipper today, and I would be the one responsible for sending his whole world crashing down. Here goes nothing.

"Sleepover? Katie never made it last night. I figured she decided to stay in. I was calling to ask if she had left yet. She hasn't answered any of my calls."

There was a long pause on the other line, and I could hear the phone hit something. He must have dropped it.

"Sheriff?"

I heard the phone being fumbled, and a little bit of static was going on.

"I have to go Amy," and he hung up.

Mission accomplished. I was all ready for school and needed to see how Mark was doing. I would be surprised if he was able to get any sleep at all after the long night he had. He would definitely take a stronger liking to Katie down the road.

We had yet to tell our parents about Katie. We figured breakfast was the perfect time. They would be furious, and not because Mark grabbed another girl. They didn't care about that. In fact, they relished in having new girls to take their turns getting out their anger and frustration on. They would be pissed off about the little fact about the new capture being Katie. Yeah, they were going to blow a fuse.

I went across the hall and saw that Mark's door was wide open.

"Mark? You in here?"

"Yeah, brushing my teeth Ames!"

I went inside and waited on the suede couch. Mark emerged from the bathroom moments later, looking kind of nervous. I completely understood. We both knew in our hearts that mom and dad wouldn't be okay with this, but there was no choice now. It was too late.

"Ready Mark?"

"Guess so. Let's do this."

We both walked downstairs to the breakfast table together. Mom and Dad were already elbow deep in their pancakes and bacon. Oh, boy. This was going to be fun.

"Hey Mark, hey Amy! Come eat some breakfast before school. Amy, is Katie picking you up today?" My mom smiled and looked at me. She loved Katie and loved her mom even more.

"She can't."

"Well that's okay, Mark can give you a ride. When is she going to come over love? Your father and I haven't seen her in quite some time."

"She's already here." Mark chimed in and looked down at his plate.

Oh boy.

"Well if she's here, then invite her down for breakfast. I didn't raise y'all to be rude." My mom scolded, and my dad looked at both Mark and I with suspicion plastered all over his face.

I decided to speak up.

"Can't. She's uh… downstairs with Anna and Tara." I closed my eyes, knowing what would happen next.

My mom spit out her coffee, and my dad froze, his bite of food still on his fork in midair. "Tell me you're joking. Tell me you're FUCKING joking Amy."

Mark and I knew better to respond to that. We both knew our mom well, and when she told you to tell her you were just kidding, it was because she knew you weren't and was trying to buy time before she blew a lid.

The entire mood at the breakfast table had shifted immensely within minutes. My mom stood up and stalked off to the key office. She was going to check for herself. I decided to follow and leave my brother to deal with the unbearable silence of my seething father.

This was worse than bad.

As I followed my mom and her ridiculous paced fast walk, I could hear her mumbling to herself. She was furious, and I didn't think it was good if Katie had seen her. I don't think Katie truly knows what is going on, but I had no doubt that those bitches Anna and Tara had already woken up and spilled the whole truth. Their version of the truth anyhow.

I vowed to tell Katie my side of the story, to make her understand. She had to know that she was never a viable option for this from the beginning, and that she simply left us with no other choice. None of my family would have wanted it this way, if that wasn't clear by my father and mother's outburst. *Understand I never wanted this Katie. You're my best friend.*

Maybe we could swear her to secrecy. Maybe we didn't have to keep her chained up. *Even you know that's bullshit. She won't leave those girls here.*

I sighed as we got to the familiar back door. My mother unlocked all the padlocks at a feverishly slow pace. She had gone from screaming, to mumbling, to now eerily calm. That couldn't fare well.

We both walked down the familiar steps to the big iron door, and my mom's hands were visibly shaking as she unlocked the chain lock. I could tell she knew it wasn't a joke, but desperately prayed it was. Me too mom, me too.

My mom slowly swung the door open and was met with three wide eyed girls staring back. My mom covered her mouth and ran upstairs. I forced myself to look at Katie. *That was a mistake.*

Katie stared back at me, tears brimming her eyes. She was able to speak, but all she said was, "Amy." I couldn't bear it. I turned and slammed the iron door shut and locked it.

I stomped up the stairs, furious. We never should have taken the tape of those idiots mouths last night. God knows what horror stories they concocted and how many lies they fed Katie about me and my family.

I just needed to set Katie straight, but later. Right now, I had to go to school and put on the best act of my life.

By the time I finished locking up the other door, my mom was nowhere in sight. Maybe it was for the best. I couldn't face her right now or handle the disappointment that was clear on her face ever since this morning. I needed to find Mark, and we needed to go- now.

What have you done Mark?

I only hoped our time away at school and work for the day, would allow my parents some time and space to process everything.

Please.

I found Mark standing by the entry way, ready to go. We looked at each other, but neither said a word, which was fine. We went outside, and I climbed into the passenger side of Mark's car after he unlocked the door. No breakfast and silence it would be. What a great morning today was becoming.

The drive to school took slightly longer than usual, mostly because for once in his life, Mark drove *below* the speed limit. I knew that it was only because he was upset, but he needed to pull it together. No one was more upset about Katie than me. If he started acting differently, people would notice.

They always noticed in Prairie.

Moments later we pulled into the familiar large brown gates of Prairie High School. I was so glad I actually got all the homework done that they had assigned last week, but quite frankly it was nothing short of a miracle.

We got out of the car, still not saying a word to each other, and Mark went his separate ways.

I was surprised to find everyone staring at me as I walked through the gates. What was going on?

I barely made it through the front door before I spotted Sheriff Johnson talking to the principal. He turned and saw me before I had the chance to hide. Shit.

"Amy!" Sheriff Johnson called my name and motioned for me to join them.

I pulled on my best sad face and walked slowly over to them.

"Come inside the office Amy," my principal said and moved me inside. Sheriff Johnson followed and closed the door.

"Where is Katie, Amy?"

13

Katie

I can't believe Amy. I couldn't fathom the idea that she would be able to come down here, see me chained like this, and not help me. Sharon too! *Did I know this family at all?*

Getting the hell out of this place would be a lot harder than I originally thought. I prayed my dad had already noticed my absence and was rallying the town of Prairie to come to my rescue. This family did a hell of a good job covering their tracks, and I had no doubt that they had done a good job erasing the events of last night.

You have to do this on your own.

Surely the girl I had seen as my best friend still had some of that girl left in her. I refused to believe that she could turn cold hearted at the drop of the dime. Or maybe she was always this way, and I had been blind to it. I hoped that wasn't the case. If it was, then any hope I had of escaping on her love for our friendship was up in flames.

Would they torture me the way they had these other girls? Or would they make me watch? Any of the million possibilities floating around in my head were driving me nuts. I couldn't sit here and let my mind wander all day, but I was left with no choice. All I had to stare at in this iron room was the two messed up girls sitting in front of me.

I still couldn't come to terms with all of this. A family full of torturers seemed less likely than pigs falling from the sky in a town like Prairie. They were the most well-known and respectable family as well, but that could have a lot to do with Amy's dad Paul controlling most of the town's finances.

Dad.

Oh god. My dad. He had probably already noticed that I was missing, and I was sure the Puntzer family did an excellent job of convincing him I was never here. I hoped he could see through their act, but I knew that was next to impossible. How many times had I been in this house lately, not knowing what was going on in this room? How many times had they tried to call for help to no avail? I felt sick to my stomach with anger, frustration, and fear.

"Overthinking won't get you anywhere." Anna spoke, eyes clearly fixated on me.

"I can't help it. I was close with this family. I just can't believe it," I mournfully sobbed, fully caught up in my overwhelming emotions.

My heart lurched in my chest. I know these girls probably thought I was naïve, and I probably was too. I was thinking about my dad. He and I lost so much when my mom passed unexpectedly, but we were finally starting to repair. We were starting to heal- together. This would ruin him. I thought of him and knew it would keep me strong.

I don't want to die here.

"We need to get out of here." I turned towards the girls, hoping they knew of some way to get out. I didn't see any exits beside the large door with chains, but maybe they knew something I didn't.

"Nope, no chance. The only way out is through those doors, and they're locked." Tara looked defeated, and so did Anna who agreed with her by shaking her head.

These girls had fully given up. They simply laid down their arms and accepted that they just might die in this place, at the hands of this family. I understood, but I wouldn't accept it. This would not be the place I died. I just needed to figure out how.

I figured everyone was out of the house given it was a Monday. Apparently the Puntzer's are all about appearances, so I knew they would be at work and school putting on a great facade.

The chain fastened around my ankle was long. I started crawling towards the door just to see how far I could get. I was able to get within four feet of it. Not close enough. Maybe it was close enough to hurt whoever came through the door next. I didn't care who it was.

I looked around but knew there was nothing here. They had carefully made sure that they didn't leave… oh I don't know- a knife or anything sitting around. Smart family.

I thought of screaming, but Anna and Tara deduced that the room was soundproof. I figured it was true given that I had never heard them. Plus, they said that Sharon threatened to cut their tongues if they screamed. Lovely.

What about George?

Oh shit, I almost forgot about George. He was the Puntzer's gate attendant. He had to have seen them bring my car in last night with no sign of me, right? I hoped he did. They made all their workers sign NDA's. Amy had drunkenly admitted it to me at a party last year, but I thought nothing of it at the time. If he had seen something, he would forego the agreement, wouldn't he?

Just then I heard the door unlocking. Oh god. Then, I heard the now familiar sound of the clanking chains. The door swung open wide, and Paul stepped in- anger plastered all over his face. He took one look at me and turned away suddenly. An emotion was obvious on his face- but passed as soon as it came. Sadness? Anger? I had no clue anymore.

Instead of me, he set his sights on Anna and marched towards her angrily.
"Stand up. Now."

Anna scrambled up and stood up straighter. I had never thought of Paul as being a scary man. He was always a good father to Amy and Mark and had always found ways to make me laugh when I was down about my mom. I didn't recognize the man standing in front of me, and I was scared too.

He unlocked her wrist chain and bent down to attach it to her ankle instead when he dropped back. She had hit him. She started for the stairs and was soon out of sight. She didn't hit Paul hard enough because he stood up and stormed off to find her.

He had left the keys behind, but they were far from me. I looked at Tara who had also noticed the keys.
"Grab them!"

Tara bent down and went to reach for the keys when Paul came storming back in. He was followed by a sobbing Anna who was being held at gunpoint by Sharon. Oh god. Don't hurt her.

"I told you what would happen if you tried to run again Anna. Not very good, is it?"

"No... I'm sorry." Anna pleaded with the both of them, tears running down her cheeks. I couldn't let this happen.

"Stop!" Both Paul and Sharon turned towards me, laughed, and faced Anna again.

"Knees." Sharon instructed Anna, and she willingly obliged.

Oh my god. They're really going to kill her.

Sharon aimed the barrel executioner style, and with a single round, Anna was gone. A strangled sob escaped Tara's lips, and I felt myself break. I had just watched someone get murdered. Any one of us could be next. Sharon had gotten blood on her shirt and looked disgusted when she noticed the tiny red flecks. "Clean this shit up and bury the bitch." Sharon spoke to her husband, turned around, and started a brisk walk up the stairs.

Holy shit.

I couldn't stare at Anna's lifeless body any longer. I forced myself to turn around. I was visibly shaking, and I didn't want to give these sickos any more satisfaction. I could hear as Paul scrubbed the floor, and the repetitive water pour. I could count at least ten more posts on my half of the never-ending room. Ten more victims? I hoped not.

After what seemed like hours on end of cleaning, the smell of bleach hit my nostrils and I heard a zip, and then small thuds as what I assumed to be Paul taking Anna up the stairs. I don't care why they did this, or what Anna had done- she didn't deserve this. Tara didn't deserve this. I didn't deserve this. If they thought I was on a war path before, they had another thing coming.

I didn't grow up with the Sheriff as my father to be left with no skills. I knew how to mentally break and manipulate someone. After today, I wouldn't view these people as my family and that included Amy. They were my captors, and I would view them as such. That was my little secret though. I knew there was one set of heart strings in particular that I could pray on, and that was Amy's.

Let's hope this works.

"Tara are you okay?"

She didn't answer but continued crying. In school, I don't think the girls ever knew each other particularly well, but you bond fast in a place like this, and it had been just them for so long. That coupled with the newfound sense of fear that Paul and Sharon placed in both of us when they murdered Anna right in front of our eyes.

I felt an overwhelming sense of guilt. I saw that they had lost all sense of hope in getting out of here, and rather than accept it- I built them up to think we could escape. Anna died trying to get out of here, and I feared more than anything that would be my exact same fate.

You know they would kill you, with no hesitation.

I knew that, and I needed to accept it.

I had no concept of time down here and felt like I was going crazy trying to figure out what time it is. There were no windows to provide outside light, and there wasn't even a clock. These people thrived on making their victims suffer. It was eerily quiet down here, and that was only broken by the soft sobs of Tara. No light beside the small dim one, and no noise.

Dad, where are you?

How long would it be till I was found? It was the waiting game that was tearing me apart. Waiting for Amy to come in and hurt me, or Paul to make me undress or even Sharon to come down and put a bullet between my eyes. Mark was the catalyst in all this, and his family thrived on it.

Just then, I heard the door once more.

Please be Amy. Please be Amy.

No such luck. It was Mark. He looked and me and made a beeline. He knelt down beside me, and took my hands into his, staring at me with tear brimmed eyes.

Oh, the sociopath has feelings. Go figure.

"Katie, you have to know that I never wanted this. You gave me no choice."

"Is this a sick joke Mark? There was always a choice. You could have chosen not to kidnap and torture girls. Your parents could have chosen to not be fucking psychopaths, and don't even get me started on Amy. You guys are sick. I can't even look at you." I forced myself to turn away.

Mark dropped my hands and stood up. His mood had done a clear 360 and he was now staring at me with cold eyes, and a hard demeanor.

"So be it." Mark then turned and walked out of the room, locking it as he went.

Nothing more came for a few hours, and I patiently waited to see if Amy would visit. Better yet, where was dinner? Did they plan to starve us to death?

The conversation was dismal, and it only made me feel more alone in here. I spoke too soon, because the door unlocked and Paul came down with a tray full of what looked to be bread, and deli meat.

He grabbed a paper plate, grabbed a generous handle of what they called food, and set it in front of me. He did the same for Tara but with a smaller amount, and a rough toss of her plate on the floor in front of her.

"Enjoy." He turned and stalked off, but to my surprise didn't lock the door.

Instead I heard two sets of footsteps. Amy and Mark walked in the room holding a girl I recognized from school. Kim Meyers. She was out cold, but my suspicions told me Mark used his handy dandy syringe.

They brought her over to the post next to mine, rather than Anna's old post. Amy grabbed chains and locked the girl's wrist to the post.

Without another word, the two walked over to the door. Before they left, Amy turned around and looked at both Tara and me.

"Enjoy your new houseguest."

14

Amy

Sheriff Johnson looked mad. Really mad. I knew Mark would leave some evidence that would get all of us caught. He was the idiot of the family... clearly. I knew better than to confess before I knew what Sheriff Johnson knew, so I played dumb.

"I have no clue Mr. Johnson. I wish I did," and I broke out into a very real sob. This whole situation really sucked.

"Does Katie have a boyfriend? You can tell me the truth. If she ran off with some boy, I would want to know now." He looked at me, hope clear in his eyes. Oh, I could use this.

"Well, she did tell me about some boy she had met, but I don't know if they were that serious for her to run away..."

"Thank you, Amy for your honesty. You will notify me if she gets in contact with you?"

"Of course, Sheriff. Please find her." I reached out and hugged him tightly.

And the Emmy goes to...

Sheriff Johnson returned a squeeze, and I saw him wipe a tear out of his eye. Part of me felt bad, but I also knew what I needed to do. I needed to protect my family, so I couldn't waste time caring about him or his.

I stepped out of the office, and ran straight into Mark, who had looked like he saw a ghost. "What did they say? Do they know?" Mark's eyes were practically bugging out of his head. This kid did not know how to handle situations without going into a stress case. He would be the death of this family. "No, Mark. But they will if you act like this. Chill *out*."

I grabbed his arm, hard, and pulled him away from the still open door. He would get us all caught if he didn't keep a cool head. Katie was tearing him apart, which was ironic, given that he was the one who decided that she was a liability, and then took care of said liability all on his own without any consultation from the rest of the family.

I wanted to protect Katie as much as the next person, she was my best friend. Blood was thicker than water, and I wouldn't let our friendship deter my judgement any longer. She was our victim. That was all she would be to me from now on. If I let my feelings get the best of me, then this whole scheme would fall to shit. My family had too much to lose. "Mark, I need to go to class. You need to go and act normal. We will talk after school." I pushed him towards his class, and turned to walk towards mine before he could get another word in. He was driving me crazy.

Something needs to be done about Mark.

I couldn't hurt my brother though. I just wish he was able to have more of a clear head, like the rest of us. Didn't he understand that the whole family would be implicated? In court, they don't give out medals or no prison time for the family members who are "less guilty". I don't know what he was hoping to accomplish.

I knew that rumor of Katie's disappearance was spreading through school, and had reached the ears of every student, teacher, and worker in this damn place.

It was only a matter of time before I was hit with the tough questions. I needed to be prepared to answer them.

No, I didn't see Katie last night. I wish I did.

Showtime.

I walked into the Chemistry class and was met with a room full of stares. Some were comforting, some were empathetic, and some were curious. I don't know which of those felt like the worst.

Mr. Aryn started off his boring class with a lecture on the weekend. He droned on and on about the dangers of drug and alcohol use…

You forgot kidnapping.

He then got straight to the point and asked everyone to pass their papers forward. We all did so, like clockwork, and then started our remaining thirty-minute lecture on atoms and bonding. Funny. He starts the lesson on the subject he just required us to have knowledge on. School was useless.

I have never been so grateful to hear the bell ring. One girl in particular never tore her eyes off of me for a second- Kim Meyers.

She had always been nosy, but today she took on a whole new level. I decided to finally give her "the look" and she turned away, obviously embarrassed and very red faced.

Bitch.

I hurried over to my next class- Calculus. That class wouldn't be half bad if it wasn't for my god-awful citizen hero seat partner- Johnny. Last time we spoke was the first day of school, and he very blatantly expressed his desire to "find" those girls, and that he was already looking. Yeah, good luck buddy.

The investigating didn't fare well for Katie.

I took my seat in the back, and Johnny wasn't there yet. I breathed a sigh of relief, and said a silent prayer wishing with all my might that he was out sick for the day. I looked up towards the door as I heard a commotion. It was him. He walked right into the edge of the door, quickly recovered himself, and made a beeline for his seat next to mine. His hair was messy, and not in the cute way. His eyes were bloodshot, and if my sense of smell was correct- he was completely drunk.

Drunk on the second day of school. Bold. He turned my way and stared at me. It wasn't a casual few second stare, but rather an intense "this is weird now" stare.

"Can I help you?"

"Your best friend is missing, and you look like you are completely fine. Weird." He looked me up and down, taking in every inch of me, studying me. That sounded a little like an accusation to me, so it was time to shut that shit down.

"Do you know how hard it is for me? I waited and waited last night and this morning for my friend to never show up, only to realize she was missing. She was supposed to be with me last night. I could have protected her. You have no idea how that feels, do you?" I looked directly at Johnny, my eyes filling with tears.

He must have bought it because he simply turned away and opened his book. Was that why he was drunk today? I knew the town was upset about the disappearances of Tara and Anna, but they didn't get sloshed over it. Maybe his little investigation had hit a dead end, and drinking his sorrows away was his choice of moving on.

I wouldn't get involved in his self-destruction regardless. That was his cross to bear. Mine was trying to keep the three girls in our room, in our room. No one could ever find out about them. It was Monday, which meant it was Anna's day.

I was glad. She had been very smart with her mouth lately, and I have all this pent-up energy and stress I was just dying to get out.

I spent the rest of the class in a comfortable silence, relishing the moments I didn't have to hear Johnny's droning on about his work. Thankfully, he seemed pretty shut down after my verbal smackdown.

The bell rang, and I heard the familiar chirp of my phone. It was a group message to Mark and myself from my mom. It was only two words.

Mom: Anna's dead.

15

Mark

I re-read the text my mother sent over and over. People were rushing by me, desperate to get to their next class. I couldn't focus. I was in my own little bubble, and I could hear my blood rushing in my ears.

Anna was dead.

My mother didn't give any specifics and kept it short and sweet. I knew she was still mad about Katie, and now I was mad at her. I don't know who killed Anna, but it was either my mother or my father. Neither of those options were acceptable to me. Anna was one of our better victims and taking her out was a bad choice.

I wanted to punch something. I must have been standing in the middle of the hallway because people were bumping into me left and right. One girl in particular practically knocked me on my ass. "Watch it!" I turned to say to the girl who hit me, and realized it was nosy ass Kim Meyers.

Nobody liked Kim, and for good reason. She always seemed to be in the background, watching, and observing. I always had a bad feeling about her. Now she was in my way, and I wasn't having a good day.

"You watch it. You are the one standing in the hallway like some freak!" She practically spit the words at me, her voice dripping with venom.
Bad move.

Kim should consider herself very lucky that I was pressed for time, and not in my right mindset today. I needed to find Amy. This little bitch Kim could wait until later.

I pushed past Kim, practically knocking her to the ground. She opened her mouth to speak, but I gave her a look that shut her up instantly. Do not mess with me today.

I maintained a fast pace as I searched the hallways for Amy. She had to be freaking out too. I know that my mother wouldn't kill without reason. It is much harder to dump and properly dispose of a body, than it is to keep them hidden. I would rather keep these girls forever than risk trying to bury a body undetected.

What were my parents thinking?

I spotted Amy easily. She was standing at her locker, with her head ducked down, and face in her phone. Her eyes looked puffy, like she had been crying. I felt instantly guilty, and then worried. Who was making my sister cry?
This whole day was a mess.

I made my way over to my sister, and she didn't notice until I touched her shoulder. She jumped.

"Are you okay?" I looked down at her phone, which was open to messages.

"So, I take it you read Mom's text…"

She looked at me, mouth gaping. I understood her feelings. It didn't make sense. We needed to go home and talk to them. Sitting around this dump would do nothing. I grabbed her hand, and we headed out to the field.

There was a spot under the bleachers where we could talk without fear of being heard.

We reached the secluded spot, and both did a once over of the bleachers. No feet. We needed to make sure no one was around, as we discussed how Anna went from alive to dead in a matter of a morning.

"What the hell happened?" Amy looked furious, and freaked out, but I knew she was more scared than anything. A death was not good right now, especially with the whole town on edge after Katie's disappearance.

"I don't know Ames. She must have tried to escape again." I put my head in my hands and sighed. Anna had a track record of trying to escape, and I remember vaguely my mother threatening to shoot her if she did again.

I continued, "Maybe mom followed through on her promise and shot Anna."

Amy opened her mouth to speak but was interrupted by footsteps coming down the bleachers. Shit. Shit. Shit.

Kim rounded the corner and faced us with a grin on her face, and her phone in hand, obviously recording everything we said.

"I knew you guys had something to do with it. I'm going to turn this into Sheriff Johnson right now." Kim turned around and started off towards the school.

"Mark, do something!"

I knew it wasn't smart, but I always kept a syringe on hand in case of something like this happening. I pulled it out from my bag and sprinted. I caught Kim around the ankles, pulling her down to the grass, and sank the needle in her neck.
And she was out.

We were still in hot water, because now we had to drag Kim's unconscious and heavy body to our car without students, faculty, and oh yeah, the sheriff noticing. There was a small patch of forestry behind the school and it would be hard, but doable to bring the car around there and then load Kim in the back. Amy grabbed Kim's backpack.

"Amy, come with me to drag her in, and then wait with her while I get the car. This way nobody will see."

My sister agreed with a nod, and as I grabbed Kim's arms and started pulling her into the trees, Amy reached down and grabbed Kim's phone. She played the video back which ended when I came up behind her abruptly and took her down.

"Delete it Amy."

So, she did, and the walk to the edge of the trees was filled with uncharacteristic silence. We were both chatter boxes by nature, but Kim had never been one of our targets. But, like we were taught, family preservation was our only goal, and Kim sought to destroy that. To destroy us. It was only a matter of time, before she would need to be dealt with.

School was almost over for the day, so I wasn't worried about skipping classes. I knew what my parents would think, but honestly, given that we were the "closest" with Katie, us skipping out on school wouldn't look too suspect on the day she was pronounced missing.

They would have wanted us to eradicate this little problem.

We reached the edge of the trees, and I reminded Amy to stay with Kim until I got the car. I rushed out and headed towards the school. I nearly ran into Sheriff Johnson.

"Woah there, bud. Slow down." He laughed, and I knew it was especially hard for him to do so, on a day like today.

"Sorry Sheriff. I was just letting the office know I would be leaving today."

"Everything alright, son?"

"Yeah. But Amy is a mess today, and our parents thought she could use a little time at home."

"I understand that. I have hope we will find her. My Katie is smart. Do you want an escort?"

God, no.

"I think we will manage but thank you Sheriff. I have faith we will find Katie too." I gave him a small smile and headed into the office.

After a long ten-minute discussion, I convinced the office that Amy wasn't with me to sign out because she was sick and throwing up in the bathroom. They finally gave us check out passes, and I headed out, keys in hand.

I didn't want to get reemed for not having passes. It wouldn't look right. So now that I had them, I headed out to the parking lot, and drove the small bend over to the edge of the forest.

At first glance, I didn't see Amy, but that was good. I honked to let her know I was there, and I got out to open the trunk. I had a small blanket back there which was key for hiding Kim. I ran over to the edge and saw Amy struggling with pulling Kim's dead weight.

I grabbed Kim's arms and Amy got the legs. I looked around once more to ensure that no one was around, and we quickly pulled her into the trunk and covered her well.

We loaded into the car and started home. "What a day huh?" Amy started laughing hysterically, and I knew the events of the past two days were getting to her. Usually we were more careful than this, but both times we were offered no choice. Well, there was a choice, and I chose to stand by my family. Always.

"Yeah. Try and play it cool for Mom and Dad."

We pulled up to the familiar gates, and had George buzz us in. We parked right by the back-basement door, so we could slip in Kim easily. The door was open coincidentally, and we ran into my dad who looked equally shocked. I told him we would explain later, and we carried Kim down the stairs.

We brought her in, chained her wrist, and Amy turned towards Katie and Tara.

"Enjoy your new houseguest."

And we left without another word.

16

Katie

Amy's words were on a constant loop in my head, as I struggled with the silence that I found myself basked in. This room was quiet as is, and Tara wasn't much of the type to try and strike up a conversation. Kim was still out.

My interactions with Amy were very limited, but it gave me a lot more insight into who my best friend really was. She was a disgusting, immoral excuse for a human being. They all were, and the worst part was that the only way I would get out of here, the only way I would survive- was to act like I still loved them.

I wanted nothing to do with this entire family, and I hoped I had the chance to escape soon. I needed to create a plan, but it was hard. There was no constant down here. There seemed to be no solid schedule that I could base my plan off of. Everything was haphazardly done, like they were winging it a little. Maybe I could use that.

Tara didn't even look my way again since they brought Kim, and I found myself feeling glad. I couldn't face her, or anyone for that matter. This room, this Iron Room, had a way of making me feel so bare and exposed. I was vulnerable, and I didn't like it.

I couldn't help myself from thinking about my father, and everything he was going through.

I'm so sorry.

Clank. Clank. Clank.

I looked to my side, and saw that Kim was waking up. I couldn't understand why they took her. I remembered her vaguely from school but that was it.

I glanced at Tara, hoping she would step up to the plate and be the one to explain to Kim what had happened, but she had her head buried in her knees.

Looks like it's me.

"What happened? Where the hell am I?" Kim frantically shifted her body and was trying to pull the chains off her hand.

"Calm down, please. I'll tell you everything." I had no idea what to say to someone who had just been kidnapped, given that my welcome party wasn't exactly... welcoming.

She didn't say another word, but rather just stared at me. Terror was clear in her eyes, grief plastered across her face. I sympathized, and I knew those emotions all too well. I hadn't stopped feeling them since I was kidnapped and thrown in here. These people were ruthless, taking anyone who they deemed a threat to them and their perfect family.

What do I say here?

"I just got here, but Tara... and Anna both told me that the whole family is in on... whatever this is. I don't know why they took you, but I'm sorry." I felt an overwhelming sense of guilt regardless of whether it was my fault or not."

"But Anna is dead... right?"

"Yeah she is..."

"I overheard Amy and Mark talking. I had my suspicions about them, so I followed them and recorded them. I was heading to the school to show your dad when they caught me." She started to cry, and I had no way of comforting her.

My dad?

"My dad was at the school?"

"Yeah, he was talking to kids and the principal."

My heart.

I felt crushed. I knew in my heart that my dad would obviously look for me but hearing about it only made it worse. I wanted more than anything to reach out and assure him I was okay. I felt like a little girl all of a sudden, vulnerable, and wanting my dad. I lacked comfort, and this place made sure of that.

This place thrived on creating an uncomfortable, and cold environment. This family relied on torture to keep their victims in line, and to satisfy their own psychotic cravings.

"I'm sorry you're here, Kim. I know you were only trying to help."

"You too, right? How did you end up here?"

"I was getting too close to the truth, so Mark drugged me, and I woke up here."

My truth was met with a range of silence throughout the room. In some ways, Kim and I were similar in terms of the reasons why we were taken. We knew too much.

The crazy part was that I didn't truly feel like I knew anything, not at that moment in time anyhow. I only said that I wasn't going to stop looking for Anna and Tara, and that was enough for the niceties to go out the window, and for Mark to decide that I had become a liability and needed to be taken care of.

Like clockwork, my thoughts were interrupted by the familiar chains unlocking and a swing of the iron door. To my surprise, Sharon walked in. She was followed by Amy, who kind of hung back by the door not saying or doing much.

No words were said, but Sharon walked over to Tara and kicked her in the side without warning. Tara had no time to recover from the blow because Sharon delivered another one, right to the side of Tara's face.

Stop it!

I wanted to protest and opened my mouth to speak but no words came out. I was dumbfounded, at Sharon in general and at the utter lack of respect for these people down here. Jesus Christ. They treated all of us like...

Prisoners. Isn't that what you are Katie?

I finally found my voice, but not before I felt something connect with my cheek. I was rocked back to the pole and looked up at my attacker. Amy. She had slugged me right in the face.

I had an upper hand on the other girls, in that I had my chains around my ankle rather than my wrist. I swung my leg out far, catching Amy's and she toppled over next to me.

I swung and connected, over and over, hitting until I couldn't anymore. Amy was bleeding and pulling herself away.

"You fucking bitch! I was your friend, and you put me down here. You're all nuts!"

Sharon had stopped her brutal attack on Tara long enough to realize that I beat the hell out of Amy and marched over to me. She helped her daughter up off the ground and stepped right on my ankle. I felt and heard a crack, and the pain was excruciating. *She broke my ankle.*

Amy hobbled off, using her mom's shoulder as a crutch. They headed towards the door. Before the two exited, Amy turned around and delivered a final menacing glare.

Yeah, you're screwed now.

They slammed the door and locked it. I was pretty sure my chain would be switched from ankle to wrist now, but knowing how sick these people were, they would probably opt to keep it around my ankle now that it was broken. How the hell would I escape with this?

Hitting Amy over and over was the greatest feeling. I am not one for violence, nor have I ever been, but after she hit me, the rage came out. This family has lied to my face and played niceties with me for years. Meanwhile, they had some sick torture show going on down here.

And I was the new victim.

17

Amy

My mom helped me up the stairs, locked the door, and I leaned on her while we walked to the house. I could feel blood pooling in my sneakers as it dripped from my face.

I couldn't believe Katie hit me.

I'm more surprised that she had it in her.

Unfortunately, there was no room in the iron room for vengeance, on us at least. My mom was angrier than I was, threatening to kill Katie the next time she saw her. I knew it was only because my betrayal hit the hardest out of all of us.

I only hit her because I had to. While I welcomed the unloading of anger onto these girls as I see fit, Katie was only a means to an end. It was a requirement. She should have never been in this place.

I was nursing a killer headache, and my face went slack. I think she may have broken my nose, but I have had worse. I think my mom broke her ankle on the way out, and I felt slightly bad. I mean, she kind of deserved it after that attack, but still.

My mom was in kind of a bad mood all day, but it brightened to my surprise when she found out we had a new victim joining us. My dad was also slightly excited, but still stewing about Katie's capture. I had to fill them in on Sheriff Johnson's little impromptu visit to the school today.

It wasn't out of the ordinary, given that was what he also did when Anna then Tara went missing. It seems like with his daughter, he would be out conducting a search party, but he was following procedure to a tee. I knew he was probably torn up inside about the whole thing, but there was nothing we could do- not without breaking up our family and everything we have worked for.

We got into the house, and my dad took one look at my face, and freaked out.

"What the hell happened to Amy's face?"

"That little bitch Katie got her on the floor and punched the crap out of her. That's what happened! But don't worry Paul, she got her own."

"She's angry, Sharon! What do you expect?"

"I expect her to fall in line like the rest of them. We don't support vigilantes in this house Paul. I'm sure the broken ankle she's nursing right now will only make that message that more clear."

My dad walked away fuming. He had expressed earlier today that harming Katie in any shape or form would be detrimental and that she should remain untouched. We couldn't do that though. It had to be done.

My mom pulled me into the bathroom off to the side of the kitchen and began cleaning the blood off of my face. She deduced that it had all been coming from my nose, but that it wasn't broken.

I'll probably be sporting a black eye tomorrow though.

Once my mother was done with her assessment, she left me to deal with the thoughts raging in my head.

Everything was falling apart.

My mom and dad could be heard shouting at each other from the other room. They never usually fought, but coincidentally had been doing it a lot more as of late. I wonder why. Mark was still holed up in his room, beside himself.

The thing with Mark is that he understood what had to be done, and he would do it without question. His emotions were hard to control, and sometimes like today, they got the best of him. I usually was able to pull him out of it.

I headed up to his room, dead set on cheering my brother up. There were times, not often, when I myself felt conflicted, but I also knew that these girls deserved it. They all did. Maybe not Katie, but it was too little too late.

I reached his room and knocked softly on the door. Sometimes Mark took a nap in the middle of the day, so if he was, I didn't want to wake him. No answer. I cracked the door open and sure enough he was out like a light. I closed the door softly and went into my room.

Maybe a nap wasn't a bad idea. I laid my head down and dozed off.

I dreamed of the time Katie and I decided to cut class and spend the day out by the river. Life was good. Her mom was alive. We were drinking and watching the stream pass by. I miss it.

"Amy, wake up."

I woke up to my mom shaking me awake. I rolled over and glanced at the alarm clock, it was 5:21. I was asleep for two hours, clearly exhausted from the events of the day.

"It's dinner time baby."

I clutched my stomach, not realizing how hungry I was. I didn't eat much at breakfast due to the commotion, and lunch was absent. I smelled my mom's famous meatloaf wafting through the air.

I pulled myself out of bed and joined my mom in walking down the stairs. I noticed that Mark's room was wide open. He must have already been downstairs.

My mom seemed to be in lighter spirits compared to what happened that morning. I was assuming her and my dad finally patched things up. We were all at a standstill when it came to Katie and what to do with her.

It was causing a rift in this family that was distracting us from our work. We needed to all get along in order to do what was necessary- what was right.

We should be in a happier mood, all of us. We had a new victim after all! It is a surprise that it didn't happen sooner. Kim was always nosy, and rarely made friends. She was a loser.

When we walked into the dining room, the spread was stretched from both ends. The meal was complete with mashed potatoes, green beans, chicken filets, pasta, meatloaf, and even rolls. My mom really knew how to roll out all the good stuff.

My dad was sitting at the head of the table per usual, and he seemed to be in a better mood as well as my mom. Mark was in his usual seat opposite me looking well rested. I was so glad to see my family getting along.

My mother and I took our seats, and my dad opened his mouth to make a speech.

"I just want to express my gratitude for all of us to be able to sit around this table tonight. For us to go through hell the past few days and come out of it better than ever- and as a family. I know we have all had different views on whether or not Katie should be here. I want you two to know that your mother and I spoke it over and agreed that Katie will stay here. We simply cannot risk letting her go. She will need to straighten out her behavior. Any other attacks on any of the family members, and she is gone. Now I want everyone to enjoy the meal that was made, and remember this: What we do, we do together as a family. Always."

My dad took his seat, and right on cue we all tucked into our meals.

This delicious dinner was a welcome distraction from the world of troubles I felt immersed in. I enjoyed every sinful bite, and my worries melted away. I was sure to be in for a world of homework tomorrow after dipping out early.

I needed to clear the air with Katie. I wanted to talk to her after dinner and knew my parents wouldn't be okay with it.

So, I would wait until later.

I knew after dinner my mom brought food to the girls. I would have to wait until everyone turned in to bed. I ate the rest of my meal in silence. We all had copies of the keys for the doors, but I would need to fly under the radar for this plan.

Once I finished dinner, I passed on dessert. I couldn't spend another minute with my family acting like I was okay with Katie being here. I knew she had to be, but I wanted to talk to her. I had to tell her I was sorry, and that I never meant for her to end up here. If she knew the truth, and saw I was still the same person, maybe she wouldn't hate me as much.

I planned to take my keys and go out through the back so George wouldn't see anything. He did sign an NDA but had undying loyalty to my parents and this family. If he saw me doing something sneaky after dark, he was sure to spill the beans. I didn't want to be the subject of my parents never ending questions.

I excused myself and headed up my bedroom. Thankfully for me, my parents went to bed early. I was sure that the staff was cleaning up the kitchen now, and that my mom was preparing a bad meal for the girls. I wished Katie could be in this house- with us.

Her attack on me today only furthered my earlier thought that she could potentially be one of us, join our group. I was sure I could convince my best friend of her true potential once I was able to talk to her alone.

Plus, two prying eyes and listening ears.

Yeah, those bitches.

I laid down in my room and turned on my laptop. I should do some homework, but rather decided to indulge myself in an episode of Paradise Hotel. It was a new show, and I loved all the raunchy and crazy drama. It made me feel better about my own life.

Tyler is hot!

I had set an alarm just in case I fell asleep. I set it for eleven o'clock. It didn't seem that late, but my parents turned in around nine thirty and I figured eleven was a great time to attempt this.

I was halfway through the episode, when Mark knocked on my door.

"Come in."

He opened the door, smiled, and came and sat on the edge of my bed.

"I wanted to just make sure that you were okay. You seemed off at dinner."

"I'm fine. Just wanted some time for me."

He didn't say anything but regarded me carefully. My brother and I were always nothing but honest with each other.

I could tell he didn't believe me, but I didn't really care.

He looked over at my laptop and laughed. "This garbage?"

He hated reality television shows, and that only made me love them more.

"Yes Mark, this garbage. Now please leave and let me enjoy it." I laughed, knowing he wanted nothing more than to get away from it.

"Let me know if you need anything, Ames."

He shut my door softly and I could hear his feet padding across the hallway. The door shut. I didn't want to have to lie to him, but I needed to. I didn't really know where Mark stood at this point in time in terms of Katie being here, and Mark was already sort of a wild card. I didn't know if he would support me or turn me in. I needed to keep a distance and sort my emotions about this out by myself first.

I pressed play, and sure enough started to drift off again before the episode was over.

Beep. Beep. Beep.

My alarm was going off, and I shut it off in a panic, praying that no one had heard it going off. The only person who truly had any chance of hearing it was Mark, and I doubted it. Still, I wanted to be safe, and waited another five minutes before leaving my room. I left a few pillows under the blankets, and softly closed my door.

I was heading down the stairs slowly, taking it step by step. Thankfully, we had no creaky boards in this house. I got all the way to the back door, did a quick look around, and was glad to see that there was no one there.

I padded across the grass and pulled my keys out of my pajama pants when I finally got to the familiar door. I unlocked it, headed down the stone steps, and unlocked the large iron door.

When I swung the door open, I was greeted with one pair of eyes- Katie's.

The other two were sound asleep, and I found myself feeling internally grateful. Usually I liked my subjects to be sentient and receptive, but I wasn't here for that. I was here for my best friend, who I knew without a doubt now hated me.

I just had to change that.

"Katie…"

"Amy, don't. You made it pretty clear that this friendship was done when you let your brother kidnap me and stick me down here. You cemented that when you came in here and clocked me."

I hung my head down in shame. She was right. I had no choice though!

"Katie, I had no choice. My family and I…"

She cut me off. "You and your family are a bunch of rich losers who have nothing better to do."

I walked towards her and bent down keeping a safe distance in case she wanted to go full John Wick on me. I opened my mouth to speak, when she spit in my face. Literally.

I pulled myself up, realizing any friendship we had was truly lost. I needed to stop thinking of her as such.

"You really shouldn't have done that, Katie."

18

Mark

I was unsure of what my sister was doing, but she was sure as hell up to something. I heard her come inside ten minutes ago, and she slammed her door pretty hard.

Who was I kidding? She went to see Katie. I wasn't sure of their status at this point. Either they were still friends or hated each other's guts. I knew Katie was probably upset with Amy, with all of us really.

Maybe Amy was done with her. Something like this could surely sever a friendship, but I hoped that Katie and I could remain friends, or more than that.

I had come up with a plan. It wasn't a rather good one, or very effective, but it needed to be done. This business my family and I have going on has nothing to do with Katie, and I never should have brought her into this world. I made a mistake, and I was the only one who could fix it.

If I did this, my family would hate me forever. They would probably kick me out, or worse we would all be cell mates in prison.

I wanted to wait at least another hour or so before I headed out to the basement. I hoped that the other two girls would be sleeping so it would give Katie and I a chance to finally talk. I needed Amy to be asleep when this happened, so I figured the waiting game was my best bet.

I decided to kill time with a book. Reading was my favorite pastime, and I settled on something scary as a way to pull me out of my current nightmare- reality. I opened up the tattered, old book and started reading.

I had read and re-read this book so many times, and I never grew tired of it. The story, the characters, and the dialog pulled me in and kept me there until the very end. Truth is, I had lost the time to sit down and read a good book especially since I first took Anna.

Who knew having kidnap victims would be a full-time job?

Not me, that's for sure. I feel like since my family and I started this whole thing, I have lost part of myself along the way. Sure, I hate when girls treat me like crap or disrespect me. I like to watch them get tortured sometimes. That doesn't make me a monster though? It doesn't make me invalid of having feelings? I have feelings towards Katie, real ones, so I can't be all that bad right?

I was about to do something for the greater good, putting aside the very real and very serious consequences that it could potentially have on my family. That made me a good person.

Before I knew it, I found myself lost in the world of necromancers, werewolves, and witches. The supernatural fantasy world was one of my absolute favorite genres. It never failed to interest me, and this series was one of my favorites.

Mom and Dad had always insisted on getting me brand new copies of the books, but to me there was nothing better than the smell and feel of an old book.

When I saw that I was about two hundred pages in, I decided to call it a night- with the reading. I still had something I needed to do.

I put a bookmark in and tucked the book into the shelf on my reading corner. I slid on my converse, pulled on a dark hooded sweatshirt, and very carefully opened my door.

I practically tiptoed out, and all but held my breath going down the stairs. Sneaking around was hard when you were six foot one.

I reached the bottom step after what felt like an hour long walk and breathed a loud sigh of relief. Hard part was over. The nice thing about having freshly groomed and well-maintained grass was that it was soft and practically silent as you walked across it.

I opened the back door and closed it with the utmost care. I did a brisk walk across the large yard, mostly because I knew my parent's bedroom had a clear line of sight into the backyard, and I didn't want to screw my chances up now. Not when I was so close to making things right.

You got this.

I finally got to the all too familiar back door. I opened it with my keys and tiptoed down the steps. If they were all asleep, I didn't want to wake them, only Katie. The other two could go to hell.

I got to the big iron door and rolled my eyes at the chains. These things always make a ruckus, and that was the last thing I needed right now. I made a mental note to ask dad to switch these out, but who knew if he would ever talk to me again after tonight.

I was able to get the chain undone, and I crept inside. To my surprise, Katie was the only one awake, and she looked mad.

"Two for one deal, huh? I already told your sister."

Amy came here, like I thought.

I walked over to her and sat down. This was a risky move given that she nearly beat Amy to death. I decided to take my chances, knowing that deep down in Katie's heart, that she could never truly hurt me.

"I wanted to talk."

"About what?" Katie looked disgusted with me, and I will admit that it bugged me way more than it should.

"That I'm sorry for everything, and for what I did. You don't deserve to be down here. You deserve to be free, and I took that from you. But I want you to know that I trust that you won't say anything about us to anyone."

"What are you talking about?" She looked confused, and I realized my mistake. I didn't even tell her the good news yet.

"Where are my manners? I left out the best part. I'm letting you go."

"You are?" She looked overwhelmed, but I was sure she would have jumped for joy had she not been shackled down and with a broken ankle.

I can't believe my mom did that to her.
"I am. But there's something else."
"And what is that? What more could you or your family possibly want from me?"
"They don't know. But I love you Katie. I want us to be together."

She looked puzzled for a moment, and then considerate as if she was mentally picturing the idea of the two of us together. It can't come as a shock to her, given that practically anyone and everyone in this town knows the magnitude of my feelings toward her.

Katie was such a beautiful light, and people liked her not because her dad was the Sheriff, but because she was genuinely an amazing person. I loved her so much and had since the day I saw her. "I would like that, Mark. Let's get out of here before anyone sees me."

I realized she was right, and that our talk had gone on far longer than I originally planned. I started to unshackle her, and I helped her to her feet. She leaned all her weight on me as she tried to get up the stairs with essentially only one good foot.

We made it all the way to the top, and I helped her sit while I locked up the door downstairs, and the one upstairs. It took me about a minute, and I was finally locking up the door when I felt something hard crack down on the back of my head.

I fell forward, clutching the back of my skull in pain. She tricked me. My only stipulation of letting her go was that we were going to be together, as a couple. If she didn't want that then she wasn't getting out of here. I knew I had to get up, but the pain shooting through my entire head made it nearly impossible to get up, but I had to.

I managed to pull myself up off the wet grass, discouraged knowing she probably got a good head start. I remembered her ankle and laughed to myself. *Biting the hand that fed you? Not a good choice Katie.*

I sprinted towards the front, knowing that was really the only way out. Katie was soon in my line of sight, and she was almost about to clear the front gate when a hand shot out of the gate attendant box and grabbed her. *George.*

19

Katie

I was almost there. I could see the gate.

I felt an arm grab my shoulder back, and all those promising thoughts slipped away instantly. My initial thought was that I didn't hit Mark hard enough, but when I turned to the side and saw George, the gate attendant holding me, my heart sank.

He was in on this too.

And I had just blew my last chance at getting out of here. I didn't play it smart. I laid all my cards on the table much too early, and now there was no way in hell that Amy or Mark would willingly be my ticket out of this hell hole.

"Leaving so soon?" George sang voice full of malice. His eyes looked glazed over, and his grip on my arm was starting to hurt.

"I'll take it from here George." Mark came over, hand rubbing the back of his head.

"And risk the chance of letting her get away again? No thanks. In fact, I think I will let your parents in on this one. Might have a shot at getting a raise. Gate attendant to kidnap capturer should come with a steady pay increase, no?"

Mark looked extremely irritable and pushed his hair out of his face. The back of his head looked bloody, and my heart panged with guilt. I knew I shouldn't feel guilty, but I was nothing like these people. I didn't crave violence. Hurting anyone, even if they did deserve it, felt wrong.

"Sorry about the head Mark."

His eyes shot to me, clearly still pissed about the whole thing. He didn't even give me the satisfaction of a response but started to head into the house with George pushing me to follow.

Let's wake up Mommy and Daddy Psycho. Fun!

George seemed absolutely delighted with himself, like a little boy on the river with his dad for the first time, who caught his first large fish. That's exactly what I was. The fact that George was the one to stop me before I was able to escape would be seen as a victory, one worthy of a prize. I'm assuming George enjoyed the cash prizes best.

We walked into the giant foyer, and neither George nor Mark had the pleasure of waking up Sharon and Paul. They were already awake- and angry.

"Would someone like to tell me what the hell is going on? Mark why are you bleeding? Why is George away from the post? And why the hell is Katie free?" Sharon looked from Mark, to George, and then to me. If she was expecting me to speak to her after I have seen her little shop of horrors, she was out of her mind.

Mark was the first to speak but was cut off swiftly by George.

"Allow me, Mrs. Puntzer. Mark tried to free Katie, but she turned on him and tried to hit him in the head. She was able to get all the way to the gate, where I grabbed her." George finished up his story with a bow, and I wanted more than anything to wipe that little smug look of his face.

If my ankle wasn't broken...

I had forgotten about my ankle until now. Adrenaline and fear will do that to you, I guess. It was now a sharp throbbing pain, and George was putting a lot of weight onto that side of my body.

"Is this true Mark?" Mr. Puntzer looked at his son, who looked guilty.

"Yeah apparently this is what happens when you kidnap someone out of love... or was it purely fear Mark? Fear that I was getting too close to this sick family torture shop?" I opened my mouth to further my verbal beatdown but was interrupted by a harsh slap delivered by Sharon.

"Shut your mouth. Paul, take Katie back to where she belongs- her room with the other sluts."

I couldn't believe my ears. I mean I could, because at this point every horrible thing this family continued to do really wasn't shocking me. Rather, it was furthering my assessment I made when I first realized where I was. They're all nuts.

Mr. Puntzer grabbed my shoulder and kept a firm hand as he walked me back to the room. He was taking his time, making sure not to put any weight onto me. If I was crazy, I would have thought he was trying to avoid hurting my ankle further. But those who tortured people had no empathy, and Paul tortured people. Him and his sick family tortured girls for their own enjoyment.

He unlocked the door, and I had to stop myself from breaking down. To be this close to freedom, even after a short period of time, and then have it taken away from you was soul crushing. I felt weak, vulnerable, and terrified as I spent my days locked in this room with these girls.

I would not allow myself to cry in front of Paul, or any of them for that matter. They were not worth my tears, and I would be damned if I let any of them see that I was absolutely broken inside. I was hanging on by a thread, and that was the hope that I would one day get to see my father's face again, to hear him laugh once more.

I had dug my grave so deep with both Amy and Mark, that there was zero chance of reconciliation and sure as hell no chance of them trying to help me- not that Amy ever did.

He pushed me into the room and shackled my arm.

This time, both Tara and Kim were wide awake, and staring at Paul most likely trying to figure out what his next plan would be.

Don't worry girls. They all want to hurt me now.

I knew that the next time one of them came down here, it would be to hurt me. I needed to mentally prepare myself for that and create a new plan.

I knew I couldn't rely on them to get me out, but instead myself. I would take whatever they wanted to do with me in stride, and not mouth off. I had to let them think they had won, and that I had accepted my role as their prisoner.

Not that I would ever be okay with playing house with sociopaths.

Paul turned to leave, but then did a three sixty and crouched down next to me, keeping a distance of course.

"If you want to survive here, you keep your head down, mouth shut. Got it?"

His voice lacked anger or malice but was firm. He meant what he said. What I couldn't figure out is if it was said to help me, or to warn me.

He headed outside, and I could hear him locking the doors.

"What happened Katie? Tara and I woke up and you were gone?" Kim had a single tear rolling down her cheek, and I knew she was scared. I was too.

"Mark tried to let me out, and I turned on him by attacking him with a rock. I made it all the way to the gate before George got me..."

"Who is George?" Tara meekly spoke, and I was taken aback given that she rarely said anything.

"Their gate attendant."

Both girls let out a whoosh, and I knew what they were thinking. It was exactly the same thing that flew through my head, as I saw whose arm was holding mine. We're screwed, because we don't have a single person on this property who would help us.

"We have to do something. We need a plan." Kim looked around, waiting for confirmation from either Tara or myself.

"I'm in," I said without an ounce of hesitation. If we were able to put our brains together, I knew we would be able to come up with a plan that had the potential to be solid enough to spring all of us from here.

"Don't you get it? There is no "out of here". This is it. Anna never got to leave, and neither will we. They will use us until we're not needed, and then it's light out."

Was Tara actually right?

I knew Tara had spent more time down here than myself or Kim combined. But how could she lose every shred of hope that there is a chance we can get out of here? Maybe any she had was lost when they killed Anna right in front of us. Whatever Tara's reasons were, while they were understandable, needed to be changed.

This plan, whatever it may be, would only work if all three of us worked together. There were five of them including George, and three of us. The odds were already pretty bad, and our chances slim. Our chances would be absolutely obliterated if Tara refused.

"Tara, we really need you on board." I attempted to plead with her, but it looked like it was useless.

"On board with what? Do you even have a plan Katie?"

"Well, not yet. But we just need time."

"Time for them to kill us. You're not getting it. I can't listen to this anymore. I need to go to sleep."

Leaving us with that, Tara laid down facing away from us.

We needed her help.

Kim looked at me, shrugged, and followed suit by laying down on the ground. I knew I should probably get some sleep too, as I was suddenly overcome with exhaustion, but I was also simultaneously wide awake.

I laid down and forced myself to close my eyes at a half assed attempt at sleep. With my eyes closed, I still found myself facing the same horrors I had whilst awake.

My head was a constant loop of tonight's antics- Amy seeing me, spitting in her face, Mark's visit, realizing I had a shot of getting out, hitting him...

...and George grabbing me. In a way, it was good knowing where he now stands in terms of my disappearance. He was on their side and would definitely not hesitate to halt my escape efforts again. This run in tonight offered me a chance at thinking smarter.

Next time, I would run the other way. The woods were thick behind their home, but it would allow me the chance to have plenty of coverage should I need to hide and find my way to an open road before George, or anyone else saw me.

Now the only issue was trying to get out again.

There was no doubt that these psychos would be amping up appearances down here, and I was sure that skeevy George was doing a perimeter check right now to ensure that the little captives were right where they needed to be.

I couldn't wait to see this family in handcuffs. Being prisoners... like me.

My eyes fluttered back open, as I found myself unable to keep them closed anymore. The room was now pitch black, and I realized that the small little light on the wall was time sensitive. It was either that, or they were controlling when it went on and off. Given that there were no windows down here, it could get kind of dark like all the time.

Somehow, the light went off right when it was about time to go to sleep, I'm assuming. I don't really have a keen sense of time down here anyways.

I stared up at what I assumed to be the ceiling in absolute shock. These past few days have been such an absolute whirlwind, that I found myself unable to properly process all the emotions going through my mind.

Perhaps that was a good thing, as it allowed me to focus on anything other than my dad. The feeling of captivity, of having no idea what happened next, possessing zero control, it was the worst torture of all.

Knowing who put me here was worse.

I rolled my head over and noticed a small red down on the wall. Better yet, it was a red dot coming *out* of the wall. A camera.

They were watching us.

20

Amy

Seems to me like it turned out to be *quite* the night yesterday after I turned in. I was woken up by the sounds coming from downstairs. Apparently, Mark had snuck out to be with Katie, better yet, to release her.

I don't know what the hell was going through his head. In what way did he think that this could help us? Katie would without a doubt run straight to her dad and uncover all the secrets she thinks she knows about us.

Funny thing is that she doesn't know half of what she thinks she does. She knows what we allow her to know.

I had hoped there was some chance at reconciliation between my best friend and I, but the spit I got in my face last night proved otherwise. That was fine. Now, I could focus on what we needed to do without my judgement clouding my mind. As of right now, there was not a single girl in the Iron Room that I cared about. They were all the same. Business.

Weirdly enough, the oddest thing of last night's spectacle was the fact that George helped out. I knew he signed an NDA drafted by my parents, but I was sure that "retrieving kidnap victims" wasn't a separate clause. I still didn't know if he knew fully about what was going on or felt the need to help out last night.

Whatever George's reasons were, my parents were keeping their mouths shut regarding the whole situation which was fine by me. The less I knew the better. My parents thrived on secrets, and sometimes I felt best to leave it up to them. I was stressed out enough with all that was on my plate.

I had to go to school today and face the mob. There would without a doubt be a ton of questions, weird stares, and people wondering why Mark and I left early yesterday. I reminded myself that I was supposed to be the grieving best friend.

Keep your head down and look sad. Easy.

I dressed in my best attire, as I always did. No outfit was complete without bold jewelry, so I decided to wear my dangly diamond earrings today. Over the top? Probably. Did I care? No.

Most people decided to drown their sorrows with food or booze. Me? I always opted for an overdose of fashion.

After I was ready, I headed downstairs for the mandatory family breakfast. I could breathe easy knowing I wouldn't be the subject of Mom and Dad's persecution, today at least.

Usually I would wait with Mark, and we would go down together. Today, I was a little upset with him and his stupidity that was causing issues for us. We would crumble if one of us started to make mistakes. Making them accidentally was one thing, but deliberately? Come on Mark.

Walking into the dining room brought me a weird sense of dread. Mom and Dad were already at the table, looking terse and the mood was tense. Mark looked down and ate his food, no words being said. *Maybe McDonalds would be a better option today.* "Amy. So nice of you to join us. Take a seat." My mom motioned to the last open seat, and I cautiously took it. She was eerily calm.

"I wanted to talk to everyone about last night. Mark made a grave mistake that could have proved quite disastrous for all of us. He knows he made a mistake, and from now on, we will only go into the room in pairs. That way there will be no "helping" these girls. Am I clear?"

We all nodded in agreement. My mom meant business, and we knew that. I only hoped that Mark was serious and truly meant what he said when he told my mother that he realized last night was a mistake. Next time, we wouldn't be so lucky. *Thank god for George.*

My mother continued,

"Now, both you and Mark need to go to school today. Look sad. Be believable, and for the love of God, do not take any girls today. That girl suspected you guys. You need to be a lot more careful, lay low, and especially keep a low profile. Most everyone will think you're grieving. But Katie and Kim are not the only students trying to investigate."

With that being said, I excused myself and went to grab my book bag, and phone. I waited by the front door for Mark to finish his breakfast, so he could take me to school. I didn't need to be late.

Time passed slowly, but finally Mark was at the door, keys in hand.

"We have to talk," Mark said as he opened the front door.

"No kidding."

I went outside and headed to the passenger side of his car as he locked the front door.

He pressed the unlock button on his remote, and I climbed in. I don't know what else he felt that he could tell me. I knew all I wanted to know. He risked everything we have built, and the freedom of this family over a stupid little crush. She was my best friend, and even I wasn't thick enough to believe that she wouldn't screw us over.

I buckled my seat belt as Mark stepped into the car. He started it and threw the car into reverse before finally speaking.

"I'm sorry Amy. I know I made a mistake."

"Do you though? You could have destroyed our family if she actually got away. I know you feel guilty for taking her in the first place, and I don't know if it's the room, the situation or if Katie was always this way, but she's changed. She doesn't care about us, Mark. We cannot care about her."

"I know that now."

He rubbed the back of his head, clearly still sore. Katie has a better arm on her than I thought.

"There's something else Ames."

"And that is?"

"She saw the camera." Mark looked nervous, and his knuckles grew white as we grabbed the steering wheel that much harder.

"How do you know?"

"I was watching the footage from last night, and she turned and looked directly at it. The sensor light was off, so I assume it was the bright red light that tipped her off."

I considered the new information carefully, only to realize it wasn't that much of a big deal. So, Katie knew about the camera… who cares?

There was nothing she could do about it, and any information she learned down there about us would only die with her later on.

You're not thinking of killing her.

Of course, I'm not thinking about it. But it is a very viable possibility. If Katie continues the way she is, trying to hurt us and get out then it was inevitable. I didn't try to look too much into the future, but where did this whole charade end? Maybe in a few years when Mark and I were at college, my parents would stop. Surely Katie's future didn't have a promising end or guarantee at this point in time.

"Maybe she will act accordingly now, knowing her actions are on film."

The rest of the ride was silence. Mark may say that he is on board with everything but adding Katie to the mix has put a chink in his armor. It is destroying him, and as long as I wasn't around when he blew up, all would be fine. He would be okay… I knew he would.

Mark was a truly complex personality. He wore his heart on his sleeve, but if you disrespected or ignored that, he turned lethal. I guess our entire family was like that. We were all able to put on a good front. But our actions and intentions were almost always sinister.

You're completely fucked up.

We arrived at school and I felt the familiar sense of dread begin to trickle in. Mark and I went our separate ways as soon as he parked. We both just needed some time to ourselves to process everything and do some reflecting. Mark and I had always been really close, so I knew exactly what was going through his head right now. He was struggling, but he had before, and he always came out on top. I had faith that my brother would continue to do the right thing for our family.

I had faith in him… always.

I knew Kim's mom had to realize she was missing. Yet, nobody had said anything so I knew I would hear about it today. There was no trace. We made sure of that when we destroyed her phone. I did note that Sheriff Johnson's car was in the parking lot, so he would surely be making his rounds to see all the teachers and talk to them. Hopefully a correlation between the time she went missing, and Mark and I's sudden absence wouldn't be drawn up.

Chemistry time. I took my seat and waited for Mr. Aryn to start his lecture about… chemistry stuff. I tuned out in the class and will be the first to admit that I used the internet to help cheat my way through his long homework assignment last night. I knew that Chemistry wasn't my strong suit, and that was okay with me.

My passion was writing, and anything in the English department. I just needed to fake it until I made it… "it" being my diploma.

Per usual, Mr. Aryn had us pass our previous night's homework up towards the front, as he collected all of them and slid it into a folder labeled "Period One". He then turned on the overhead projector with his book under it.

We continued the rest of the class period doing group reading. My group was okay, and I could hardly call it group work considering the fact that we all read silently, and then completed the in-class questions on our own.

Better for me anyways, I hate small talk.

The bell rang, and I was already on my feet heading out the door. Mr. Aryn had let us know that since it was his anniversary today, that he would share the love with no homework.

Gee, thanks.

I was in the hallway, and like expected, everyone was in small groups huddled, probably talking about Kim, nonetheless.

We did you a favor! She was a nosy wannabe who had zero social skills.

I headed into my next class, Calculus. The class itself was not that bad if not for my idiot seat partner.

Johnny.

He was sitting in his seat, actually looking smug. I had no clue what he was feeling so smug about, but I have no doubt that he was about to let me know.

I sat in my seat and he turned to look at me. "What?"

"Nothing." Johnny laughed, and turned back to face the front of the room where the teacher had started her lesson. I threw my attention fully into the lesson plan and was completing some bookwork and problems when she came by my seat, and gave her approval letting me know I was indeed on the right track.

At least something in my life is going good for me.

I could feel Johnny's eyes on me, and I was trying my hardest to avoid giving him the satisfaction of me looking. I continued to do my work dutifully until I couldn't take it any longer.

"Seriously Johnny. What the hell is your deal?"

"Did you know that I am a great voice impersonator?" He laughed.

"No, nor do I care. Your point?"

"My point Amy, is that it was so easy to call the phone company and convince them I was Sheriff Johnson wanting to see Katie's phone records…"

My throat went dry, but I kept my cool.

"…and imagine my surprise when your brother was supposed to meet her in a dark park at eleven at night. In fact, I will place all my bets that he was the last person to see her."

21

Mark

I don't know what was so important to tell me, that I needed to be late to my third period class. But here I was, waiting for Amy by the bleachers. Our parents had been pretty clear this morning in making sure we both knew to act as normal as possible.

I looked to my left and saw Amy approaching. She looked panicked, and the worry began to set in. If something was really wrong, I would want to know. "Ames, are you okay?"

"No." Amy handed me a paper, and I wasn't sure what exactly it was supposed to be. It seemed like a bill from a phone company, but I flipped to the backside and saw that it was the past few messages between Katie and I where we clearly discussed a plan to meet that night.

Holy shit.

"Where did you get this?" I prayed to God that my sister got it herself, and that someone didn't dig this up.

"Johnny Antin."

Johnny Antin? That freaking creep? Why would he ever go to such lengths to find Katie's phone records? Was he searching for the girls too? Did he show this to anyone else? Was he threatening to tell? Did he always suspect me, or did this start it?

"Mark…"

I crumpled the paper, shoved it in my pocket, and started towards the school.

"Mark!" My sister yelled my name, but there was no talking any sense to me right now. If Johnny was trying to start a war, he just did.

"I'm going to take care of it, Amy!"

I stomped into the school, sweeping the halls for Johnny, but alas no sign of him or anyone for that matter. Third period started, and I knew he was in Band, so I hoped this was the period he took it.

Heading over to the band room, I made sure to watch out for any teachers, or worse, Sheriff Johnson. I didn't need to get a late pass, not right now.

Finally, I reached the room, and peered through the glass. He was sitting in the back room, looking gaunt as usual. He appeared to be slacking off as he was one of only students to not be actively practicing.

Loser.

I opened the door, and peered my head in. I pulled a blank white piece of paper out of my backpack and waved it loosely in the air at the teacher.

"Sheriff Johnson wants to speak with Johnny Antin."

Mr. Gordon looked at the obviously fake note, at Johnny, and at me.

"And he sent you?"

"I was just in there." I tried my best at creating a sad face, so Mr. Gordon would believe that this was nothing more than pure honesty.

My luck seemed to be turning around because he gestured for Johnny to get his things. Johnny eyed me suspiciously, and I realized he probably knew something wasn't right, but he chose to get up anyways.

Why was everyone in this school so damn nosy?

This kid was so incredibly lucky that my parents issued a "no more kidnapping" ultimatum, and that we only took girls. But his luck could always change. After all, I was the "wild card" in my family.

We got into the hallway and walked in silence for a moment, before I pulled him into the boy's bathroom.

"Hey man, what is going on?"

I shoved him against the wall and grabbed him by the throat.

"I'll tell you what's going on. You're going to keep your nosy ass mouth shut about those text messages. I didn't see Katie that night. She never showed. If you start spreading rumors, not only will it create problems for me, but it will create them for you."

"Ah. I see your sister came running to her brother with my findings. I'm guessing that means you guys actually *do* have something to lose from this leaking. Would hate for that to happen…"

"You're lucky I don't kill you right here, right now. Keep your mouth shut."

I released him and headed out of the bathroom. I went straight to the office and spun some crap story about how my stomach was upset and I was in the bathroom, so I needed a pass for class. The secretary bought that, and I strongly considered nominating myself for best liar, because I was getting good.

I went to my class just in time to hear the History teacher drone on and on about The Declaration of Independence.

Should I be taking notes? Nah.

My thoughts of my girls at home took over. I really did have a good group. Perfect, untouched. Kim wouldn't have been my first choice, but I have never been one to complain. Nevertheless, they weren't only mine.

I did worry about Katie. I was angry, sure, but my sisters and my parents had a whole new level of vengeance that they would without a doubt take out on her first. Due to my parent's new rule of pairs down there only, I hoped whoever I went with could curb their anger when it came to her.

I still love you, Katie.

The bell rang, and it was finally time for lunch. I was starving. All this plotting, threatening, and scheming had taken a toll on my stomach and I was the first person in line to get the weekly bowl of Chili Mac.

I was just about to tuck in when Sheriff Johnson came up behind me, with no other than Johnny Antin trailing behind.

In the Sheriff's hand was a paper, that I had no doubt was a second copy of Katie's phone records. "Come with me son, and we can clear this up quick."

22

Katie

I sat, sulking, all morning. I was in a rut. How would I ever get out of this god forsaken place?

Cameras. They have fucking cameras in here! I don't know if they are for surveillance, or so these sick bastards can rewatch what they did to us on a constant loop. At this point, I had zero understanding of this family.

I knew Amy was a pointless person, and that Mark was willing to sacrifice his family's trust to help me. Granted, he did so as a way for us to be together and that was not a possibility in any way shape or form.

Maybe I could do a convincing job of allowing him to believe that fantasy he orchestrated, even for a moment.

Maybe Mark was still my ticket out of here…

They may have cameras… but if I was able to get out for even a second, then I would be able to get through the forest. So, I needed a precise plan that would allow me to be freed, and Mark was the safest bet. Seeing the way that he treated me, the way he reacted when I agreed to be with him, it was clear…I had him wrapped around my finger. I knew he hadn't written me off completely even after I attacked him.

The odd thing about Mark was that he came off as a ticking time bomb. He seems to have followed his worst instincts, which have in turn been fueled by his family, and now struggles to find a balance between his needs and those of his family.

The familiar noise of doors unlocking filled me with absolute panic. While I had thought I had a good strategy of getting out of here, I was only digging my own grave. I severed the friendship with Amy, and that was for two reasons. One, I don't trust her as far as I can throw her which thanks to the place that she has me in, is impossible.

Thanks to these damn chains.

Two, I am so disgusted with the person she is that I truly want nothing to do with her ever again. I wouldn't pretend to like her even if it was my ticket out. I rather die down here or take my chances with her creepy brother.

So, who was the torturer today?

Imagine my surprise to see both Sharon and Paul walk in. The parents are feeling vengeful today. They didn't even look my direction but walked straight over to Kim. Sharon delivered a punch before Kim was able to even process what was happening.

While Sharon continued a beat down of Kim, Paul yanked off her top and threw it across the room. Kim was left in nothing but her bra and pants.

Paul moved on to Tara, and repeated the same shirt removing process. He never lay a hand on her physically, which I found out. I was carefully observing the way each of them operated. Paul seemed to only be interested in sexualizing the girls, while Sharon went full blown nutzo.

Sharon let off Kim, and walked up to Tara, grabbed her head, and kneed her right in the face. *Jesus. What the hell was wrong with these people?!*

Tara was still luckier off than Kim, who was now dripping blood from her face onto her pants. My heart twisted in my chest, and I felt my stomach doing somersaults. I was never one who was able to watch people fight, because I hated watching others get hurt physically. To go from that, to now watching women get beaten daily was too much for me to bear.

The absolute lack of respect for basic human life, and the enjoyment in inflicting pain on others was this family's vice. It was immoral, inhumane, and made me feel a type of rage that I didn't ever feel I was capable of until now.

Paul had retreated to the corner of the room, simply watching. After ripping Tara's shirt, he decided to silently observe rather than move on to me. Thank god.

This couldn't last long. They hated me too much to simply let me skate by. I knew it would come at any time if not being worse than the other girls received. Of course, mine would be personal. I attacked two of their children, and I had a gut-wrenching feeling they were starting to believe I was more trouble than I was worth.

Sharon turned to me, and beelined straight over.
This was it. You can take it.

The blow she delivered to my head sent a ringing through my ears. It was a splitting pain throughout my head, but I knew better than to show she hurt me. She wouldn't break me. This family wouldn't break me.

"Does that hurt Katie?"

I didn't answer Sharon but decided to go out on a limb and engage her in a stare. I wanted her to know I was standing my ground, and wasn't afraid of her but on the inside, I was shaking like a leaf. This family had no bounds and were capable of murder. I had seen it.

"How about this?"

Sharon took that opportunity to step right on my clearly broken ankle. The pain was excruciating, and I couldn't help myself from howling in pain. The scream seemed to satisfy her deepest cravings and her and Paul began to head back. Paul tossed the girls' shirts back to them so they could put them back on, but Kim instead used it to clean up her bleeding face.

How anyone could receive satisfaction after doing something like this to young innocent people blew my fucking mind. When I got out of here, I needed to include the other two girls in here as well. I was terrified that if I was able to escape again, Sharon would retaliate by killing both Kim and Tara and I couldn't be responsible for that.

I needed to save them too.

Sharon headed up the stairs, and Paul turned around to face me. He didn't say anything but rather mouthed the words, "Good job."

For what? Letting your psycho wife obliterate my ankle?

Probably. Paul was full of alternate meanings and I didn't have the time or the energy to try and decipher it.

This ankle would be a surefire problem if I were to escape. I knew I would be able to put zero pressure on it. Maybe that's what Sharon's plan was. Break me enough that I have no chance of making it out of this room on my own accord.

My ankle was throbbing out of control. I was so distracted by the pain that I didn't hear what Kim was saying to me. Everything was being made to background noise. You ever hear those stories of people blacking out because they are in so much pain? I would actually opt for that right now.

"Did you hear me Katie?"

"I'm sorry Kim, what?"

"I said we need to get out of here."

"I know. I have a plan." I had finally decided on my safest bet out of here. I couldn't take any more of this mentally, and physically draining hell hole. The Iron Room was draining the life and the fight out of me.

"What are you going to do?"

"I'm going to seduce Mark."

23

Mark

I felt myself begin to panic. Then it turned to anger. I was seriously going to kill Johnny. Where he got off thinking he had the upper hand blew my mind. I had the ultimate upper hand. I knew where the girls where, whereas him and everyone else in this lame town were chasing their tail in circles.

Useless, pointless people.

Sheriff Johnson was the only redeemable guy in Prairie. He was really laid back, and he seemed to genuinely care about everyone here while everybody else was simply pretending. This wasn't some close-knit town like everyone thought.

If it was, why didn't anyone offer to drive Anna home when she was stumbling drunk in the street? Why did they leave her to her own demise? I was the one who extended the kindness despite her spitting in my face every chance she got.

I was a nice guy, turned sour from the treatment of these shitty townspeople.

Prairie had never had a scandal like this before, ever. These people welcomed it. They didn't really care about the welfare of Anna, Tara, and all the others. It was all a façade. They simply needed some fresh gossip, and this was the talk of the century. It was all thanks to me.

Johnny was screwing with not only me, but my family. And that was dangerous.

He's done.

"I'm sorry Sheriff. I don't understand what's going on."

"Well, Johnny here and I ran into each other as he came out of the bathroom. He said you attacked him. Is that true?"

I looked over at Johnny, who looked smug. An idea came to mind.

"Yes, sir."

"I'm sorry?" Sheriff Johnson was clearly caught off guard, not expecting me to own up to it.

"I did it. But only because he tried to grope Amy."

Johnny's mouth dropped open, and I felt satisfaction bloom.

Yeah, I can play dirty too, bastard.

"Is that true, Johnny?"

Johnny opened his mouth to protest but was interrupted by Amy.

"It's true, Sheriff. I was so upset that I came to Mark, and he flipped out." Amy was leaning against the open office door.

"They're lying, Sheriff!" Johnny began to stammer apologies, and I knew we had him. Sheriff was already closer with Amy and I due to our tight family friendship. Two of us attesting to the same story was sure to dispute any bullshit that came out of Johnny's mouth now.

"I think I have heard enough. I will be informing the principal of this." He began filling out the paper he had in his hand. I realized then that it was a report form that the principal used. It wasn't the text messages. Johnny hadn't gotten to that. And he never would.

Sheriff Johnson dismissed all of us but held Johnny back so they could wait for the principal to figure out a punishment or course of action.
"What the hell dude? You can't go around assaulting people!" Amy shoved me.
"I told you I would take care of it, didn't I?"

I didn't want to listen to her anymore. It hurt because all this commotion surrounding Katie's arrest was really tearing up my relationship with my sister. We had always been close, but that can easily falter especially when you feel like you are constantly being ostracized for your mistakes.

Lately my entire family had been ripping me apart. People make mistakes. I always had the best intent through everything I did, and it was never enough for them. I was never smart enough, never mean enough, never calculated enough to satisfy my family, but more importantly Amy. I was tired of being treated like a liability and especially like a disappointment.

If it wouldn't hurt me in the process, I had half a mind to stop trying to fix everything. That would teach them. It would teach them just how much I do for them, and I would finally get the damn appreciation I desperately deserved.

I stalked off, unwilling to listen to Amy anymore, and needing to get to my class.

The rest of the school day dragged on by, and I was so excited to just go home, and let my worries drip away. Strangely enough, I felt an urge to see Katie. Rules were rules, and my mom had been extremely clear about them. Pairs only. I was the untrustworthy one, the "wild card".

I didn't care. I needed to see her. She made me feel better.

Katie was the love of my life.

"Ready to go home?"

Amy.

I didn't say anything but unlocked the door and climbed in the car. Amy followed suit.

"Do you want to talk about it?" I could tell Amy felt bad about earlier, but quite frankly, I didn't give a single shit. If she wanted someone to criticize, she could look in the mirror.

"To you? No, I'm not in the mood to feel fucking useless."

"Mark, I never want you to feel that way!"

"What end result do you think stems from constant judgement from you and our parents? I can never do anything right. I'm always screwing up, at least in your eyes. I would rather be an "idiot" than a cold-hearted bitch like you."

She slapped me across the face, and I swerved the car slightly to the left.

"Don't do that when I'm driving! What are you, crazy? Oh yeah, you are."

"Turning on me Mark? We're family." Amy crossed her arms over her chest. She was such a hypocrite. We were only family when it was convenient.

"Act like it then."

The rest of the car ride was silent, and it gave way for me to drown in my thoughts. I felt so conflicted. I loved Katie. She made me want to be good, but I wasn't. The truth is, I was similar to the rest of my family when I say that I loved watching those girls suffer. They deserved it. They were mean, nosy, and worthless. Katie was different.

She didn't deserve to be there. To wake up every day knowing she wasn't out there walking free, broke my heart. A heart I didn't know I had.

She didn't love me though. She hated me... so much so that she smashed a rock over the back of my skull. I knew that deep down she cared about me. This place we kept her in, the Iron Room, it messed with her mind. It was made to. I knew that given the chance, she and I could really be great.

My mind drifted to Katie's dad, Sheriff Johnson.

He looked in real bad shape.

The bags under his eyes were deep and purple, as if he hadn't slept in weeks, but it hadn't been that long since Katie had gone missing. His eyes were bloodshot, and his hair messy and uncombed. I felt bad for him. I knew how bad it felt to lose Katie. Him and I were in the same boat, really.

I'll get her out for both of us, don't worry.

I would see Katie tonight if it was the last thing I did.

I parked the car after George waved me in. He had this smirk plastered across his face ever since he caught Katie.

Jerk.

I would have to figure out ways around George from now on. He was my parent's new lapdog.

Amy got out and slammed the door, heading inside without another word. Her hair blew in the wind, and I could clearly see a bruise from where Katie had hit her, and I couldn't help but laugh. "What's funny?" Amy turned around. "You."

I locked up my car, as Amy continued her stomp into the foyer. She was a drama queen.

My parents were already home, as evident by their parked cars in the driveway. My mom was dressed in pearls and a fancy dress as if that somehow hid the fact that she tortured girls.

Appearances aren't everything, and I see right through you.

I saw through all of them, and I felt free for the first time in a long time. I would no longer be under their thumb. I would make my own decisions. I took Katie, and I could sure as hell release her. I didn't need to ask for their permission or forgiveness.

Amy stormed past me up to her room. "What's her problem?" My dad walked up to me, eating a pastry.

"Women." I shrugged my shoulders, and ran up my room, slamming the door.

I would see Katie tonight… her brown hair that was always so sleek and shiny, and her bright blue eyes. That brightened my mood. I wondered if she thought it was weird that her, Anna, and Tara looked alike. I had a type, shoot me.

But Katie was different.

I had faith that her and I could work things out. She just needed to see that I wasn't like them.

My mom called up to me, letting me know that we were going out to dinner tonight. Well, that would explain the pearls. She would expect all of us to dress out best and put on the best mask for the town of Prairie to see.

I hated this.

I showered the worries of the day away and dressed in a nice silver colored button up. Mom said it always complimented my eyes, and I felt the need to appease to her today given my recent transgressions. I didn't care or feel sorry for them, but her and the rest of my family needed to believe I did.

I put on a nice pair of blue jeans, and my new sneakers. I threw a little gel in my hair and tousled it to achieve that "effortless" look.

I bounded down the stairs, where my immaculately dressed family was already waiting. We cleaned up so well. You wouldn't even know we were a family of rage-fueled, kidnapping, and remorseless sociopaths.

"You look great baby." My mom planted a kiss on my forehead, and my dad patted my back.

Amy just glared at me.

We all loaded into my father's car and headed out the gate. George waved to my parents on the way out, and my dad made a right. We must be going to Giuseppe's. It was the only Italian restaurant in town, and also the nicest.

When we arrived, they came out to valet our car. Valeting a car in a town like Prairie seemed fruitless, but that was the way my family rolled.

We were seated swiftly and ordered right away. We were regulars here, and creatures of habit so we knew what we liked. The waitress came over to me.

"Chicken Parmesan please."

She put our orders in and brought out an appetizer tray piled high with various types of breads, dips, and a nice bruschetta. The restaurant was nearly empty, so our food came out within fifteen minutes. The conversation was light, minimal, and we all tucked into our food immediately as a way to avoid conversation with one another, I'm sure.

"I just wanted to say thank you to everyone for your group efforts lately, and I feel that all of our adversities we have overcome, we have done so together, and that it has made us stronger. I am glad that we are all on the same page." My dad raised his glass for a cheer, and we all did the same, one by one.

When it came time for mine and Amy's glasses to clink, she looked me in the eyes, and whispered.

"I'm sorry."

"Me too." I forced a smile, and it felt fake.

Anything to get through this dinner and home to my girl.

Thankfully the remainder of the dinner was free of any more speeches, and we got home by 8. I went straight up to my room to peel these clothes off myself. I liked being comfy more than anything. It wasn't long before there was a knock at the door. I walked over and opened it.

Amy. Who else?

My sister was relentless in her efforts to patch whatever issues we had. I didn't want to patch them, and I thought I already did a good job at convincing her at dinner that we were okay.

"I wanted to say sorry again Mark. I didn't know that I made you feel that way. My only intention has always been to protect our family, and you are part of that family."

"Don't worry about it. I know. It was just a trying day for me. Sorry to take it out on you."

I turned around and headed back in my room, desperate to avoid this conversation.

"You sure you're okay?"

"Yes Amy, just really tired. Don't forget I kind of beat someone up today."

My sister laughed, and I knew that she had fallen for it. I could always distract her with humor.

"Okay, I'm going to lay in bed, I love you."

"Love you." I heard my door shut and let out a sigh of relief.

Just a few more hours, and I could see her.

I laid in bed and turned on Netflix. I picked a romantic comedy, as I was feeling particularly sentimental right now. *The Ugly Truth.*

Seemed fitting. Girl pushes away guy, only to realize they were right for one another all along.

The movie was over, and it was 10:15. I slipped on a pair of shoes and stepped into the hallway. I carefully closed my door, being cautious about making noise.

I walked over to Amy's room. I pressed my ear against the door and heard loud snoring.

Thank god.

I walked downstairs, did a look around, and went out the back door like last time. But this time, I had to be extra careful when it came to George. He may be out on the lookout, but also wouldn't leave his box so I would just need to avoid being in his line of sight.

I tiptoed across the freshly wet grass and reached the back door.

I could hear my pulse crashing in my ears, and my heart beat a million miles a minute. I unlocked it extra slow, trying to avoid a ruckus.

I cascaded down the staircase to the next door. My girl was right on the other side.

I opened it, and all three girls were asleep. I couldn't believe my luck. The other girls slept like logs. It did play to my benefit though.

I walked over to Katie, sat on the cool ground next to her, and then carefully started shaking her shoulder in an attempt to wake her.
God, she looked so beautiful.

Her eyes peeled open, and rather than freaking out upon seeing me, she smiled. My heart soared and I knew my suspicions were correct.
"Hey…" Katie sounded sleepy, and it was the sexiest thing ever.
"Hi beautiful."
"Mark… I'm sorry."
"I know. I am too."
"I just panicked. This whole situation is kind of insane." She looked at me and squeezed my hand.
"Trust me Katie, I know. I probably could have gone about the situation better than I did."

She shrugged her shoulders and continued to gaze at me. I continued.

"I want to try again. But, once I break you out, I need a plan. That will take time."

"I figured as much. But, thank you. It means so much." She spoke softly while squeezing my hand. I felt on top of the world.

Her pretty blue eyes sparkled even in this dark room. The moonlight had cascaded in and paired with the sensor light that was dimming down, she looked like a dream.

Suddenly, she leaned in and planted a chaste kiss on my lips.

This is more than I could've imagined.

"I want to try too, Mark."

24

Amy

I'm fine Amy.
Just tired.

Something was going on with Mark, and something had changed within him. My brother who was always so dead set on protecting our family was slipping away in front of my eyes, and I had not a single clue on how to stop it.

Yesterday he seemed uninterested in speaking to me at all. I felt bad that I had hurt his feelings. I never tried to make Mark feel like an idiot.

Technically speaking, he was. That doesn't mean I wanted him to feel that way. It's no secret that Mark had been messing up a lot lately. He was careless, and continuously chose to act on emotion rather than using reason and logic. People who are sloppy always leave trails. Trails get us caught, and we will all be implicated if this goes horribly wrong.

I loved my brother, and I always would. I just wish he took more initiative when it came to maintain all that we have built together as a family.

Maybe he's changed his mind.

No, Mark would never do that. He's the one that takes the girls in the first place! While this is definitely a family effort, Mark chose the first girl, Anna. He was the one to acquire the tranquilizers through the black market.

This may have been a family thought out plan, but Mark, and his feelings towards specific girls was the ultimate catalyst.

Yesterday and the close call with Sheriff Johnson was getting to be too much. I mulled over what to do all night long. Part of me wanted to tell my parents everything… the text message receipts, Johnny, the Sheriff- but I didn't want to get Mark in any more trouble.

Deep down, I worried that my brother might be playing both sides. It made me furious to think that some girl would have a strong enough effect on him that he would turn against his family. I didn't know for sure and didn't want to make accusations. I figured I would use this car ride to school this morning as a way to sus out where his head was at.

Like every other school morning, I dressed myself, and headed downstairs for our morning breakfast.

Today it was yogurt, fruit, and granola which made sense. Every time we went to Giuseppe's, my mom swore up and down that it made her gain weight which was only rectified by a light breakfast. If my suspicions were correct, we would also be having soup for dinner.

Oh joy.

Breakfast this morning carried a very light and easy conversation. Mark's mood seemed to have shifted a complete 180 since last night. He seemed happier, and more easygoing with all of us. Most sisters would be happy that their brother was in a good place, but not me. Mark's ups were really good, and his downs were really bad. If… *when* his ups turned into a down, he would fly off the handle.

I finished, excused myself, and sat in the foyer waiting for Mark per our routine. He usually finished right after me but took his sweet ass time today. I was anxious to get him alone in the car and drill him about where this newfound source of happiness was coming from.

Finally, he appeared out of nowhere, and we headed outside. He unlocked the car and we both climbed in. He could barely get his side door closed and the car started before I spoke.

"Spill."

"Spill… what?"

"Why the hell you're so chipper this morning… spill."

"Why can't you be normal, and just say you're happy for me? That you are happy that I am happy. Oh wait, you can't do that can you?" Mark looked pissed off, and I realized I may have overstepped.

"If you are really truly happy Mark, then I am glad. I'm just curious what or should I say who… is the source. That's all." I shrugged my shoulders, hoping he would be willing to open up.

"Nobody, Amy. I am just happy."

Liar.

I knew he didn't plan on letting me know who or what he was doing. I would simply have to figure it out on my own. I sat in silence the rest of the ride. I needed time to think and utilized the silence to my benefit.

"I'm tired of fighting with you. I don't feel like you're on my side anymore, and I don't trust you." Mark finally spoke as we pulled into the parking lot.

He can't trust me? I can't trust him!

I wanted to reply but struggled to find the words. Before I had the chance, Mark parked, turned off the ignition, and stepped out of the car.

He stalked off towards the school, and I was left standing outside the car looking like an absolute idiot. He stopped, turned around, and I felt my heart soar thinking he changed his mind. My heart immediately sank when I saw him lock the car.
He hates me.

This was working out to be a crap day. My brother was angry at me, and honestly, I couldn't decipher what the exact cause of that way. I didn't know how to fix it, mostly because he won't allow me to. He sees our relationship as being finished, and I feel like I'm in a rut.

My brother has always been my closest friend, and biggest confidant. But lately, we have not been connecting at all. Something has been causing a huge rift in between us, and earlier I had simply written it off to be the effect of Katie's arrival.

But now I found myself forced to question if it was maybe something more.

The bell rang, and I was torn away from my debilitating thoughts because I needed to get to class. This crazy situation the past few days had completely thrown me off my axis, and I felt like I was struggling to find my focus and recenter again.

I rushed off to my first class, and so began the rest of the agonizing school day. Surprisingly enough, Calculus was actually pleasant because Johnny decided to cool his jets for once. He didn't speak to me, or even look my way once. I had hoped it was because the threat from Mark yesterday was enough to send him running with his tail between his legs.

Or he could be gathering more evidence.

I decided that I would push those worries to the back of mind, better to be dealt with at a different time. I had enough stress on my plate with my withering relationship with Mark.

When the school day was finally over, I waited by his car. I would make things right between us, whatever it took.

He came out smiling, locked eyes with me, and his smile turned into a frown.

"Hey brother. I wanted to talk to you."

"About?" Mark reached the driver's door and unlocked both doors.

We both climbed in. I buckled my seatbelt, and I grabbed his hand before he could turn on the car.

"Us Mark. You're angry with me, and I don't know how I am supposed to fix it."

"I just… ugh." He put his heads in his hands, clearly frustrated. He elaborated.

"Amy, I don't want a part of this anymore."

Are you crazy?

"Why the hell not?"

"It doesn't make me happy Ames."

"It used to, so what changed?"

He sat there quietly, mulling over what to say. The battle between the truth and a lie was clear on his face.

"Katie."

I couldn't help but to laugh right in his face. Katie… the same girl that beat me bloody and smashed a rock over his skull.

"You're pathetic."

I didn't want to hear anymore nonsense, so I turned my head facing out the window and stopped talking altogether. Mark was so idiotic that it honestly blew my freaking mind. Katie didn't care about any of us, and especially not the guy who kidnapped her! I knew from the moment that he drugged her... that she would become a huge conflict of interest. He had strong feelings for her before all of this happened, but now he felt responsible, and even guilty.

This had to stop... and the only way to do that was to kill the source- Katie.

25

Katie

I hadn't had a shower since I got taken, and I desperately needed one. After that kiss with Mark, I felt the urge to get in a shower and scrub my skin raw. He made my skin crawl and pretending to so much as care about him was practically killing me.

Drama was never my best class, but I deserved a damn Oscar for my performance. "Well, is he a good kisser?" Kim asked laughing, clearly pleased that it was me and not her who had to take one for the team.

I shot her a stare that shut her up instantly. I had told the girls that the next time Mark came down, to pretend to be asleep. Mark would never try anything with those girls watching. He was so scared of his family finding out about his little transgressions, that he wouldn't risk it. I needed him to fall completely in love with me- fast.

I couldn't last any longer in this cold Iron Room. It was pretty dark, all the time, even with the small light. There was nothing to stare at, no pictures, nothing. Just each other. I looked around the room and felt my heart sink in my chest. The camera.

I wasn't sure how the systems operated but knew that his parents at least had some access to its footage. What if they saw Mark come down here last night? Would they disallow him access? He was my ticket out of this place. I just needed to find a way to get both Kim and Tara on that pass as well.

I didn't know if Tara and Anna confided in each other while being held down here together, but Tara never talked to Kim or myself. She kept to herself, as she did before she was here.
I would never be able to leave them here.

I found myself constantly worrying about my dad. I was the one being held in a confined space, chained up, and beaten, but I worried about him. Without me, my dad was all alone. I didn't know if he had been eating or sleeping properly, and it was really wearing on me. I wanted more than anything to get out of this place and see him again.

My ankle still hurt like a bitch, courtesy of Sharon. Mark had slipped me some aspirin last night when he came down, and while it helped, aspirin was no match for a broken ankle. It especially didn't do much when the ankle had been stomped on not once, but twice.

I was comforted with a small sense of satisfaction in knowing that when I eventually did get out of here, my dad would nail her ass to the wall. He could make sure this family never had the chance to see the light of day ever again.

I had offered them all a good amount of time to see the ways they were wrong, but they all chose to continue torturing and kidnapping, not to mention killing innocent girls. I knew the what, where, how, but struggled with the why.

Why did they do this?

I knew it was the afternoon. Paul brought down bread and a banana for each of us earlier. We were allotted two small meals a day. No lunch. I assumed that was primarily because they were all at work or school during the day, but it might also be a ploy to keep us weak.

While I despised doing it, I was anxious for Mark to return tonight. I needed him to believe I was on his side, and in doing so- I had to kiss and play pretend. It was more painful than my ankle, and that is saying a lot.

I screwed up the last time Mark let me out by showing my cards too early. This time, I would let Mark accompany me all the way home and then turn on him. I needed to be safely off the property first. What could I do about the other girls though?

If I left them here, there's a chance the Puntzer's could retaliate and hurt them. If I took them, Mark wouldn't be for it. He probably wouldn't even be for it in the first place.

My head hurts.

The door creaked open, and I instantly knew it wasn't Mark. I didn't even have to look. Mark wouldn't risk coming in here in broad daylight, not with Amy or his parents' being home.

Amy.

"How are you girls enjoying your stay?" She laughed coldly, and turned, her eyes fixed on me.

"Just wait until I get out of here." Kim threatened, and Amy's head snapped quickly and sharply.

"Is that a threat? You won't get out of here don't you get it? You will all die at some point, just like that whore Anna."

Kim stayed silent, which was wise because Amy seemed to have a quick temper these days.

Amy turned back to me, eyes glazed, and fists balled.

"You especially Katie, because trust me when I say your time here is limited."

Amy turned and walked away, locking the door on her way out.

What was that supposed to mean?

My time here was limited? I knew she wasn't talking about an early release, or a release from here at all. She was threatening my life. A few days ago, I would have believed Amy to not be capable of ever hurting me, but recent actions proved otherwise. She meant what she said.

Rather than feeling scared, I was furious. I was tired of being treated like garbage or disposable. I wasn't, and they would soon see that. In no time, I would outsmart all of these idiots and have them locked away for life.

I had never hated people more in my entire life than I did them.

Anna was dead. I wasn't able to save her, and I felt responsible for her death. I would hold that on my conscience forever. If I was able to save these girls, I would feel like this was all worth it, even if I died trying.

I did want to live, mostly for my dad. Knowing I would be reunited with my mother, shall these psychos decide to kill me brings me some sense of comfort in this scary place, but I want to live. I want to see my dad again.

I knew Amy was furious and had completely written me off ever since I spit in her face. I also knew that today she seemed even angrier, so something had ticked her off. I hoped Mark hadn't spilled the beans about us. If she thought I had any chance of turning her brother around to get him to release me again, then she would kill me herself.

She cared more about familial preservation than anything else, or anyone else.

I'm counting on you Mark.

The minutes felt like hours, and the hours like days in this room. Finally, the door opened, and rather than another beating, it was Sharon with our dinner. She was different from her husband in that she threw our food in front of us like we were animals. Paul placed it in front of us nicely. Sharon tried to demean and break us in any way she could.

It wouldn't work.

Dinner tonight was a vegetable mush and some kind of weird chili. It was like prison food, delivered with a side of violence.

Sharon didn't say another word and headed out. The lock on the door sent us all into an eating frenzy. This tasted like gutter trash, but it would have to do. They gave us little enough food that we were absolutely famished by the time each meal came around.

We would have eaten anything at that point.

In terms of hydration, the delivered two bottles with our breakfast, and three with dinner. Buckets were a few feet away from each of our posts, for our use. Knowing that this was all on camera, and they had full unbridled access twenty-four-hour access to it made me absolutely sick to my stomach.

Being demeaned and violated every single day was wearing on me. I had no idea how Tara had survived this long. The beatings weren't the only form of torture that this family delivered.

We all ate in silence, and when we finished, Kim turned towards me to speak.

"Do you think Mark is coming back down tonight?"

"Definitely. He thinks I like him. Hook, line, and sink. It shouldn't be much longer now."

"We can only hope so." Kim started chugging her water.

Tara looked at me, shook her head, and turned away. She didn't think I could do it. But I could, and I would. I would get us all out of here.

Kim and I spent the remainder of the evening talking, with Tara listening, but never chiming in. Kim decided she was tired and was going to actually turn in, and Tara followed suit. I debated going to bed for real, or just staying up until Mark came.

I went with the latter, and sure enough it couldn't have been an hour later before Mark came walking in. I closed my eyes when I heard the chains being unlocked, but that was only to make sure that it wasn't Amy, or their parents.

He looked so happy.

He was all smiles walking in, as if he was waiting for this moment all day. He sauntered over to me, sat down, and immediately took my hand into his. His sandy blonde hair hung loosely in his face, his green eyes dancing with excitement.

"I missed you." He rubbed his thumb back and forth over my knuckles.

"I missed you too, how was your day?"

"Could have been better. Amy was really on my case." He shook his head, clearly annoyed with his sister.

That makes two of us.

"Tell me about it. She came in here today, guns blazing, upset with me." Her threat remained fresh in my brain.

"What did she say?" Mark was growing increasingly upset.

"Nothing you need to concern yourself with. I'm just glad you're here." I smiled at him, and he returned a grin. Mark was reasonably attractive, and I was surprised more girls weren't interested in him.

I still found it hard to fake an interest, because everything he did made my stomach churn. I had morals, and a pretty face wasn't enough to make me turn away from them. I was better than that.

Mark leaned in and kissed me. It was different from yesterday. This one was more passionate, more needy. He grabbed the side of my face and pulled me in closer. It started to get hot and heavy when I heard Amy's voice.

"What the hell is going on in here?"

26

Mark

"What the hell is going on in here?" My sister was standing in the doorway looking furious. She beelined for Katie and slapped her in the face.

I found myself shoving my sister back. "Leave her alone, Amy. I mean it."

"Oh, please. Give me a break Mark. You cannot actually think she *cares* about you. You're not that delusional!"

"You're the delusional one. Just because she hates you, doesn't mean she hates me. I'm actually a good person, whereas you are just a miserable *bitch.*"

My sister charged me, and raised her hand, but I grabbed her wrist. I shoved her back, hard, and she fell back onto the cold metal floor.

She got up and ran up the stairs, without a doubt on her way to tell my parents. I had to stop her. I looked down at Katie who looked terrified.

My girl.

"I'm so sorry. I am going to fix this."

I leaned down and planted a chaste kiss on her then ran upstairs. I left the door open but there was no way for them to get out, not that Katie would want to anyways. She was happy here, with me. I saw Amy about to enter the house, so I called her name.

"Stop!"

She turned around, eyed me up and down looking disgusted, and yanked the sliding glass door open heading inside.

Hateful bitch.

I sprinted faster and caught up to her in no time. I yanked her arm as I reached the door, "Don't do this Amy."

"I have to Mark! You're going to get us all caught! I bet you were planning to release her again, weren't you?"

I didn't reply, which gave my sister all the confirmation she needed. She looked sad, pulled her arm away and headed to my parent's room. This was bad, really bad. My parents would not look past this a second time.

I needed to fix this, and fast. I had my keys still in my pocket, and I ran back outside and sprinted to the back-basement door, still wide open. I jumped down the stairs taking two at a time, and beelined for Katie.

"C'mon, we have to get out of here. Quickly."

She didn't hesitate and held her wrist up for me to unlock it. I took her hand, and ran upstairs, not even bothering to give a final look to the two other girls staring at us open mouthed and wide eyed.

We made it out and I could see my parents and Amy emerging from the house.

We need to run.

I squeezed her hand and pulled her towards the forest. If I attempted to go through the front, George would stop me instantly. The forest was our best bet, because we had ample hiding room above all.

I couldn't believe I was doing this. They would never forgive me.

We were sprinting, and I could tell Katie was getting winded. She was supposed to. That was why my parents fed the girls so little. Plus, Katie hadn't really been up and about much obviously, and her legs were crapping out on her right now. There was also the ankle which I had no doubt was killing her, especially if the adrenaline hadn't kicked in yet.

We were lucky in the sense that we had a pretty good head start on my other family members. But we were outnumbered so we had to play this smart.

"We should hide somewhere good and wait for them to go in the different direction."

Katie nodded and I found a small hidden hole beside a tree and a large brush bush. The hole provided enough room for Katie to hide, while I stuck my legs in and covered my top half in the bush.

I could hear my family members getting closer and closer, and I couldn't make out what they were saying but heard a murmur of voices. I prayed to God they weren't planning on splitting up but was confident in the place I chose to hide.

If Katie and I continued running, they would have sectioned off and caught us without a doubt. The patch of forest behind our home wasn't much, and it connected off to a highway. If they weren't able to find us, they would simply think they lost us.

I could tell Katie was nervous about Tara and Kim, who we left back there. I couldn't understand why. They weren't her friends, and they certainly didn't care for or respect her the way I did. They were horrible people, and that's why they found themselves down there.

Katie never belonged there.

I would do everything it took in my power to ensure that Katie never had to step foot in the filthy god-awful room again. It was too disgusting for her perfect, and pure soul. Her hand was still intertwined with mine, and she was shaking.

In the moment I felt furious with my family. I was furious that they were scaring her so badly, and that they wouldn't allow her the chance at freedom. I had fucked up by taking her and made a poor choice. This was me trying to right my wrongs and attempt a chance at being happy…with Katie by my side.

Amy's words rang fresh in my mind, but I pushed them to the side. Katie cared about me, and Amy was simply jealous that her best friend no longer thought the world of her anymore. My words were true. Amy was a cold-hearted and calculated bitch. She had my mind so messed up for so long, and I was finally able to see the truth. My family was horrible.

I could hear my family closing in. Sure enough, it sounded like they had all devised a plan: divide and conquer.

I could hear my father off to the left of me, calling out my name.

Amy was off to the right, calling Katie's name.

Oh yeah, let me just poke my head out and respond. Morons.

I had faith, because my family didn't have two brain cells to rub together combined. My mother sounded like she was right on top of us. She was calling my name and trying to reason with me. "Mark, I know you messed up baby, but it's okay. Just come out, and we can talk about it. We will let Katie go."

Yeah right.

Katie squeezed her hand around mine tighter, and I placed my other hand on top of hers in an attempt to comfort her. She had seen sides to my family recently that she didn't know existed. It scared her.

Meanwhile, I had known them my whole life, and nothing they did scared me. I was horrified at their characters, but their threats were usually baseless.

Except for the threat they made to Anna.

Right. I could hear my mother growing closer, and I felt a pang of worry that they might see me. I wasn't able to say anything to Katie with fear of being discovered, but remained holding her hand, and I felt her hand relax in mine.

We were getting out of this.

I heard my dad approaching.

"Did you find them Paul?"

"Do you see him with me? Of course not."

"Don't be smart with me. I figured you darted them, and they were still over there." My mom sounded exasperated.

Darted them? Shit.

My parents had tranquilizer guns on them. This was worse than I thought. Katie and I had to remain hidden for as long as it would take. It might even be our safest bet to stay out of sight until morning. If we were even grazed with a dart from the gun, we would be out like a light. My parents had invested in these a while ago, when Anna got out of her chains and ran.

My parents were moving the chain from her wrist to her ankle when she punched my mother. My dad was changing Tara's at the time, and Anna made it all the way outside before they caught her.

Thank god for Amy that day.

"Well I didn't Sharon. Where's Amy?"

"Right here." My sister was with them.

"Maybe they got out to the road. Let's head back and see if George saw anything." My dad urged my mom and sister that we weren't out here. Truth is, he was just simply too lazy to search and really didn't think I was capable of getting too far.

I heard my mom and sister agree with my dad, and then I could hear three pairs of footsteps retreating back to the house.

I still felt our safest bet was to wait until morning, but Katie may not like that plan.

"We need to get out Tara and Kim." Katie started to whisper to me, but I squeezed her hand hard.

"Shhh. We can't."

She didn't say any more, but I knew she wasn't going to drop this. I would not run the risk of losing her freedom for two low class girls. The world was better off without them.

How could she not see that?

I checked my watch. It had been an hour since my parents left. I wanted to start heading out to the main road now. It was no more than a five-minute walk, and we would be running.

"Katie..."

"Hmm?" She sounded like she fell asleep.

"Let's go." I stood up first and helped her out of the hole. She dusted herself free of leaves and dirt. I stepped out of the brush and we started a fast walk. She squeezed her eyes in pain, obviously due to her ankle.

Just a little bit farther, baby.

I started to pull her hand harder when I heard voices, and it turned into a run when I realized my parents never left.

"There they are Paul!"

Katie and I were sprinting though the lush greenery, while my family was not far off behind with tranquilizer guns.

The main road came into sight, and I felt my heart soar. This was it. Once we got out of the forest, we could use the highway to get help. The highway wasn't far from the station, where I knew for a fact that there was an officer stationed there twenty-four-seven.

Our feet reached the edge of the concrete road, when I felt my arm tug down. It was Katie. She had fallen to the ground in a heap, and I saw the dart sticking out of her neck.

No.

I tried to pull her up but was hit with a sharp pinch in the back of my neck and I was out like a light.

I opened my eyes, and I was in my bedroom. What the hell happened? Was that all a dream? I looked down at my feet which were caked in mud and stuck with leaves.

Not a dream.

Oh god, where was Katie? I remembered the darts, and both of us dropping. I closed my eyes, incredibly disappointed.

I failed her.

I started to cry, realizing what had happened. Katie was back in that god-awful room. And I was in my room… chained?

I lifted up my arm only to realize I was chained to my bed post. I started yanking on it feverishly trying to get the wood of the bed frame to snap.

"Wouldn't do that if I were you…" Amy walked into my room carrying a water bottle.

"Why am I chained?"

"You're a liability now Mark. One that we can't afford."

"What? What are you guys going to do… just keep me chained up?"

My mom and dad entered the room.

"Until we can be sure you're on our side again. I just left the school a message. Sick with the measles… such a nasty sickness."

They were going to keep me in here and lie to the school about some made up sickness.

I was now a prisoner in my own home.

27

Amy

As far as I was concerned, I didn't have a brother anymore. I was so disgusted with his lack of respect or even love for this family. What the hell was he thinking yesterday?

He was fully prepared to throw away everything he loved, including his family, for some annoying chick with mommy issues.

She used to be my best friend, but no longer. Mark was my brother biologically of course, but there was no love there.

How could there be after what he did?

Thank god we invested in tranquilizer guns after Anna's first attempted escape. Who knew they would come in handy down the road as Mark tried to free one of the captives? He was such a complete and utter moron. Katie didn't give a shit about him, and I can't believe he was so blinded by a pretty face that he couldn't see it.

We spent the better part of the night looking for him, until Mom devised a plan to hang back and act like we left. We knew if Mark thought we were gone then he would deem it safe to come out- and we would have him and Katie.

I could care less about Katie at this point, but if she was able to successfully get away, we would lose everything.

And it would all be Mark's fault.

When we finally got Katie back in her chains where she belonged, and Mark into the house, my mother couldn't stop sobbing. She was upset with Mark, herself, and overall just angry at the whole situation. Different from me, she wasn't able to write Mark off so easily even though he betrayed every single one of us.

At the end of the day, he was still her son, and that meant something to her... and my dad. I thought after what he did, they would be so angry that they might kill him.

No such luck.

They thought it over alone and came to a decision that they felt would best benefit everybody involved. We all agreed that Mark had become too emotionally involved and needed to be removed from the situation. Enough time away from that room, and the clouded perceptions it brought, would surely reunite Mark with his old self.

I had gone downstairs after locking Katie back up and retrieved a spare set of chains. Mark's frame was steel enforced beneath the beams, and it would be sturdy enough to keep him in there. We added another security measure in the extra locks we added onto the *outside* of his door.

He wasn't getting out without us.

Mom felt it best to leave a message with the school filling them in on Mark's illness that came over quickly, and that he would need to be on bed rest for two weeks. They would send homework home for him that I would pick up, and no one would suspect anything.

Luckily enough for me, I now had to face the hordes of gossip at school- alone.

Mom was letting me drive Mark's car, even though I didn't have a license yet. The only person in this town who had any authority to do something about it was Sheriff Johnson, and I can safely assume my lack of a driving license would be the least of his worries.

I still felt bad for him in a way. Katie on the other hand, not so much. When we were best friends, she was always timid, kind, and compassionate. Being here only brought out her true self, which is a combination of being calculated, rude, and unappreciative all rolled into one.

Now that I knew how Mark truly felt about her, and how far he was willing to go to be with her, I knew she had to die.

It's the only way to save my family.

With her out of the picture, Mark has no other girl to play hero for, and we can finally settle back into our life.

This whole Katie mess had thrown us off balance, and out of center.

I glanced at myself the mirror and was surprisingly impressed. I was able to clean up pretty good, even for someone who was up half the night reinforcing her brother's door, because he tried to run away with one of her captives. Yeah, I know it sounded crazy.

"Amy! Come down here." My mom yelled up, and I collected the rest of my things for school and headed downstairs.

Breakfast would be missing one this morning, and I didn't really care all that much. I wish I was able to see the look on Mark's face when he realized he was now also a prisoner. That served him right. What he chose to do with his freedom was atrocious and could have easily ruined our family.

I was glad he now knew what it felt like to be isolated and alone, as he had made me feel recently.

I walked into the dining room, and my mom's face was clearly terse. She had taken this Mark situation harder than any of us, and I knew it was because she was struggling with her emotions on it. Truth is, she didn't know how to handle it, and was facing an internal battle.

"Sit. We need to go over what you will say when people ask about Mark."

"Nobody is going to ask about Mark..."

"Yes, well, if they do, tell them that he has a nasty stomach bug. Don't forget to add that it may be a few weeks before he is feeling back to normal. I don't suspect this detox will take that long, but we must prepare."

"Okay, mom."

She smiled, clearly happy knowing that she got her point across. Her mood did a complete three-sixty and she clapped her hands together.

"I have something that will cheer you up pumpkin." She smiled at me, got up, and ran into the other room, coming back holding her iPad.

She hovered next to me, handing me the iPad. She leaned down and whispered in my ear.

"I thought you would want to see Katie's reaction when she woke up and realized she didn't escape." My mother laughed and sat back down to resume eating her breakfast.

I pressed play, anxiousness blooming in my stomach. The video started, and Katie was lying on the floor, still clearly unconscious.

You could see her start to stir, her brown hair splayed against the metal floor.

Finally, she sat up, rubbed her eyes, and realized the chain connected to her wrist.

She looked absolutely panicked. She looked over at the other girls wide-eyed and started to cry. She then looked down at her purplish blue, swollen ankle.

Serves you right for trying to escape.

She then laid her head down in her lap, still clearly sobbing.

The video ended.

My mom was looking at me, smiling, and I handed the iPad back to her.

She was right, that did make me feel better.

My dad rolled his eyes, finding humor in my mom and I's exchange, and stifled a laugh as well.

Things were so much easier… so much *better* without Mark around.

"I have to get to school. I'll see you guys later… love you."

I was met with a chorus of "Love you too" as I made my way to the front door, keys in hand. If Mark knew I was about to drive his baby right now, he would blow a freaking lid. This car meant everything to him, and that made it that much more satisfying that I was about to get behind the wheel of it.

I unlocked the car and slid into the driver's seat.

This felt awesome.

I stuck the key in the ignition, starting the car. The engine began to hum with power, as I thrust the gear shift into reverse.

Slowly, but surely Amy.

I backed the car up ever so slowly and held the brake as I shifted back into drive.

I pulled up to the attendant box, and George came out, clearly taken aback.

"Where's Mark?" George was laughing, knowing full well Mark would never let me drive his car.

"Sick." I shrugged my shoulders and gassed it as George let the gates open for me. I started cruising to school, confidence growing as I drove.

I really should get my license.

I found Mark's sunglasses and slid them over my eyes.

I continued my cruise down the open road, until the school came into view, and my mood simmered. Nothing to put you in a shitty mood after a great morning, like going to high school. I was so glad to almost be done with this place and all the judgment, drama, and issues that came with it.

I parked the car perfectly between the two allotted lines given to us. Mark had his own specific spot since the beginning of the school year, when he was lucky enough to snag it at registration.

It also may have had something to do with Mom and Dad's generous donation to the school once again.

Having money did have its perks.

I locked the car, heading into school. Per usual, I was met with a lot of judgmental staring, and obvious whispers. These people truly had nothing better to do with their lives.

I was sure that the absence of Mark who was usually joined at my hip was also a cause for gossip. In Prairie, everything was a cause for gossip.

I settled into my first period class seat as Mr. Aryn took the time to set up his PowerPoint presentation which was guaranteed to be a snooze fest.

I felt myself dozing off from sheer boredom, and due to the lack of sleep I got last night. Another thing to thank Mark for.

The bell rang, and I finished writing down the homework assignment in my planner.

I stood up, collected my things, and mentally prepared for mind-numbing Calculus. School wasn't my forte, but third period Creative Writing was my favorite.

Katie and I had signed up for it together.

I pushed that manipulative bitch to the back of my mind as I stepped into my math class. Johnny was perched in his usual seat, looking surprisingly sober.

I headed to the back and took my seat beside him without a glance or a single word.

"Mark seems to be missing today. That wouldn't be because he's with Katie?"

This kid had a death wish.

"Not that it is any of your business, but he's sick." I wouldn't entertain this bullshit, but couldn't risk someone else hearing it, and spreading gossip.

Johnny didn't reply, but simply tut-tutted, and started on the problems the teacher was vigorously writing on the board.

I figured that burying my thoughts in equations was also the way to go and followed suit.

Creative Writing was the best class of the day by far, but no story I wrote could outdo the one I was living in right now. If it wasn't my life, I wouldn't believe it.

The rest of the day droned on by.

When the final bell rang, I practically sprinted to Mark's car, eager to get home and kick my feet up.

What a hard week so far, and it was only Wednesday!

I started the car, turned to grab my seatbelt, and nearly had a heart attack at the sight of Johnny Antin standing outside my driver's window.

I rolled the window down.

"Can I help you?"

"Where are you going Amy?"

"Home. Now stop being a creep before I file a restraining order."

I rolled the window up before he had the chance to reply. I threw the car in reverse and got the hell out of there.

He really did make me uncomfortable and I wasn't sure if it was because I knew he was onto me, or because he might know more than he should.

I was casually driving, slower than usual, at an attempt to take in my surroundings. When I got home, I would be forced to deal with my actual problems, and I wanted to pretend for a while longer.

I needed to stop for gas and pulled into the nearest one. A silver Chevy pulled in behind me, and I thought nothing of it.

I also didn't worry too much when the same car pulled back out behind me as I was leaving.

I knew I was being paranoid, but I didn't care.

I did a test.

I made a right. They did the same. Another right… same result. I made another two rights, completing a full circle.

It wasn't until I realized that they were still behind me that a harrowing truth set in.

I was being followed.

28

Katie

Defeated. Confused. Angry.

I can't even begin to describe the feeling of having freedom so close within my reach, to having it snatched away in the blink of an eye.

I have no clue what happened to Mark, and that both equally terrified and worried me because he was my ticket out of here.

I had never felt so alone before.

Kim and Tara respected my not wanting to talk this morning, and quietly let me process everything. So many things were going through my head, since I woke up back in this room this morning. *Would Sharon come down here and shoot me like she did Anna? For escaping?*

I guess I can't even call it an escape, but rather a lack thereof. All I remember was seeing the open road, feeling elated and also having my ankle in a lot of pain. Then it all faded to black.

My heart started beating out of control, listening for every small noise I could, terrified that each one would be someone unlocking the door to come down and kill me.

We tried to get away, and we failed. I had no doubt there would be harsh, and cruel consequences to follow. That was this family's style after all. I guess I would wait for Mark to come in tonight, and maybe he would be up to making a new game plan. *Don't fail me now Mark.*

The door unlocked, and I felt myself visibly tense up. I mentally prepared myself for the very real possibility that this could be one of the last moments of my life.

I love you dad.

It was none other than Paul who sauntered in the door. He had our food on a tray. Three plates. Okay, maybe they weren't going to kill me.

Or it was your last meal.

Paul placed a plate in front of Kim, then Tara, and finally me. He looked me in my eyes and shook his head. I guess he was disappointed in me, and I couldn't find a shit to give. Screw him, this psychotic family, and the horse they rode in on.

I was so tired of being here, and more fed up with the fact that they felt they had a right to keep me here. They were horrendous people and didn't deserve to have another day of blissful freedom, while I sat here, as a prisoner for a moment longer.

I kept telling myself that they would receive their karma. It did slightly take the edge off, but I also was a realist who knew that the world wasn't a perfect place where those who did wrong always paid the price for it.

Paul delivered one last final look to all three of us, and head upstairs. Maybe Paul decided we were all more trouble than we were worth. Maybe we would all be on the chopping block because of Mark and I's mistake.

My stomach clenched.

I had done nothing but get people hurt since I got here. Anna would have still been alive if it wasn't for me. I hated myself.

I wasn't in the mood for food of any kind, but I knew I needed the sustenance, and forced myself to take a bite.

Bread, and fruit. They really did try and give us the bare minimum to keep us alive, but not strong. Maybe it was my fault that Mark and I weren't able to get away last night.

Or it was Sharon's fault for breaking my damn ankle.

I wondered why she didn't come downstairs herself this morning. Knowing full well what kind of person she was at this point, I found myself genuinely surprised that she passed on the opportunity to revel in my botched escape attempt.

Maybe she was waiting until dinner time.

"Are you okay Katie?" Kim's words broke my thoughts, and for a small second, I was grateful. Despite these horrendous people that kept us here, I was my own worst enemy right now.

"Not really. But there's nothing I can do, can I?"

Kim just gave me a small smile, and weirdly enough, Tara also looked sympathetic. She had to watch Anna try and escape twice, to which the second attempt resulted in her death, in front of our eyes. She knew exactly what it was like.

I stopped eating when I felt like I couldn't possibly stomach anymore food. Eating the same thing every day was hard enough, and each bite today felt like swallowing sand. I had a pit in my stomach over the whole thing last night, and not seeing Mark was throwing my anxiety into overdrive.

As much as I thought he was a piece of crap for what he did to not only me, but every other girl he has taken, he seemed to be the only one who gave a damn about me. I needed him, even if it was hard to admit it.

"I need to get the hell out of here."

"You tried. They won't let us leave- ever." Tara spoke, and I knew she was right. They would not ever let us leave. I didn't care though. I would die trying to escape again before I spent another day, another week in here.

I closed my eyes for a small millisecond to regain focus, and I was out. I was absolutely exhausted from the previous night, and whatever they gave us to knock us out still felt like some was leftover in my system.

When I opened my eyes, it was dinner time. *Did I sleep the whole day?*

Tara and Kim were already feasting their dinner plates which look to be haphazardly thrown. *Sharon was here.*

Mine was thrown in front of me, obvious by the fact that half the food was off the plate. She was such a bitch.

I started eating in silence, only just realizing how famished I was. There was a fresh bottle of water in front of me, and I started chugging that as well. I don't remember getting water this morning, probably a punishment for trying to escape.

They were nothing if not creative.

When I finished my flavorless meal, I turned to Kim.

"Was I out all day?"

"Yeah you were actually slipping in and out of consciousness, mumbling about Mark. It's okay. You were tired. Sharon brought the food down ten minutes or so ago."

"Did she say anything?"

"Just that she would be back. You know what that means."

I did know what that meant. She was feeling particularly evil today and wanted to inflict pain on us. I knew Mark wouldn't come down for that, but I only hoped he would come down later tonight.

Unless they were angry with him, which I knew without a doubt that they were. He was their family, but he had clearly chosen me last night over them, and that had to sting. Maybe his punishment would be no access to see me.

In that case, I was screwed.

"Yes, I do." I shook my head, and mentally prepared myself for what was to come.

It couldn't have been more than an hour when the door opened. I braced myself and expected the worst. What would be the worst?

You dead.

I really hope not.

I knew Sharon would be the one coming down, but accompanying her was her little psycho in training, Amy. Those two were cut from the same cloth in every way imaginable. The whole family was horrible, don't get me wrong. These two however, had a special taste for violence and demeaning women.

"I'm sure you both know that our little Katie tried to leave us last night. We all know that everyone in this room sans my daughter and I knew full well of whatever plan that it was. Therefore, everyone will be punished." Sharon started walking toward Kim.

Oh god, no!

"No… please don't!" Kim pulled her arms up cover her face, giving Sharon full access to her stomach which she greeted with a blow.

As Kim doubled over in pain, Amy ran over and delivered another hit to the side of her head. Sharon grabbed her hair, pulling her head back, as Amy delivered punch after punch, bloodying Kim's face.

I can't watch this shit.

I turned away, to which Amy of course noticed. She walked over to me and rather than hitting me, she stood behind me, grabbing my head, and holding my eyes open.

Cruel bitch.

"Oh no Katie, you have to watch. See, you *caused* all of this. You." Amy let out a cold laugh.

"When I get out of here, I'll make sure you and your whole family never see the light of day again." I forcefully turned my heads, deadlocking with Amy's eyes.

"Whole family, huh? Even your little love Mark? Oh, you don't really like him though, do you? Such a shame… that he's being punished for someone who doesn't even love him back."

Punished…

Amy could clearly see her words affected me and continued.

"Yeah, Mark is now a prisoner as well. He gets to stay in the main house of course, but his regimen is quite similar to you whores. Two meals a day, constantly chained, oh and he gets his very own bucket as well!" Her eyes danced with excitement, and I was able to truly see the depths of her depravity.

She wasn't just hateful towards me, but everyone who got in her way. Even Mark.

"Are you that vile of a person that you don't even have loyalty towards your family? You make me fucking sick." Just like last time, I ended my sentence with spitting in her face.

She wiped the spit off, infuriated. She punched me, sending my head sideways, to which I felt Sharon rush up and kick me in the ribs.

Don't go for the ankle, please.

They stayed away from my ankle, but only to batter my body and leave me bleeding everywhere else. Finally, Sharon ceased and moved on to Tara. Amy bent down and grabbed my face, so I was forced to look at her.

"You have seemed to forget who the hell is in charge here. You see, I control your fate. Whether you live, die, eat. Don't fuck with me Katie. You're on thin ice." She shoved my head and it hit the back of the post where I was chained at.

Satisfied with their beatings, Amy and her mother headed towards the door. When they reached the door, Sharon began to head up as she wiped the blood off her face with a handkerchief. Amy grabbed the door and began closing it before she turned and looked at me.

"Remember what I said Katie. I will kill you myself if you step out of line again. And that's not a threat. It's a promise."

She slammed the door shut, and Kim and Tara began to cry, as they used their clothes to mop up the blood dripping off of them.

This was agonizing, and I wasn't referring to the pain.

They were mentally trying to break us.

And I'm not going to let them.

29

Mark

They were treating me like the trash we kept down in the Iron Room. They only brought me two meals today, not even allowing me to use my bathroom in my room. My chain only went so far as to let me use the bucket they so generously left for me.

I can't believe my family would be so angry with me as to treat me like the filthy girls I capture. I was better than them, and I think my family felt this tactic best to help me remember who I was.

I was remembering all right. I was a part of this family, held to the highest esteem, and I wasn't like that garbage. I was more furious than anything that they would choose to treat me as such.

Amy had been a real pain in my ass lately, and I was even more infuriated when I saw the footage from today. I still had my iPad with me, directly linked to the camera in the Iron Room. It gave me full access to watch in current time, as well as past.

I watched what her and my mother did to Katie, and I was enraged. How dare they treat her like dirt and literally kick her while she was down?
I didn't want to be a part of this family anymore.

They thought keeping me in my room, chained, and imprisoned like this would bring me some sense of clarity. Well, it did. I don't think it's the kind they hoped for though.

The only thing I am able to truly see now is just how toxic and horrendous my family is. It's okay to treat Tara and Kim like this, but the way they were able to turn on Katie at the drop of a dime blows my mind.

Katie is our friend.

The truth had become quite clear to me- my family was willing to kill anyone who got in their way.

Maybe even me.

Being able to at least see Katie brought me a small sense of comfort. I hated seeing the way my family treated her but was glad to see my dad didn't partake in this.

Amy was all big and tough, but what if Katie didn't have the chains on? Would she be so strong then? Katie kicked her ass before, *while* chained up. Not only was my sister weak minded, but she was weak physically.

That's probably why she loved torturing these girls so much. She had no control in her everyday life, letting people walk all over her. In the Iron Room, Amy had all the power against multiple defenseless women.

I had wished more than anything that we had audio in the room, but it was solely the camera. Seeing Katie spit in Amy's face was the highlight of my morning, which otherwise was quite dull.

I saw Katie talk to Kim a lot more than she did with Tara. Tara didn't really talk to either of them, or she didn't say much at all. She had always been like that- meek and awkward.

I felt like I was going stir crazy in here. I needed to get the hell out. Now.

My bedroom door opened and my sister sauntered in.

I hate you.

"We need to talk." She looked nervous and was wringing her hands.

"I don't really care to speak to you. As far as I'm concerned, you and I are done Amy."

"You don't mean that. We're family." She sat down on the edge of my bed and I had an urge to lay her out after what she did to Katie.

I didn't even justify that bullshit with a response and stayed silent. She continued to stare at me, and I finally realized she wasn't leaving.

"What is it Amy?!"

"I was being followed today."

"I'm supposed to care?"

"This is serious Mark. It was Johnny."

"Johnny followed you where? At school?" I was a little pissed off, that he had heeded my warning. Once I was out of this prison lockdown, we would have another talk, one that was a lot less nice.

"No. I was driving… my car, and I saw him behind me. I pulled across the road sideways, and he wasn't able to pass. He got out of the car, so I asked him why he was following me."

"And?" My sister was the slowest storyteller, and I had very little patience as it was.

"He warned me. He said that he knows there's something going on with our family and that we're connected to the missing girls. He said he's not going to stop until he found out the truth. I told him he was insane, and I got back in the car." Amy let out a long breathe, almost like she had been holding it in for a while.

I carefully mulled over this new information. Johnny was dangerously close to the truth. In fact, I wouldn't be surprised if he found those girls any day now. But that was no longer my problem. With me locked up, anything concerning the girls was none of my business, excluding Katie of course.

"Say something Mark."

Why are you still in my room?

"I hope he finds the girls. And I can't wait to see you get led away in handcuffs."

Amy's jaw dropped and she slapped me across the face.

A one trick pony I see.

"Get the hell out of my room."

"Don't have to tell me twice." Amy stomped towards the door, and slammed it shut. I could see tears streaming down her face. I can't believe I ever considered her family. We were different in every sense of the word, and I couldn't even stomach being in the same room as her anymore.

I laid my head against the pillow. My head felt like it would explode any moment. I needed to get out of here. I couldn't be a prisoner in my own home. I wondered how my Katie was doing.

I pulled out my iPad again, and slid onto the camera app. There she was.

She was sitting there, eyes closed. Part of me was bummed out because I wasn't able to see her beautiful blue eyes, but her brown hair looked gorgeous as ever. God, she really was the most beautiful girl in the world.

My girl.

I rubbed my thumb over the screen, aching to touch her. I wondered if she missed me the same way I did her. Even as we were running through the forest, the chemistry was palpable, and the connection was absolutely electric.

We belonged together.

I couldn't find my phone anywhere, but I knew the iPad could message people through apps. I got onto Facebook and looked up a name.

Johnny Antin.

I friended him, and impatiently waited for a response. He must have been on, because he almost immediately accepted it. Once I received that notification, my finger tapped the message icon, and I started typing.

Mark Puntzer: Hi Johnny. I know this is really weird. My sister just came in my room about how you followed and threatened her today. The truth is, you are right. Katie, Kim, and Tara are all locked in an Iron Room which is completely soundproof. I tried to rescue Katie and now I am chained up in my room. I need to get her out, and I need your help.

He read the message as soon as I sent it, and several minutes went by before I saw the typing icon.

Johnny Antin: Is this a joke?

Mark Puntzer: No, I wish it was. I need to think of a plan. I'll message you later with the details. My parents are pissed. I don't think Katie has much longer.

Johnny Antin: Okay man. I'll be waiting.

I deleted the messages and hid the Facebook app behind a bunch of other ones in the rare possibility my mother was crazy enough to search my devices. It was hard to see the sweet mom I grew up with turning into a person who would chain her own son in his room.

I didn't care about the consequences that would surely follow if the girls were released or found anymore. I would serve my time, however long that may be, as long as it meant I was able to be with Katie.

Knowing her, she might even find it noble or attractive that I would be willing to sacrifice my freedom, even if for a little bit, just to one day be with her.

I knew she loved me. I just knew it. I checked my iPad. 6:24.

My door cracked open, and my mother pushed her way in carrying a tray with my dinner on it. Meatloaf with mashed potatoes, and peas. My favorite.

Nothing like a good home cooked meal to fix the fact that you locked your only son up.

"Mark honey, I have dinner."

"I see that."

"Are you going to be upset with me forever? That's not very fair."

"And this is?" I held up my chained arm.

'Mark, that was necessary. We simply do not know where your head is at these days. It's a precaution. But you are my son, and I love you."

"Is this how you show your love? A bucket? Two meals a day? You're punishing me. I'm not one of your little captives. You seem to have forgotten that." I shook my head. I couldn't look at her. I couldn't look at anyone in this family anymore.

"Mark…"

"Just leave the food and go. Please."

I heard the clatter of the plates, footsteps, and then a door opening and closing. Finally.

I turned my attention to my dinner and started feasting at the speed of light. I was starving, and the stress of my family only exacerbated that.

I cleared the plate within five minutes, and then lay in a food comatose watching Law and Order reruns for an hour after.

I got lost in a few movies and started hearing my mom and dad go to bed. I checked the time. 11:04. Yeah, everyone was turning in for the night for sure. I heard Amy padding down the hall, followed by a door opening and closing.

I pulled up the camera on my iPad once more. Katie was awake now and talking to Kim.

I wish I could hear what you're saying.

Katie turned towards the camera. She was mouthing something, and I was desperately trying to make out what it was in the dimly lit room.

I…love…you? I love you?

I replayed the footage and confirmed that was indeed what she was trying to say. My heart swelled three sizes bigger, and I felt a grin spreading across my face.

I knew it. I just knew it.

Maybe it wasn't meant for you.

Well who the hell else would it be for? Everyone in this house abused and tortured Katie, but not me. I laid everything on the line and risked the love of my family for this girl. I would do it all again too, given the chance. I was just elated that she had realized the true depths of my love for her and returned those feelings.

I need to get her out of here. And I need help.

I closed down the camera footage and opened Facebook messenger once more. I typed compose, selected Johnny Antin and started typing.

Mark Puntzer: I was thinking about it, and I definitely need your help. It will be a challenge. Our gate attendant is in on everything and will not let the girls escape.

Johnny Antin: I don't care. I want to help.

Mark Puntzer: Glad to hear that. Now here's the plan...

30

Amy

I decided to take a risk, and slammed on the breaks of Mark's car, turning it to the side. Whoever was following me was blocked off. They had no choice but to get out of the car.

I parked and turned off the ignition. The person in the other car stalled theirs, and opened the front door, stepping out.

Johnny Antin.

I shouldn't be surprised, but I am.

Why the hell was he following me?

He started to walk towards the car, and a small part of me started to panic, unsure of what he was about to do.

"Why are you following me?"

He was getting closer and closer until he walked right up to the driver's door of Mark's car.

"This is your brother's car, isn't it?"

"And? You followed me over a car?"

"No, I followed you because I was trying to see where you're hiding the girls." He eyed me suspiciously, casually glancing towards the backseat. As if they would be there!

"What girls, Johnny?"

"You know what girls. I'm going to find them and expose you."

With that being said, he turned and started off back towards his car.

"Why don't you stop trying to be a hero Johnny?"

He stopped dead in his tracks, and I wondered if he would come back. He simply turned around, looked me right in my eyes, and spoke.

"Because Tara deserves a hero. She deserves someone to save her. They all do."

Tara?

He turned back around and got into his car. I started Mark's car back up, fixing it so I was right side on the road again. I continued on my way home.

He didn't scare me. I mean, I didn't think he would physically hurt me, but his threats about finding the girls sounded pretty real. He hasn't let up since the first day of school when I met him, and I feared he never would... not until he found them.

I can't believe that after all this time, that people still pretended to care. They didn't. They wanted to act like they were helping, just so they could sleep at night. Their efforts were useless. Take me for example, I know exactly where the girls are, and I sleep awesome at night.

I felt myself visibly shaking, and I mentally chastised myself. I was in control. I wouldn't allow myself to be feel weak or be intimidated by Johnny.

Breathe Amy. Breathe.

My hands were gripping the steering wheel so hard that my knuckles were turning white. I needed to get this anger out. And I knew just the way.

I pulled up to the gate of my house, and George buzzed me in. I parked Mark's car, and headed inside nearly tripping over my mother's purse on the way in. She was home early.

"Mom? Are you home?"

"Yeah hon. I'm in the kitchen."

I walked into the kitchen to find my mother leaned against the island with her head in her hands.

"What's going on? Are you okay?"

"Would you believe me if I told you I had the worst day? Marcy at the office was giving me crap again, and everyone else seemed to try and get on my bad side."

"Right there with you, Mom."

We looked at each other, an unspoken understanding passing between us. She grabbed the Iron Room keys out of her purse, and we headed out there.

"I already brought them an early dinner."

"Yeah well they can starve for all I care."

My mom unlocked the door, and we headed downstairs. I could feel the excitement building, as it always did before a session.

When we stepped into the room, my mom started in on Kim. She always started with the girl closest to the door and worked her way down. Sometimes I would join in and help, and other times we would hurt different girls at different times.

I helped her with that one, when to no surprise, Katie started mouthing off. I had already been feeling resentful towards her lately and beating the absolute shit out of her is exactly what I needed.

Before I knew it, I was wailing on her. My mom started in too. She was no longer my ex best friend, but the bitch that brain washed my brother into turning on his own family. She couldn't be trusted at all.

I made sure to leave her with a warning.

Katie's time here wasn't promised, and after what she did, it was also limited.

My mom and I headed outside, feeling a million times better than we did when we stepped into the room. There was something about taking out your stress and anger in a physical way that really brought you a sense of inner peace.

All the worries, and pent up aggression that had been slowly building the past few days was released, and I felt whole again.

We could never lose this room. Or the girls.

When my mom and I got back into the house, we went our separate ways to wash up before dinner. I stepped into my bathroom, turning the shower up all the way. The steam began to cascade throughout the entirety of the room, enveloping me in it.

I loved hot showers, and today I felt especially dirty after being caked with blood.
Katie's blood.

I stepped into the boiling shower and gasped at the stream hit my back. I began to cup water in my hands, and rinsed my face thoroughly making sure every last drop was gone. I decided to wash my hair as well, knowing that would make me feel even cleaner.

I did that quickly, washed my face, then body, and turned off the shower. I stepped out and was completely in steam. I used my hand to wipe the mirror and began taking my makeup off with a wipe as I simultaneously started wrapping my hair in a towel. I wrapped my body with another, and opened the door letting all the steam out and feeling the instant rush of cold air.

I closed my bedroom door and started to dry myself.

When I was finally dressed, I raked a brush through my hair and headed downstairs where the smell of meatloaf was already starting to waft through the air.

Mark's favorite.

I wrinkled my nose in disdain. Why my mother decided to reward Mark with his favorite meal was beyond me. He had betrayed us last night, and nearly cost us everything we have built and worked for.

My mom gestured me into the dining room. "Take a seat love. I'm going to grab the rolls. She shuffled into the dining room.

It was only my dad and I sitting there, and it settled into a comfortable silence. My dad and I were close, but not as close as my mom and myself. I had felt a rift especially between him and I lately, similar to the one with Mark.

"How was school today Amy?"

"You know, same old. How was work?"

"Same old."

Someone please save me from this conversation.

Right on cue, my mom rejoined us in the dining room, carrying a plate of hot rolls fresh from the oven.

"Sorry about that. You guys can dig in."

I took a bite of the meatloaf, and it was wonderful. My mom always used her grandmother's recipes for the meatloaf, and every single time it turned out amazing. Truth be told, she didn't exactly cook the meals herself, our chef did. It was still a family recipe though.

"Did you get your homework done?" My mom was trying to create conversation, even though I had told her earlier I didn't.

"Nope. They gave us a free day."

"Well, isn't that lovely?" She smiled and continued eating her dinner. Like me, she was always relieved and in the best mood after a visit to the Iron Room. My dad and Mark were wary when it came to physical abuse of the girls, so visits were always better when it was comprised of only her and I.

I did feel like a weight was lifted off my shoulders, but still was mulling over what Johnny said today.

He has to be feeling pretty confident that we have the girls, or he wouldn't go to the lengths of following me home. What exactly did he plan to do when he got here?

He wouldn't make it past the front gate, let alone be able to get the first, and second door open to where the girls were. Then, how would he make it unspotted with three girls in tow? His plan was baseless, and it would only get him hurt.

Even though I was still pretty furious with Mark, he always provided great insight. I planned to fill him in on everything that happened with Johnny after dinner.

Once I finished my food, I excused myself and headed upstairs, straight into Mark's room. "We need to talk."

"I don't really care to speak to you. As far as I'm concerned, you and I are done Amy." Mark looked angry with me, and I couldn't understand why. He was the one that turned his back on us.

"You don't mean that. We're family." I sat down on the edge of his bed.

He didn't answer or reply, but just stared at me blankly.

What was his deal?

"What is it Amy?!"

"I was being followed today." I braced for his reaction.

"I'm supposed to care?"

Yeah? You're my brother!

"This is serious Mark. It was Johnny." I knew full well that would set him off, especially since Johnny and Mark had already had a physical altercation earlier.

"Johnny followed you where? At school?" He looked upset.

"No. I was driving… my car, and I saw him behind me. I pulled across the road sideways, and he wasn't able to pass. He got out of the car, so I asked him why he was following me."

"And?"

I rushed into an explanation of everything that was said between Johnny and I earlier this afternoon, trying to not forget a single detail. Rather than reacting, Mark continued to sit there in silence.

"Say something Mark."

"I hope he finds the girls. And I can't wait to see you get led away in handcuffs."

My jaw dropped open, and I delivered a hard slap to the side of his face.

Mark was out of control.

"Get the hell out of my room."

"Don't have to tell me twice." I pushed open the door, making sure I slammed it on the way out.

Where the hell does Mark get off? I chose to forgive, well sort of, everything that he did yesterday. I chose to put my ego aside and try and confide in him like I used to, but naturally he turned away and acted as if he didn't give a shit about me.

Maybe I needed to realize that it wasn't an act. I have always been someone who wasn't big on words, but rather actions, and his actions proved my point. He didn't care about anyone in this family.

I sat on the edge of my bed and laid my head against the pillow. I put my head in my hands, frustrated at the lack of communication my family had. Usually, we never would talk about what was on our mind or what was bugging us, but now, Mark hadn't stopped. He had no problem telling me just how horrible of a person he thought I was.

Fine by me.

Mark would really hate me after I killed his little girlfriend.

I had been stewing over the idea of killing Katie for a while now. At first, it was only because she was becoming a liability. Now, it would be even sweeter if I was able to spite Mark in the process.

I would kill Katie tomorrow.

31

Katie

It was clear that Mark wasn't going to come down here anymore, and I struggled with the why. Was it because his family forbade him? Was it because he was angry with me? Or did they do something to him in retaliation for what him and I did?

Feeling bold last night, I turned towards the camera before bed and mouthed the words "I love you." It was a lot easier than saying it to his face, because I didn't have to see his sickening reaction. I had no clue if he would even see it. I don't know how their camera systems worked and he might not even have access to it.

Or maybe they killed him.

I wouldn't put anything past this sick family as this point, but I knew without a doubt that if anyone could kill one of their own children, it would be Sharon and Paul. She was truly messed up in the head and justified all of her horrible actions.

In any case, I wanted to make sure that if Mark is alive, that he thinks I am still loyal and in love with him. I need him to help me out of here since there is really nothing that I can do with the chains still on me.

As much as I wanted to break out and free the other two girls on my own, it was simply impossible to do so. If I was breaking out, I needed to actually get away this time or I was afraid that it would be the last thing I did. They had seemingly looked the other way both times, when Anna was shot to death over her second escape attempt.

These people kidnapped and tortured the Sheriff's daughter. Maybe they were just afraid that if they killed me, and people found out, they would be imprisoned or sentenced to death.

Isn't that a scary thought?

The all too familiar sound of doors and chains unlocking forced me to sit up straighter. I hated the effect these people had on me. I wasn't usually one to scare easily, but after all I had been through, put through, by this family- I felt terrified at all hours of the day. Every minute, second even, was spent waiting in dread for the moment they would come down the stairs and hurt, or even kill one of us.

They would probably kill me next.

Amy was the one to walk in, carrying our breakfast. She only had two plates today, unusual considering there were three of us. She carefully placed a plate in front of Kim, then Tara, and when it got to me, she just shrugged and walked out.

Bitch!

I wouldn't have guessed starvation would be my way to go. In fact, it's humorous. These people were barely feeding us enough to stay alive, and while I wasn't about to waste away on the spot, if this turned into a routine- I would be dead.

Maybe that's what they want Katie.

Amy, sure. But Mark? At this point I was sure he would die for me. But they would never let him of course. I needed to get the hell out of here.

I missed my dad so much, that some days it felt as if there was a constant ache in my chest. Not only was I aching from missing him, but I knew how much he is hurting with me gone, and that makes it even worse. All of this- the torture, the starving, the beatings, the treatment of my dad… it only adds fuel to the fire and creates a fight in me that I have never had before.

I was ready to get out of this place and was willing to fight like hell to do so.

"Here." Kim pushed her plate towards me, and it was half full of her food.

"I can't. Finish it."

"I can survive on half a plate Katie. You can't go without anything in your stomach…especially if you're going to get us out of here." Kim laughed.

I pulled the food over and couldn't help myself as I ravaged the plate. I was really hungry, as the portions given were already teetering on the smaller side.

I finished the entire plate in under two minutes, and I used my sleeve to wipe my face. I coiled back from the smell of my clothes. I smelled absolutely disgusting, and I had this family to thank for that. I hadn't changed my clothes, or showered in days, not to mention that I was caked in dried blood.

"Thanks Kim." I cracked a smile.

She just nodded at me and looked over at Tara who was quiet per usual.

"I'm trying to think of a new game plan. Mark hasn't come down since the escape. Either he's dead or they have done something to him, so we can't base our plan on him anymore."

"Our plan? Since when has it been "our plan"?" Tara looked irritated.

"What are you talking about Tara?"

"You and Mark made it all the way to the forest, and you didn't once try and come back for us. They could have killed us for your retaliation, but you didn't care, did you?"

I tried to keep my cool, but I was sick to death of Tara's behavior.

"What the hell is your problem? You have been a massive bitch ever since I arrived. Oh, and do you know why I arrived? Because I got in over my head trying to find you and Anna! Everything I do is to try and get us ALL out of here. Being in this room is no fucking walk in the park, but you and your fucking attitude DO NOT HELP. If you can't attribute anything nice, then shut the hell up."

Tara stared at me openmouthed but recovered quickly and shut it.

Finally. I was getting tired of Miss Negativity on a constant loop.

"Okay I think we're all feeling a little worn out. Let's just take it down a notch." Kim was attempting to smooth things over between Tara and I, but it was no use.

Tara didn't care about getting out of here, and she didn't care about Kim or myself. The only person she seemed to get along with was Anna, and in Tara's mind and mine, I was the reason Anna was killed.

"Whatever."

I turned away from both of them, making sure my back was facing them. I was feeling so emotionally and physically drained. Our bodies were physically being put through trauma day after day, with no real nourishment, or relaxation.

Sure, we were locked down here, but mentally we were being put through the ringer. We were forced to live in constant fear worrying when they would torture us, and who would do it.

Mark, where are you?

I looked towards the camera, and for a split second missed him. I didn't support or like the person he was, but he was kind to me. Kindness and warmness go a long way in a cold, dark place like this. While the pretending was hard, having Mark there for me brought me a sense of comfort that I so desperately needed.

I needed to get out of my own head for a while and decided to take a nap. Being asleep was better than being awake and knowing I was still prisoner in this hell hole.

I closed my eyes and drifted off to better times.

I was running up and down the beach, absolutely elated. My dad was taking pictures, laughing while my mother chased me trying to put more sun block on.

"Come here Katie!"

"Got to catch me mom!"

We ran until we dropped on the sand, exhausted. My dad walked over with two ice cream cones in his hand. One chocolate for me, and the other mint chip was for my mom.

"Got your favorites girls." He passed me a
cone, smiling down at me and my mother.

I woke up in a cold sweat, with a single tear
running down my cheek. I missed my mom so much.

I wished more than anything that she was still
alive. I didn't want my dad to be alone, especially
right now. He needed me, and I hadn't realized how
much I still need him.

A big part of recovering from the sudden loss
of my mother was being able to have my dad as my
support system. We leaned on each other in more
ways than one and found comfort in the mutual
feelings we both shared whether it be grief, anger, or
sadness.

I wiped the tear from my face, feeling
eternally grateful that I was not facing the cameras, or
the other girls for that matter. I didn't want them to
see me like this, vulnerable. I tried my hardest to put
on a strong front, especially in front of the other girls.

I was struggling beyond belief, and missing
my dad only furthered my pain.
I can't do this anymore.

Someone who has never gone through a
situation like this- one where you're ripped away
from everyone you love, kept in a secluded, dark, and
dismal place, beaten, treated like dirt, and abused
mentally... you began to break down. Mentally and
physically, I felt broken and I didn't know that I
would be able to put myself back together again even
after all this blew over.
If it blew over.
"I'm tired." I spoke to no one in particular, but rather
putting it out into existence.

"Take another nap hon." Kim had such a soothing voice, that for a split second I actually felt that if I were to take another nap, all would be healed.

"Not physically tired. Mentally. I feel broken."

"Me too." This time it was Tara that spoke, and she sounded genuinely empathetic.

I breathed a sigh of relief, glad that my true feelings were put out there. Facing and dealing with all the emotions that I had recently was hard enough on its own but hiding them from the two people I see all day, every day, was a real struggle.

I had no clue what time it was, but it must have been dinner time already because I heard doors being unlocked.

Oh joy.

I secretly hoped it was Mark who was about to walk in the door, but I knew there was no way of that happening.

Instead, it was Paul.

He carried three plates this time, and I felt myself visibly relax. I didn't want Kim to have to eat an even smaller portion yet again, simply because Amy had a hard vendetta against me.

As usual like clockwork, he carefully set the plate in front of Kim, then Tara, and last but not least me. He turned without another word and headed outside. He started locking the first door, then the second, and then it was quiet only interrupted by the noise of all of us chewing our dinner.

We ate in silence, devouring every last morsel. It was far from good, but a turkey sandwich wasn't the worst meal in the world.

It was better than nothing.

I looked over at Kim, and really took in everything about her face. She was starting to form bruises under her eyes and had a pretty badly cut lip. Her arms were covered in bruises and her wrist looked a little bent out of shape. I glanced over to Tara, who looked even worse. She had a large chunk of her hair missing, as if it had been ripped out. She had two black eyes, a bruised cheek, and more bruises up and down her arms as well as her chest.

Courtesy of Sharon and Amy Puntzer.

Those two were sick.

Right on cue, the door swung open and who else would it be but Sharon and Amy?

They both had wicked gleams on, and they didn't even hesitate before heading to Tara. Recently, they both had been starting with Kim, but maybe they were trying to switch up their "torture tactics". I rolled my eyes and prayed that it would be quick. I couldn't bear to watch either girl suffer at the hands of these maniacs.

Amy was the first to deliver a blow to Tara's right eye. Tara leaned over, crying in protest, to which Sharon took as an opportunity to knee her in the face. Sharon grabbed her hair yanking it back with such force that she ripped out another small chunk of hair. Amy began choking Tara, and I started to see her lose consciousness.

Oh my god... they're going to kill her.

"No! Stop!" A strangled sob escaped my throat, as I watched this unfold right in front of my eyes.

"Please!" Kim started pleading with Sharon and Amy, but to no avail.

Tara's eyes rolled to the back of her head, and she fell backwards. Sharon released her hair as she fell, and Tara's head made a sickening thud as it hit the cool metal.

They turned to Kim and started again. They both were going in on Kim so mercilessly: punching, biting, kicking... you name it. It was horrendous to watch, and I decided that I couldn't. I turned away and shut my eyes, leaving it all to my imagination.

I could hear Kim's cries, followed by the sounds of low laughter coming from both Amy and Sharon.

Please God, make it stop,

Almost immediately, the beating ceased. I braced for them to hurt me and turned around. Last thing I needed was to get hit from behind.

Sharon started stomping towards me when Amy grabbed her arm. She pulled her mother close to her and whispered something into her ear. I struggled to hear but wasn't able to.

Sharon looked at her daughter.
"Are you sure?"

Amy nodded, and her mother shrugged, heading towards the door.

Amy looked at her mother, then to me, and came towards me.

Oh, she wants you all to herself. Fuck.

"Don't think that all is good and well. In fact, it's the opposite. The hard beating that they received today? Your fault. Make sure they know that when they regain consciousness. Don't sleep too well either... never know who will be showing up."

She winked, laughed, and headed outside,

I took the opportunity to steal a glance at Kim, who looked exactly like Tara. They were both laid out on the floor, unconscious, as Amy put it.
I'm so glad they're not dead.

Hard beating because of me? Was she nuts?
Yes.

No. I wouldn't allow her to put her atrocious behavior on me. That was her cross to bear. The only reason I was in this situation in the first place, is because her and her sociopathic family decided to kidnap and torture girls in our town. The only actions that caused anything were hers.

It took the girls longer than expected to wake up. For a second, I was scared that Amy and Sharon had actually killed the girls on accident... or purpose.

After what seemed like an eternity, they both started to open their eyes. The bruising on their necks was starting to come through.

I couldn't see any bruises on myself besides my ankle, but my face did feel tender and I was sure I had the same markings at Kim and Tara.

"What happened?" Tara seemed very groggy and was grabbing at her throat which was clearly sore.

"Yeah..." Kim started mimicking Tara's movements.

"It was Amy. She was choking you guys and you passed out."

"You too?"

Did I lie... or tell the truth?

"No, I'm pretty sure she's waiting until she can complete the job and kill me."

"She's not going to kill you Katie." Kim tried to be reassuring, but she failed. It wasn't her fault, but more attributed to the fact that I felt it in my bones. There was a reason she didn't attack me today, and I really doubt it was because she "had a change of heart".

I shook my head.

"How are you guys feeling?" I tried to change the subject.

"Sore." Tara and Kim answered simultaneously.

"Look, I have a feeling Amy is going to come back for me tonight. If she does, pretend like you're sleeping, please. I don't want you guys to get hurt in the crossfire of this. It's between us."

They looked unsure, but finally nodded in agreement.

We all laid there talking about everything we would do when we got out of here. It was light-hearted, fun, and honestly really nice to finally see Tara getting out of her shell and embracing the future we could have.

I could hear the upstairs door unlocking, and I motioned for both girls to close their eyes. My heart started to pound a million miles a minute as I heard footsteps cascading down the steps followed by the chain moving around. The door swung open and in stepped Amy.

"Nice to see you're awake."

"What the hell do you want Amy?" I rolled my eyes, making it clear I didn't want her here.

"You should really watch the way you speak to me Katie." Amy pulled out a gun from her back pocket.

I'm going to die.

"What? You're going to kill me now?"

"Maybe I will. After all, you spit in my face throwing away how many years of friendship Katie? Oh, and you seduced my brother into betraying his family. You disgust me. I don't even know who you are anymore."

"Is this a fucking joke Amy? My best friend turned out to be someone who kidnaps and tortures people. You let your brother throw me in here and you and your mother take turns beating not only me, but them too. I'm the disgusting one?" My words spit out, dripping with venom.

"Yeah, you are." Amy pointed the gun directly between my eyes, cocking the gun.

I'm sorry dad.

"Any last words?" Amy smirked.

I was about to say something, when the sound of the gun went off. Tara and Kim started screaming. I didn't feel any pain, so I opened my eyes only to find Amy lying in a heap at my feet, bleeding from her head.

My head jerked up to find someone standing there, pointed a gun at Amy.

Johnny Antin.

"C'mon girls. We're getting you out of here."

32

Mark

The plan was simple. Johnny was hiding in the edge of the forest by the house, waiting for my signal. I had my iPad set up with the Iron Room camera on. I would wait for someone to go down there, and then have Johnny rush in and get the girls.

I had no clue who would be coming down there, but I didn't care if it was my mom, dad, or Amy. Johnny was instructed to knock out whoever it was and take the girls.

Those idiots always left both doors open when they came into the Iron Room. They felt it was safe, given that we owned two acres of property which was heavily forested in the back, and guarded in the front by George.

While there is no gate attendant in the back of the property, there is still a good chunk of forest to sweep through, and I had to talk Johnny through navigating it. We had been using Facebook messenger as our only form of communication, since those idiots also took my phone.

I waited until someone came in the room, this time it was Amy.

I let Johnny know it was a go, and he started to head into the room.

Things started taking a turn for the worse when Amy threatened to kill Katie and kept a gun positioned in front of her eyes.

My stomach became sick with worry as I waited for Johnny to rescue them, and while Katie remained at gunpoint. My sister was absolutely crazy. How she could go from seeing someone as her best friend, to trying to murder her was beyond me.

I had no doubt in my mind that if Johnny hadn't gotten there in time, that Katie would have been dead.

Instead of knocking Amy out, Johnny shot her point blank. I watched him take the keys off of my sister's bleeding and lifeless body, and quickly unlock all three girls free of their chains. They all ran out and I'm hoping they ran straight into the forest as I instructed.

For a few more moments, I watched my sister, patiently waiting for any small sign of life.

Nothing.

My sister was dead.

My parents were going to go absolutely ballistic, and I didn't know what they would do. We needed to get off this property and fast. I had no doubt that the gunshot woke them, or alerted George, and there would soon be a manhunt on this property conducted by who other than my savage mother.

The next phase of the plan was for Johnny to come up through the back of the house with Amy's keys, and freeing me. I knew the ins and outs of this house and could probably get out with Johnny virtually undetected.

Johnny coming in to get me, was another issue.

I had guided and instructed him as much as I could through the messaging service. Now, all I could do was wait.

I hid the iPad under my leg where it wasn't easily detected, or in a direct line of sight of the door.

I heard my parents up and about, loudly thrashing throughout the house. My mother let out a high-pitched thrill, and I figured she was watching the same footage I was. I heard the back door swing open loudly crashing into the frame. There were heavy footsteps coming up the stairs, which I identified as my dad's.

He's coming to make sure I'm still here.

Still alive and kicking Dad. Wish I could say the same about Amy.

She tried to kill Katie.

Yeah, never mind.

My door swung open, and my dad's eyes were wide and streaming with tears. I tried my best to feign a similar reaction.

"Dad! What's going on?!"

"Your sister has been shot. The girls are gone. Come on." He came towards me, and unlocked my chains, freeing me. I slid off of my bed, and his eyes darted to the unlocked iPad sitting there.

Shit.

He grabbed it swiftly before I had the chance to do so. His eyes scanned the Facebook messages, and he dropped the iPad on the floor in anger.

"What the hell have you done son?!" He began to charge me, but the lamp I was now holding connected with the side of his head, sending him in a slump to the floor.

I'm sorry.

I dropped the lamp and picked up the iPad that had a visible crack running across the entirety of the screen.

Please work.

I pressed the home button, unlocking it. Thank God. I open Facebook Messenger and there was a message waiting from Johnny.

Johnny Antin: Girls are safe and hidden at the very edge of the forest. I am coming to get you now.

It was sent two minutes ago. I still had time to warn him.

Mark Puntzer: No, stay with the girls. I'll find you. My dad unlocked me, and now he's unconscious. Will explain later. Stay where you are but be careful. My mother and George are probably out searching.

I threw the iPad under my bed, it being no more use to me. I couldn't carry a big iPad while I was running through the forest.

I pulled on a pair of shoes, and a large hoodie. I lightly closed my door, in the rare case that my mother was still in the house. I started heading downstairs when I heard her voice.

"Paul?"

She rounded the corner. I thought she would be upset, or angry that I was freed. But she looked relieved, and I could see the tears fresh on her face.

She found Amy.

"Mark! Oh god, I'm glad your dad freed you. Did he tell you what happened?"

"Yes… and we need to find them right now. Dad already went searching after he unlocked me."

"Unlocked you… baby I'm so sorry. We should have never done that to you."

"It's okay. Let's go find Dad."

She grabbed my hand pulling me outside. She handed me a tranquilizer gun.

"We're going to need all the manpower we have. There are three girls somewhere on this property as well as some stupid vigilante. Don't touch him. He killed my baby. He's mine."

I nodded in agreement, knowing full well that I wasn't letting my mother near Johnny or any of the girls, especially Katie. She needed to escape. I wouldn't allow her to spend another day trapped here.

We headed towards the forest.

I held fear in my heart at the possibility of my mother actually seeing and tranquilizing someone. I comforted myself in the sense that there was only a one in three chance of it being Katie. I have to admit that I hated the fact that the other two girls were getting off scot free.

They were horrible, nosy, greedy, and the list goes on and on. Society as a whole was much better without them in it. I had done the world a favor in taking them. Katie though, she never belonged here, and thanks to Johnny, she would never have to spend another day treated as a prisoner.

We just had to overcome the obstacle that was Sharon Puntzer.

I knew that George was somewhere on this property, lurking, hoping he could catch one of them and then use it to his own cash benefit. It didn't matter if he caught one, or two, or three. As long as one person escaped, they could go to the police and blow the lid off of this whole thing.

I knew we would all be put in prison. That was fine. I didn't think it was fair to be charged for the other three girls, especially since they were menaces to society. Katie though, taking her was wrong. I deserved to be put in prison for kidnapping her and taking time out of her life like that. I had faith that if I did, when I did, serve time that when I got out, Katie would see all that I have done for her since my mistake, and realize we are magic together. *Game time.*

My mom and I stepped into the edge of the forest.

"Let's split up Mom. I'll try to find Dad. I know he's out here somewhere."

"Okay." She turned and headed in the opposite direction. I continued straight. I knew if I continued straight, I would reach the edge of the forest line which turned into a main road. Once I was out there, it would be much easier to find Johnny and the girls and then run as fast as we could.

Once I was out of earshot of my mother, I started whispering their names by every bush I could. I only said either Katie or Johnny because those were the only two that mattered.

Kim and Tara could rot for all I care.

"Katie…"

"Johnny…"

No answer. I kept walking ahead, repeating the same process. I gained more confidence with each passing moment they didn't respond. I hoped that meant they were as far away from the house as they could get.

This is good.

"Mark?"

My mom.

"Yeah? Over here…"

She came into view, looking dismal and defeated.

"I haven't found your father."

"Me neither. I actually thought that he maybe went back to the house to look for us."

"Damn it. Have you seen the girls?"

"No. I thought I should head out to the open road and work my way in." I prayed that she didn't want to come with me.

"Well, I'll probably go towards the house first. That gives me a chance to search for your father, and that way, you and I can be working at opposite ends inwards."

"Sounds good mom." She reached out and squeezed me in a tight hug. I knew she was trying to stay strong and focused despite grieving immensely over Amy's sudden death.

Amy had it coming.

I let go, giving her a reassuring squeeze. I headed towards the way I was originally heading. I could still see my mom walking the other way and thought it best to not try and call Katie or Johnny until she was out of earshot.

I continued walking straight, until not only was my mom out of sight, but I could see the edge of the forestry. I could see the main road.

"Katie… Johnny…"

Johnny stood up from behind a large bush.

Thank god.

Tara and Kim were huddled together by the bush, and Katie was standing up, wobbling slightly in an attempt to not put any pressure on her ankle.

My girl...

"Hey man. What's going on?" Johnny looked around, probably still wary of me.

"My mom headed back towards the house to look for my dad. Hopefully he's still unconscious. But we need to go. Now."

"Which way should we head?"

I looked around. The main road was right here, and I debated whether we should take our chances trying to walk it or if we should find somewhere to hide and call Sheriff Johnson.

I had a better idea.

"Let's get the hell away from the forest. We can run up the main road and find a good spot to hide by the highway and call Sheriff Johnson. He can bring cops and backup in case my parents find us."

"Good idea." Johnny pulled out his phone and started dialing the number for the police station.

I looked at Katie, who despite all she had been through, and thoroughly caked in bruises, still looked like a dream. Her brown hair was blowing in the wind, and she was looking back at me.

"Hi..." I reached out and squeezed her hand.

"Hi." She smiled and squeezed my hand in return.

I knew we were okay.

"Okay, I just called the Sheriff. He wanted all the details, but all I said was to meet us under the highway- and to bring backup. That's about half a mile from here. We need to run."

We all nodded in agreement, and Johnny and I each took one of Katie's arms to help her run without putting pressure on the foot further injuring the ankle which I was positive was badly broken.

We started into a low sprint and were running for about five minutes. Katie needed a break, so we took a breather, and stood there in silence for a few moments.

I encouraged her that it was best if we kept going. Who knew how close my parents were?

We began running once more, and within a few more minutes, the highway underpass came into view.

"Mark!"

My mom.

I turned and was immediately jolted with a shooting pain in my chest. I was knocked onto my back, and everyone stopped and turned to look at me. It was a tranquilizer dart. Damn it.

I reached into my chest to pull it out but noticed blood on my fingertips when I pulled back. I touched my chest once more, and felt the shiny bullet now lodged in it.

No, not a tranquilizer… a bullet. My mother shot me.

I looked over and my mom and very angry father were heading this way.

I couldn't risk them getting caught again.

I looked at them, at Katie, and then at Johnny.

"Go."

33

Katie

Johnny, Tara, Kim, and I were practically sprinting the remaining distance to the freeway overpass. I couldn't help but steal one final look at a bleeding Mark laying in the middle of the road. I could hear the police sirens in the distance, and my heart soared.

Dad.

I turned around to look at Sharon and Paul, who upon hearing the sirens, dashed back into the forestry.

We finally reached the underpass, and I found myself collapsing onto my knees due to the amount of sheer pain I was in. My ankle was practically useless and felt as if it was hanging on a small shred.

Johnny held my shoulders and tried to comfort me, right as my dad and five other squad cars pulled in.

The car was immediately thrown into park, and my dad came bolting out, beelining for me. He grabbed me in a huge embrace, and I burst into tears. I missed him so much, and there were definite times where I didn't know if this reunion would even be possible.

My dad held me at arm's length, surveying my probably badly bruised face and torso. He shook his head, tears visible in his eyes, and he looked at my ankle which looked absolutely horrible. He made an audible gasp, and then seemed to remember that there were two other survivors with us.

He looked over at Tara and Kim who were also crying.

My dad motioned for two other officers to help them out.

He looked at Johnny, and broke into a huge grin.

"I suppose I have you to thank for my daughter's homecoming. Thank you. Especially for saving Tara and Kim. I have to ask... where's Anna?"

Johnny looked somber, and I knew it was the question on his mind as well. Running through a forest didn't exactly provide you ample time to talk about things. They both looked to me for an answer.

"Sharon killed her." I looked at both of them.

"Sharon? Puntzer? Amy's mom?" My dad looked shocked, and I realized that Johnny hadn't filled him in on all the details when he called him.

"I'll tell you the details later, but right now, you need to go to the Puntzer house and arrest Sharon, Paul, and their gate attendant George before they try and bolt."

"What... what about Mark and Amy?"

"Amy's dead... and we left Mark back there. His mother shot him, and we left him behind on the main road. He took Amy, but he also helped us escape." Johnny was explaining the situation in simple terms to my dad.

I'm in for a round of questioning.

"Mark took you? And the family has had you this whole time?" My dad looked taken aback, and genuinely furious.

Yeah, they had the wool pulled over all of our eyes.

"It's a long story dad. Just please arrest them and I'll give you a statement."

My dad nodded his head, giving in for now at least. I had no doubt that he would want a full detailed report later.

"First, you're going to give me another hug." He reached out and squeezed me even harder than the first hug, and I found myself squeezing back. It felt so good to hug my dad again after all I had been through… and all I'm sure he has been through.

He released me, and grabbed Johnny pulling him into a hug as well. Johnny looked awkward at first but returned the hug. My dad would be forever eternally grateful to him for doing what everyone in this town wishes they had been able to do… save all of us.

I looked for Kim and Tara, but they had already been taken to the hospital. My dad informed me that I was going to be going there as well. I tried to protest, but it was no use.

"Katie, you look like someone has beaten you half to death. Your ankle is also very obviously broken. You're going. I will arrest them and meet you there. But you will have an officer escorting you, and he's not going to leave your side. Neither is Johnny, right?"

"Right." Johnny nodded in agreement, and after a final hug to my dad- Johnny, an officer and I headed down to the local hospital.

Please be safe dad.

We arrived at the hospital in no time at all, and they took me in right away. Everyone there was shocked to see me, and they even stuck me in the same room as Tara and Kim as I was being examined. I told them that I had not been raped, but they still wanted to do a full physical check. I asked Johnny to wait outside.

In fact, all three of us had to do a physical check throughout. While we were in the same room, they used small curtains to separate us into sub rooms. The checks didn't take long, and they begin examining my face and the bruises. They said they would heal, and that I didn't have too much damage in the facial region.

They explained they were going to hook me up to an IV, noting that I looked severely dehydrated and malnourished. I could hear the other two doctors telling Kim and Tara the same thing.

Tara and Kim's final checks were done, and the doctors left. The nurses for each pulled the curtains open so we could freely talk. While I was almost done being examined, I needed my ankle to be looked at. The doctor took one look at the swollen, purple ankle and said it was broken. He wanted an X-ray done as soon as possible, especially since it had been hurt twice.

They wheeled me away, and I gave a wave to my friends as I was leaving.

I wondered if it was weird that I now considered the girls I was in captivity with as friends. I don't know how you could go through something like what we did, and not come out of it with some sort of bond. We were bonded for life, and I could live with that.

Besides our obvious differences in the beginning, Tara and I had started to warm up to each other recently. Once she realized that we were really in it together, she came around. Kim had always been sweet to me from the day she was taken.

As I waited for the x-ray to take, my mind became lost in thoughts of Mark. Was it wrong to want him to be okay? I knew he was the catalyst to my coming into this Iron Room in the first place, but he also got me out. He turned against his family and everything he knew in order to save me.

That counted for something right?

It at least gave me the grounds to want him to live.

Don't forget he also took you.

Yeah, but if I had never been taken then I wouldn't have been able to get the girls out.

True, but Anna wouldn't have been dead, and Kim wouldn't have been taken.

I shook the negative thoughts away and focused on the positive. I was free. Kim was free. Tara was free.

And the Puntzer family was about to get what they deserve.

"X-ray is done. I'm going to wheel you back to the room, and the doctor will come in, in a few minutes to talk to you." The nurse smiled at me, and I recognized her as Alexis from two streets down. She was always such a sweet lady.

"Thank you." I returned her smile as she began wheeling me back to the room where Tara and Kim were waiting.

When I entered the room, they were both already hooked up to the IV and a nurse was waiting to do the same for me. Kim and Tara both smiled meekly, as they rested their heads on the pillows. It was a surreal feeling… to be safe after feeling scared for your life on a day to day basis.

We knew we were safe, and I was sure the IV was making them feel much better.

The nurse began inserting the IV needle into my arm vein, and for once I didn't flinch at the pain. *I had been through worse lately.*

A sad, sobering truth.

The doctor walked in just as the nurse switched on the drip.

"Katie… glad to see you're getting the hydration you need. I looked at your X-rays…" He stopped, and looked at the other girls, unsure if he should proceed.

"It's okay Doctor. There's no secrets between any of us anymore."

He gave a sympathetic smile and continued. "You have a comminuted fracture on your ankle bone. The bone snapped, and broke into a few other pieces. Due to the severity of it, and the fact that is was broken twice, you will need surgery. I'm so sorry Katie."

"It's okay. Thank you, Doctor."

I put my head in my hands, nervous for surgery. I had never had surgery before in my life, and the thought nearly scared me half to death, but I also reminded myself that I had been though absolute hell the past few days, and nothing should scare me anymore.

"It's okay Katie. We are going to be right here with you the whole time." Tara spoke, and Kim gave an affirming nod.

I'm so thankful for them.

"I will also be here." Johnny stepped into the room, clearly given the go ahead now that we were all fully clothed, and had our IV's hooked up.

Johnny smiled at me, Kim, and headed over to Tara's bedside, taking a seat. He grabbed her hand and squeezed it.

Well I didn't expect that.

Tara smiled at him, happiness clear on her face and I felt my chest tighten with excitement. These girls and I had been through a horrible trauma, especially Tara who was there the longest out of us three. She deserved happiness so much, and with a cute guy like Johnny especially.

Go Tara!

Johnny turned to Kim and I and explained their situation.

"Before she went missing, Tara and I were actually really close. She helped me with my homework, and I taught her how to play the guitar. It was a fair trade, but what I didn't know is how I would fall madly in love with her. When I found out she was missing, I vowed that I would do everything in my power to find her- whatever it took."

Tara smiled and leaned in to hug him. He returned the hug, and I felt like I had stepped into a private moment. I turned away, with a grin plastered on my face.

Tara and Johnny were in their own little world, and Kim and I took the opportunity to talk.

"I wouldn't have been able to mentally survive without your support, so thank you. I mean it," I said looking at Kim.

"I don't think any of us would. It helped, to have someone who knows exactly what you went through. I think we're bonded forever in a way." Kim laughed.

"Me too."

Just then, my dad walked into the room and my heart started beating a million times a minute. Did they find Sharon and Paul? Did they arrest them? What about George?

What about Mark?

I mentally slapped myself for thinking about Mark. He kidnapped me! But he also helped me to escape twice, even though the first time failed. He didn't come and see me after that, for reasons unknown, but he still took that opportunity to get Johnny to help us, or me. I didn't know how he felt about the other two girls.

"What's going on dad?"

"Well, we arrested Sharon and Paul under kidnapping charges since you haven't formally told me what happened. We found the gate attendant George and arrested him as well. However, we weren't able to find Mark."

What?

"We did circle back and find his blood on the road like you said, but the bullet was lying there so I'm assuming it was pulled out."

"What's going to happen when you do find him?"

"He will be arrested, even if he didn't do anything. He clearly knew about everything."

"But he helped us escape." I pleaded with my father.

"And I'm sure the prosecutor will take that into consideration when passing a sentence. Now, I need you to tell me everything… all of you." My dad looked around the room at Tara, Kim, Johnny and myself.

"Mark kidnapped Anna first, and then me. They tortured us with beatings almost every day. They fed us only twice a day, in unbearably small amounts."

My dad shook his head, becoming upset.

"And you Katie?"

"Mark took me Sunday night. I was planning to stay over Amy's after we spoke. I felt he was a suspect, and he wanted to clear it up. When I made it known that I wasn't going to stop looking, he stuck with me a needle and I woke up in this Iron Room."

"Iron Room?"

"That's what I call it. It's made of metal, even the walls, and it has a big iron door with chains."

"I know what room you're talking about. The doors were open. We found Amy's body in there."

I continued.

"It was weird the first day and a half. They were unsure what to do with me. But once I made it clear that I wanted nothing to do with them anymore, they started to treat me as a prisoner."

"And they gave you these…" my dad reached out and touched my bruises. He looked down at my ankle and wiped away a tear.

"You need surgery too Katie. The doctor told me."

"I know Dad, I'm safe now though. Mark helped us. He tried to help me escape once, but they caught us. That's when Amy got increasingly more violent with me. She tried to kill me."

"And who killed her?"

"That would be me." Johnny raised his hand in the air.

"Where's the gun?"

"I dropped it in the forest," Johnny explained.

"Well I will need your statement. Thank you though."

Johnny nodded. My dad turned to Kim.

"I got into it with Amy and Mark at school when I recorded them talking about it. I tried to run into the school when they caught me, put a needle in my neck, and took me home."

"That day when I went into the office to talk about Mark assaulting me, it was because I had showed Amy the receipts that I got from the phone company where it showed she agreed to meet Mark in the park that night." Johnny began to explain to my dad.

"You didn't tell me that." My dad looked shocked. *Johnny was really trying to help all of us.*

Johnny shrugged. I knew he probably felt best if he investigated himself, like I did. Except when I did, I got caught and kept as a prisoner.

"My detectives are searching the entire house now going through that "Iron Room" as you call it, and the rest of their home. Katie, what happened to your car?"

"No clue." I wondered that as well, as it was quite hard to hide a huge car. Knowing those nut jobs, they probably pushed it into a lake.

"Sharon and Amy would come in and abuse us physically every day. Paul sometimes came in and watched or ripped off their clothes in the process. Mark only came in when I was there to talk to me." I looked at my dad.

I watched as my dad shook his head in disgust. The Puntzer family was held to the highest esteem and were one of the most distinguished families in the town of Prairie. No one would have seen something like this coming.

My dad's phone rang, and he stepped into the hallway to answer it.

Have they found Mark?

The phone call took longer than I expected, lasting up to a few minutes.

When my dad finally stepped inside, his face looked somber.

Bad news.

"Did they find Mark?" I was hopeful.

My dad shook his head no.

"That was one of my detectives. They found the cameras in the room."

"Yeah I saw those. They liked to watch."

My dad continued,

"Yeah, and apparently so did a few thousand other people. Did you know that the Puntzer's were broke? The camera in the room was live streaming the abuse to the dark web. People were paying them thousands to watch you guys get beaten."

34

Mark

I watched them running away, with tears in my eyes and blood on my hands. Once the sirens started blaring, I watched my parents run away probably hoping to be clear out of town by the time the officers made their way to the house.

I couldn't be found, not like this. I pulled out the bullet, which was to the point of being unbearable. I left it on the road, as a token of my love for Katie. I had hoped she would see it and know I was okay.

I had to stop the bleeding, which thanks to my mother was profuse. I was grateful that she had shit aim from a distance, otherwise she would have had two children die today.

I pulled myself a safe distance away from all the commotion where I was still able to watch what was going on. I ripped off a piece of my shirt and stuffed it into the wound as a haphazard attempt to stop the bleeding.

I hope Katie is okay.

I had no doubt that she had already filled her dad in on everything that happened since I took her. I was sure that Kim and Tara also spewed some horror stories, painting me out to be some monster. I knew in my heart that Katie wouldn't do the same, and neither would Johnny- well hopefully.

I was man enough to know when I had done wrong, and when I messed up. Taking Katie was a big mistake. She never belonged there, and I feel personally to blame for what she had to go through every single day. My sister and mother ruined the years of friendship and throwing the familial love out of the window by treating her like one of the other captives.

But I never did.

I tried to always treat Katie with the utmost of love and respect, because she was a genuinely beautiful and kind person.

Earlier, I had decided that I would be okay with being taken into arrest. I thought it would serve as the perfect penance for what I did to Katie, and the other girls as well.

Don't get me wrong, I still despise them. I think that they exhibit horrible qualities, absolutely deemed unfit for society.

However, I have come to the riveting revelation that maybe that doesn't exactly allow for them to be beaten every single day and held in captivity.

And then there's the streaming. That part was all mom and dad. I knew that the bank hadn't been doing too good lately, with a lot of the townspeople taking out loans in return for IOU's. Our town of Prairie had been hit especially hard with a financial hardship, and in turn, the townspeople turned to my dad for help. It in turn, made us nearly broke.

I took Anna purely as an opportunity. The room had been built as a safeguard in case of national disaster but served a greater purpose in housing our occupants. Mom was researching ways to make some extra cash and came up with the idea of taking requests from strangers online on how to follow abuse requests, as well as streaming, in return for cash.

The whole family thought it was a brilliant plan, including myself.

Now, the thought of all of it made me sick to my stomach.

I hobbled through the greenery, trying to stay out of the way of the officers. I needed to patch myself up, and quick. I knew enough about crime shows, that I knew I needed to stop the source of bleeding. I should probably get checked out by a doctor, but I would need to go a few towns away to do so.

I continued walking for as far as I could when I collapsed from sheer exhaustion. I had spent most of the night walking, and it was wearing on me. I made my way to the main road and felt comforted when I realized I was out of Prairie. I decided hitchhiking would be my best bet for getting me to a hospital without collapsing again.

Or they could kill you.

I was too tired to care, and after what I did, I deserved it.

I stood on the edge of the forestry, where it meets the road. I saw small businesses nearby and not many cars on the road. But still, I persevered and held my thumb up.

I looked up and down the road, desperate for someone to agree to give me a ride, while my chest ached considerably.

Finally, after what seemed like forever, a small truck was driving towards me, and upon seeing me slowed down. The truck did a complete stop in front of me, and the driver was an older gentleman.

"You need a ride son?"

"Yeah thanks."

I opened the door and climbed in. He surveyed me, taking in the ripped shirt and the spot dripping blood as if he had only now just seen it.

"Do you need a doctor?" He looked worried.

"I do. Can you drive me to the nearest hospital?"

"Sure thing, bud." He put the car in drive and started to make a U-turn.

No, not Prairie, I can't.

"Not that hospital, please. They don't take my insurance."

"Well son the only close one beside that one is 2 miles the other way."

"That's fine with me. Please."

He continued to study me, probably thinking I was batshit crazy for wanting to go to a further hospital when I was clearly in bad shape. Oh well. I didn't care. I just had to do whatever I could to get there and get examined.

He fixed the car, continuing straight. The drive was quiet, only the sounds of the country music station filling the empty void of silence.

"So how old are you son?"

"18."

"Do you mind if I ask what happened?"

"I was messing around with my friends and I got hurt with a BB gun. I need the doctors to pull them out, it's quite a few stuck in there." I shrugged my shoulders.

Who knew I was a terrific liar?

"Some friends." The driver tut-tutted and shook his head in disappointment.

The reality was that I didn't have bad friends, but a bad family, where my mother felt it morally okay to shoot her own son in the chest and leaving him for dead.

It was also incredibly ironic if you considered the fact that just a while before she shot me, she was apologizing for how cruel the captivity was. Imagine that. My psychotic mother felt horrible about keeping me in chains in my own home but could give a shit less about leaving me shot and bleeding in the street. *She was always more concerned about saving her own skin.*

We were ten minutes into the drive. It was turning from a comfortable into an uncomfortable silence, and I thought it would be best if I at least attempted to have a lighthearted conversation.

"So, where do you live?"

"Just about a half mile out of here. You?"

"Yeah, I live back that way, and that damned hospital doesn't take my insurance. I have to hitch rides out to this other one."

"You get hurt often?" He looked wary of me all of a sudden.

"Boys will be boys you know," I said trying to incorporate a light-hearted laugh.

He could see right through me.

"You know, I have a relative that lives back there too. In a town called Prairie. You might know him."

"What's his name?"

"Well, you might know him as Sheriff Johnson."

Shit.

My heart stopped in my chest, and I thought it was over for me. Sheriff Johnson probably sent whatever backwoods relative this was to try and find some bleeding six-foot-tall kid stumbling on the side of the road.

I was so fucking screwed.

I used my better instincts to figure that I should probably play it cool, just in case the old man actually was clueless and just trying to create a conversation like me.

"Yeah, he's a cool guy. I know him. How are you related?"

"He's my son. He's such a good man. I raised him in this town we're in now, Grenado. But he had bigger dreams than this shithole of a town and now he's Sheriff over in Prairie."

"Sorry to hear about his daughter."

The old man immediately slammed on his breaks, and I realized I had said something wrong. I should have never brought Katie up, now he was going to think I knew them more personally than I had originally let on.

Play it cool.

"You know about that?"

"Yeah, everyone does. It's a sad situation."

"Mm-hmm." Just then, his phone started to ring.

He flipped open the colossal prehistoric age flip phone and answered.

"Yello."

Who the hell answers the phone like that?

I mentally shook my head.

"Yeah. No way! God is good. Mhmm. Yeah, I will definitely come. What? Say that again." He looked at me.

"I'm going to have to call you back son."

He shut his phone and pulled off to the side of the road nearly knocking my head against the glass doing so. He threw the car into park and yanked the keys out of the ignition. I kept my head facing forwards but could feel his eyes burning a hole into the back of my head.

I could see him reaching in the backseat for something out of the corner of my eye.

"Get out." I turned to my left and he was pointing a gun right at me.

Do I make a run for it?

I mulled over the possibilities and the outcomes of what to do, as I slowly but surely opened the passenger door. The minute my feet hit the grass, he jumped out of his car and rounded the front, so he was facing me.

"Turn around. Walk."

I did just as he said, walking straight forward with the barrel of the gun pressed into the back of my head. We had walked beyond the truck and were standing in the middle of a field when he gave me more instructions.

"Kneel."

Executioner style... not good.

"That was my son on the phone… would you believe it if I told you that he told me to keep an eye out for a guy who matched your exact description? He even nailed you right down to the bleeding torso. You must be Mark… the kid that kidnapped my Katie."

This was it. He was going to kill me, and I would never see Katie again.

"Do you have anything to say for yourself?"

This is your chance. Distract him.

"I do actually. You have the situation all wrong. I was the one that helped Katie escape, twice. The first was a bust because my parents got involved and then they chained me up. I could never hurt Katie… I love her."

At this point, I was fully turned around facing this man, as he began to lower the barrel of the gun that was resting between my eyes. I had a big sigh of relief waiting, but held it in. This guy was still a loose cannon.

Just then, the old man was knocked backwards. His gun was shot out of his hand, and I looked to the right where I saw someone standing with a gun pointed right at the man.

"You okay? I saw the whole thing. I called the cops… they're on their way."

"No bother." I grabbed the keys of the old man's car, climbed inside, and high tailed it out of the corn field and onto the pavement. I was speeding and going well over the speed limit. The cops in all of these towns were few and far between and I knew that their focus would be on the call they just received about a man holding a gun to a kid's head.

I needed to get to the hospital and get stitched up. The sooner I was fixed, the sooner I could hide.

I hated myself for still debating whether or not I would turn myself in. It was guaranteed jail time for the crimes I committed, and while I never hurt the girls physically, not like my mother or sister, I kidnapped them.

I knew turning myself into the Prairie Police Department was the right thing to do. It would make me a man in Katie's eyes, and at this point in time, her opinion was the only that mattered.

Within a few minutes, I could see the hospital straight ahead.

Yeah, it's amazing how far you get when you actually drive over 25 mph.

I was smart and made sure to park the old man's car out of sight. If the police came looking for it, then they wouldn't be able to find me. I don't know exactly how long it takes for a bullet wound to get all fixed up.

I walked into the hospital, and straight up to the front desk. I could already see that the waiting room was packed but I needed help right away. I couldn't wait any longer.

"Excuse me, I need medical assistance."

"Sir, please sign in and we will be with you shortly."

"No, I've been shot."

Her eyes darted up from the computer screen she was immersed in, and she pressed a button on the desk. She spoke into a little microphone, off to the side of her screen.

"Dr. Fields to the ER. Urgent."

Just then, a team of nurses, and a doctor came running out behind double doors, with a bed. They laid me down on top of it, and the doctor removed my hand from my makeshift bandage. He pulled it back slightly as they were wheeling me in, and immediately replaced it again with his hand when it began to spurt blood everywhere.

I'm going to be okay. I have to be.

"He's losing a lot of blood Dr. Fields," The nurse warned.

I could hear a flurry of voices but couldn't focus on one. Everything was becoming blurry, and then black. I was out.

When I finally opened my eyes, I found myself lying in a hospital bed, in a room isolated by myself. I laid my head back when I saw the bandages covering up my bullet wound. Thank god. When I started to fade into the blackness, I feared that I wouldn't make it.

I wanted to see Katie.

I reached out to touch the bullet wound but found myself unable to. I looked down at my arm, which was cuffed to the side frame of the hospital bed.

Sheriff Johnson strolled in the room with a grin plastered over his face.

"Hello Mark, glad to see you have woken up."

I shook the cuffs once more.

"Oh… those. Yeah. You're under arrest for the kidnapping of Anna Lewis, Tara Brooks, Kim Meyers, and Katie Johnson.

Fuck.

35

Katie

They were selling videos of our abuse to sickos online for money? My head was spinning. Mark had never let on about the reason for all of this, but that was pretty out of left field... even for this family.

My heart ached. I was really struggling with the internal battle I faced. On one hand, I was furious. I was angry and upset at the fact that each one of us girls had been mentally, and physically broken in more ways than one. We had been exploited by this family in every aspect of the word, and now to find this out... it's unimaginable.

On the other hand, some twisted, deep part of me sees Mark as the hero in this story. And how can that possibly be? He kidnapped women, including myself. He never partook in the physical abuse but allowed it to happen. He was a clear bystander, who seemed to not give a shit about whether these girls lived or died. How could I care for someone like that? *I don't know... but you do.*

Okay, I will admit, I care about Mark. It's nothing more than the "you saved my life" aspect though. Nothing about his traits are desirable to me in the slightest. My heart simply felt a large sense of gratitude to him, when my mind is telling me that's absolutely insane.

You're insane.

"Katie?" My dad was looked at me, trying to get my attention, and in turn- breaking me out of my deep dark thoughts.

"Yeah... sorry. I was just trying to process."

"That is understandable. All of you have been through a great deal of trauma, especially you Tara. I'm sorry I didn't find you sooner." My dad turned towards Tara... a great sense of empathy clear on his face.

"It's not your fault Mr. Johnson. No one saw it."

He nodded his head and turned to me.

"I'm going to make a quick call to your grandpa before you head into surgery. Let him know that you've been found."

I smiled, letting him know that was okay. All this drama and new developments allowed me an escape from reality, and for a moment- I forgot I had to get surgery.

Yeah, tough luck on that one.

"I can see you worrying about the surgery. Stop. You will be fine." Kim comforted me with a grin, and I felt for a second a sheer sense of calm.

Just then, the doctor glided into the room and let me know that the OR was prepped and ready for me.

"Can we wait for my dad to come back in the room? I want to say bye first."

"I'm here, I'm here." He walked over, planted a kiss on my head, and continued.

"I will be right here when you get out of surgery. Don't worry about Mark, I told Grandpa to keep a look out for him."

What?

I had no time to process anything, because the nurses were swiftly rolling me away. What would happen to Mark? My stomach was torn up into knots, and I must have looked visibly nervous, because the nurse addressed me.

"Don't worry about anything hon. It will be a quick surgery. You will be all better in no time at all." She smiled as she wheeled me into the OR, put the mask over my nose and mouth, and started counting back from ten.

I counted with her, the room getting darker and darker, until it blurred to nothing.

Please let Mark be okay.

I had no idea of how long the surgery actually ended up being, but I was met with a chorus of "You did great" when I woke up. As I opened my eyes, I was back in the shared room with my friends, both of which were knocked out.

I'm glad I can be in the same room of them.

Despite being in a room together already, this room, this hospital room attached different promises to it versus the Iron Room.

The Iron Room was dark, bleak, and held no promise of the future. Every day was a fight, and we had to do so chained down, with minimal food in our system, dehydrated.

This hospital room held three physically broken girls, but not mentally.

Mentally, we were all stronger than ever. This was a rough patch in our lives, one that we would undoubtedly remember forever. We were weirdly bonded in a way that would stick with us for the rest of our lives.

This hospital room held hope…and promise.

"I'll send your dad in hon. He just got back."
Back from where?

My dad waltzed into the room, in a seemingly great mood.

He reached over me, hugging me tight. I also forgotten what this had felt like. I missed it.
"I knew you would do just fine in the surgery. I'm so proud of you. I'm also glad you're awake, because I have great news." His grin practically stretched from ear to ear.
"What is it?"
I had a gut wrenching feeling it had something to do with Mark.
"We got him."
Oh god, no.
"You got who?" I asked, playing dumb.
"Mark. Believe it or not, my phone call to your grandpa did wonders. He found him wandering on the side of the road and picked him up. Mark got away, but the local hospital near there notified me. He's under arrest and will be picked up when he's better."
Poor Mark.
"And then what will happen?"
"Well there will be a trial Katie, and then they will all be handed down a sentence. Sharon, Paul, George, and Mark will all be tried for crimes."
My heart sank, knowing that Mark would without a doubt go to prison.

Sharon and Paul deserved it. Amy deserved it. George definitely deserved a little time in the slammer for halting my escape efforts, and letting the scheme go on while he knew about it and could have helped.

I know it sounded like I was defending Mark, and I wasn't. He had done some pretty horrible things, and while I don't know the specifics of everything, I do know that there would have been no girls to torture and exploit without his hand in the kidnapping.

It makes him liable, but Mark showed a different side to himself in there. In the beginning, the thought of him at all repulsed me.

But throughout everything, and the way he so blatantly put his neck out on the line for me, I was fighting an internal battle over what I should feel and what I actually feel.

You're being an idiot Katie.

"Sounds fair."

My dad sat down at the edge of my head and took my hand into his. I hadn't noticed earlier due to the flurry of everything happening, but he looked a lot older. He was sporting more gray hair, and his skin looked sallow, complete with dark circles under his eyes.

He looked like hell, and it was all my fault.

I knew in my mind even while I was down there that my dad was without a doubt running himself ragged trying to find me, Tara, Anna, and later Kim.

I had so many thoughts and emotions flowing in my head and was having an incredibly difficult time trying to separate and evaluate them. I needed a good night's rest in my own bed and hoped that the doctor would allow me to do so.

"Dad, do you think the doctor would let me go home tonight?"

"Let me grab him."

He stepped out for a moment's time, and I took the opportunity to glance at my still sleeping friends. They needed all the sleep they could get. Once wind of everything that happened got out, everyone and their mom would be in our faces wanting to know close details.

Another perk of living in Prairie.

The doctor and my dad stepped back into the room, and I braced myself for a hard no.

"Your dad informed me that you had a question for me."

"Yes… I wanted to know if I could possibly go home tonight." I smiled at the stern-faced doctor, in a weak attempt to butter him up.

"It's not hospital policy to leave after any surgery, even if it is a bone fracture."

"Please? You know my dad won't leave my side."

"Fine. The only condition is that you take a wheelchair, and that your dad stays home with you for a week. You need to come back tomorrow and a few days from now so I can evaluate the ankle."

"Deal." I reached out to shake the good doctor's hand, amused and also shocked that I got my way.

I couldn't wait to be in my own bed.

I did feel bad about leaving Tara and Kim here, but their parents had been in and out of the room all day from what I had been told, and they had family that I'm sure were desperate to get them home as well. I think visiting hours were almost over, as I didn't see either of their parents since I got out of surgery.

"That means we're leaving tonight kid."

"Okay dad. Can you grab me a pen and some paper? I want to leave notes for the girls."

"Of course."

My dad returned shortly with a few pieces of paper, and a ballpoint pen.

I started writing the note to Tara.

Dear Tara,

Thank you for everything including the support. I don't know how I would have gotten through this hell without you. You're sleeping peacefully, and I don't want to wake you. I passed my surgery with flying colors, or so they tell me. I'm going home tonight and we're leaving now. Please call me when you get home. My house number is 310-776-3458.

Love, Katie

Short and sweet, just like Tara. It was perfect. I had my dad lay it on her bedside table where she would easily see it when she woke up. I began to comprise my note to Kim.

Dear Kim,

It's amazing what we have overcome together in a short amount of time. I'm so glad that you are okay, safe, and where you belong. I know your family missed you terribly. My dad is taking me home tonight, but I didn't want to worry you or Tara, and left you both notes. Lord know what the family did with my phone, so for now if you need to reach me, my house phone works. The number is 310-776-3458. Talk to you soon.

Xoxo, Katie

Once I finished that one, I had my dad repeat the same process.

I collected all my things which were nothing, and patiently waited while the nurse filled out my discharge forms, and listened while the doctor droned on and on about the endless list of do's and don'ts when it came to taking care of me.

He handed him a printout of all my appointments, and my medications including what time to give them, and what to give them with.

He was nothing if not thorough, I will give him that.

A million hours later...

Okay, maybe one, we had everything ready to go and we loaded into my dad's car. Well technically, *they* loaded *me* since I was now the cripple.

Fun times.

The ride to my house was short, but for some reason there was a lot of traffic on the streets tonight. "You have no idea what I have been through to find you Katie... and to think that you almost died. It's unimaginable." My dad shook his head in fear...anger... I couldn't discern what. Probably both. "I know, and I missed you every day. You were the one thing that got me out of there mentally stronger. I kept the image of you alive and well plastered in my brain and it served as a daily reminder."
"Of what?"
"To never give up. You're the strongest person I know Dad." I smiled and put my hand over his.
"It hasn't felt that way... but thank you. I love you."

"I love you too dad." I smiled, seeing that we had pulled into the driveway of my house. My dad made me sit in the car while he ran inside and got everything prepared, including my bed. I was exhausted and couldn't wait to finally lay in it.

He came out, and slowly opened my door. He pulled the wheelchair out of the trunk and opened it, slowly lowering me into it. He was careful not to damage my foot, and kept it propped.

He slowly helped me up to my room, having to ditch the wheelchair, and carry me in his arms.

I suddenly was overcome with a fond memory from when I was younger of pretending to fall asleep in the car to get carried up to bed.

My mom always knew I was awake though, but she never said anything.

I miss those times.

We entered my room, and I could see that my bed sheets were pulled back so I could slide in with ease. My dad used a hooked slim pole he had lying around to hook a wrap under my foot and over the clips of it, so I didn't put too much pressure on it. To further ensure so, he added two pillows underneath, so my ankle wasn't pulling too far down or too far up either.

He flustered around me making sure everything was perfect.

"Do you need anything? Name it."

Oh boy...

"You're going to hate me, but I would love a shower."

"Well lucky for you, I also have a shower chair. I knew it would come in handy someday."

He headed into the bathroom to set it up and helped me into it. I was still fully clothed, except for my shirt. I had to leave my foot hanging out of the tub anyways since the dressings weren't able to get wet right now, so that was fine. I would take what I could get.

I smelled like shit.

The shower didn't take long, given the fact that I could not really wet my legs. I washed my upper body, and somehow managed to wash and condition my hair. I finished this bootleg shower off with a face wash, and it gave me a refreshing feeling. I pulled a towel from the rack, and dried off, putting on a top and new pajama pants. I was brushing my hair when my dad knocked and then walked in.

"Need some help?"

"Yes please. God, I forgot how good a shower feels."

My dad didn't reply, and I remembered how hard it must be to think of everything I went through.

He helped me into bed, and covered me with the blankets, planting a kiss on my head.

"I have a water right here in case you get thirsty, and the wheelchair next to your bed if you have to pee. Here's a bell in case you need me, and I will be right here. Goodnight, I love you."

"I love you too." He walked out, shutting off the lights.

The feeling of being in my bed was as close to heaven as I had ever been. Part of me wanted to watch television and celebrate my freedom, but the other half was exhausted.

I chose sleep, and I slipped my hand under my pillow when I felt the hard edge of a box. I sat up, and turned on my bedside lamp, pulling my pillow off the bed.

Sure enough, there was a small jewelry box. I opened it and there was a silver chained necklace with a sparkly "K" on it. Attached to it, was a note. It read,

Katie,

You've been in the Iron Room for two days now, and I have come to realize what a big mistake I have made. I should have never taken you, and I promise I will get you out if it is the last thing I do. You are the only thing that matters to me right now, and this necklace is the symbol of that. I'm leaving this here in hopes that you see it when I figure everything out and find a way to help you escape. Whatever happens, just know that I love you.

-Mark

Oh my god.

36

Mark

It didn't take long before I was out of the hospital and spending my days in a jail cell waiting for the trial. I had a good defense lawyer of course, and I was genuinely surprised that my mother paid for one, given that the last time I saw her... she tried to kill me.

Who knows? Maybe it was my dad who paid for the lawyer. Anyways, everything we did to obtain that money was certainly a group effort, so the money was just as much mine as it was hers.

She was always greedy.

My lawyer thought it best if I did an insanity defense and convinced the jury that I was mentally unfit to stand trial due to reason of insanity.

I knew in my heart that I wasn't insane by any shape or form, but I would do whatever it took to make sure I got out and made my way back to Katie.

A part of me began to wonder about the realness of everything we shared. She was in such a dark situation, and a small part of me worries that all the emotions were a facade to get me to help her escape.

I knew Katie's character pretty well, or at least I thought I did, and it didn't seem like her to do something like that. She wasn't the type of girl to mess with anyone's emotions simply for her own personal gain.

She was a good person, inside and out.

The trial started today, and I couldn't have been more relieved. I thought that I had a good defense, and a lot of our case was also riding on the fact that while I may have been the catalyst in kidnapping the girls, I never laid a hand on them otherwise.

If the insanity defense failed, we would need to convince the jury that I was forced to do this and kidnap the girls in order to help my family make money.

Which was pretty much true.

In fact, I was waiting in my cell to have the lawyer meet me with a suit he picked up from my home.

I had been told that the police finally opened our house back up after it had been closed off for a thorough examination. Apparently, everything had been taken into evidence, including the iPad, which I felt quite nicely helped my defense.

The correspondence between Johnny and I clearly showed how desperate I was to get the girls, well Katie, out. There was also the evidence of chains they found in the room, with the bucket I described when I gave them my statement.

Sheriff Johnson wasn't very happy with me, but he didn't seem to hate me either. I thought he would, give that I had taken Katie in the first place. But Sheriff Johnson seems to see the side of me that I have been striving for. I want to be someone who Katie is proud of, and not what my family has morphed me to be all my life.

I wanted to be better for her. She made me better.

More than anything, I wanted to be done with this trial so I could put all the mistakes of the past, in the past. I don't think I wanted to be associated with my family anymore, and I know it comes off as being incredibly cold.

It's hard to have love for someone who saw you as disposable and tried to end your life. I don't want my mother in my future, especially if I want one with Katie. She abused her, and that would not be someone I associated with further beyond this, regardless of familial connection or not.

The sad truth is I never wanted any of my family hurt. I had grown to loathe Amy, mostly because making the mistake of taking Katie forced me to finally take a good, long look in the mirror and realize all the wrong doings I had done out of anger, and for the good of my family.

I grew as a person through the whole experience, while my family didn't. If anything, they got worse and it only brought the truth to my eyes.

They were monsters.

But I would have never wished any of them dead. So now that I have had time to process everything that happened, I allow myself to mourn for the sister I lost.

When I think of Amy, I don't attach all the horrible things she did to her memory. Instead, I choose to honor the seven-year-old girl who wouldn't stop taking my Legos and blaming it on her teddy bear. I honor the innocent, warm hearted, and bold spirited sister I grew up with- the one that wasn't tarnished by my parents and their selfishness.

"Mark, please step forward." The officer commanded me sternly.

Time for the trial.

My lawyer came into sight holding a suit as promised, and he looked upbeat.

That was a good sign.

I stepped out of my cell and the officer had me hold my hands in front of myself while he unlocked them.

My lawyer and I were given time in an office so I could change, and we could discuss strategy before heading to the courthouse.

In Prairie, we had a small courthouse that was only ever used for small traffic violations. Like I said, nothing bad ever happened here. This was a big deal, and there would be a huge amount of people turning up for the trials, with a lot of opinions.

I had no doubt over the level of hate that the townspeople of Prairie now held towards me and my family. It didn't bug me, or even upset me in the slightest. I knew what I did was wrong. While I felt that I had learned a valuable lesson, it is truly up the jury and the judge. If they think I also deserve prison time, then so be it.

Katie made me want to take accountability for once.

I subconsciously wondered if she would show today for the trial. I'm sure it was all over the local news. My lawyer had given me the rundown of the day. My mother would go first, followed by my father, George, and then myself. Depending on how everyone plead, the length of each trial was really up in the air right now.

Little did my lawyer know, I had a different plan in mind.

I finished getting dressed, and my lawyer felt it best if we discussed the plan at the courthouse as we were running late. The drive from the station to the courthouse was brief, and quiet.

When we finally arrived, I could barely see the doors to the entrance because there were mobs of people, and I wasn't exaggerating.

They were buzzing like mosquitoes, eager to get their fix.

I knew I was in for a rude awakening, so we pulled around the back instead, where an officer who was friends with my lawyer was waiting to let us inside.

Thank god for that.

We got inside, and I was surprised at the crowds of people inside as well. They were all starting to file into the courtroom, and it was for my trial. Mine started in fifteen minutes, and my lawyer and I needed to brush up on our statements and go over his line of questioning once more.

That means that my mother, father, and George already went.

As we were walking into an empty office to talk, I surveyed the crowd. I could have lied and said I was looking to see what kind of turnout it was, but there was truthfully only one person I was looking to see.

Katie.

When we got inside the office, my lawyer closed the door behind us swiftly and motioned for me to take a seat.

I did so quickly and waited for him to start.

"So, Mark, why did you take the girls?"

"My parents were broke, and we needed a source of income. They instructed me to start taking girls which we would later use as a broker for ransom money."

Lie.

"And at any point, did this plan change?"

"Yes sir. My parents realized they could make more money selling and taking requests for torture videos on the dark web."

"Did they ever have you abuse any of the girls?"

"No sir." I tried to keep my calm, and not seem like I was out of sorts in the slightest.

"In fact, you tried to free one of the girls."

"Yes sir. I tried to free Katie, but my parents hit us both with tranquilizer darts. They then chained me in my room, with no way of getting free or having access to the girls. I messaged Johnny Antin in hopes that he could help with me an escape plan for all of them. That's what he did."

"Did you tell Johnny Antin to shoot your sister Amy?"

"Absolutely not."

"Do you wish that he hadn't shot her?" My lawyer looked at me carefully, very obviously looking for a reaction to that one.

"Of course. But she had Katie at gunpoint. It was a do or die situation."

"And how do you know Katie was at gunpoint?"

"Well, I had the camera wired up to my iPad. I could see everything that went on in there but was unable to do anything about it."

This line of questioning is pointless. No one cares how much less guilty I am than the others.

"That should be good for now Mark. Their prosecutor will then cross examine you. I need to reiterate to you the importance of keeping your cool and maintaining a calm headspace. They are looking to poster you as a volatile young man. You will show them that you are not but were merely a byproduct of your parent's wrongdoings."

"Got it."

Satisfied with my agreeability, we headed out of the room and down the hall to where I would await what my future would hold for me. Regardless of the "impartial" jury and judge, I knew who the true judges were. The entire town of Prairie would be my judge, jury, and if need be... executioner.

I stepped into that room and felt the glare of a hundred eyes staring directly at me.

I knew what they were thinking.

Kidnapper. Sadist. Sicko.

I was all of those things, but I didn't want to be. I would use whatever outcome this trial had in store for me to undo all those horrible words associated with the name Mark Puntzer. I wanted to be a better man.

Think of Katie.

I recognized more than a few faces from around school. In the first row, there was a girl who I sat with in science class last year. I spotted a kid named Gabriel who I played soccer with after school a few years ago.

It would have felt a lot better recognizing all these faces if I knew they were here to support me, rather than come to watch my head on a stick.

My lawyer and I made our way to the table and waited for the judge to enter. I took this moment as an opportunity to look at my jury. The jury was comprised of people of all races and genders, varying in age. I knew that didn't matter. Regardless of skin color, gender or age group, people knew what I did was wrong.

It was up to them to decide if I should be punished for my crimes.

The judge finally filed in, taking a seat his designated podium. He looked angry already, and it hadn't started yet. I wondered if he had been presiding over my parent's trials as well, or it was just mine.

You know what you have to do.

"Please stand." We all followed suit.

"How does the defendant plead?" The judge looked from me, to the lawyer, and then back to me.

"Not...." I cut my lawyer off.

"Guilty, your honor." There was a round of loud gasps erupting from the courtroom, as well as a sour look from my lawyer.

"Mark, what the hell are you doing?" My lawyer whispered to me angrily, and very clearly confused.

"Okay. We will have a small recess, and then a sentence will be handed down." The judge banged the gavel, and my lawyer yanked me by my arm clear out of the courtroom all within seconds.

He pulled me away into a hidden corner, and his face was lit with fury.

"What do you think you're doing? You kidnapped four girls. You WILL go to prison."

"I deserve to." He rolled his eyes and pushed me away from him.

"Whatever, it's your cross to bear." He waited patiently with me for the remaining ten minutes in the recess. I knew he was upset with me, especially since he felt that he had a strong enough case to get me no jail time at all.

What kind of man would I be if I ran from this?

We headed back inside for sentencing.

I made my way to my seat, with my very solemn looking lawyer trailing behind me.

We sat, and the judge entered.

"Please rise for sentencing." So, I did.

"In the four cases of kidnapping in the second degree, you have pled guilty. I have reviewed the evidence submitted by the defense as well as the prosecution and have reached a decision."

The judged paused, then continued.

"Mark Puntzer, you are hereby sentenced to 2 years at Highmore Psychiatric Facility. I hope you get the help you need son."

37

Katie

Two years in a psychiatric facility? What was the judge thinking? Mark wasn't crazy. He was just raised by crazy people... there's a clear difference there.

When my dad told me the sentence today, I was shocked. I was sure for a second that Mark would receive jailtime, but my dad had told me about the amazing lawyer Mark had hired, and I held out a small sliver of hope that he might avoid jail altogether.

But never once did I consider the possibility of a psychiatric facility. Mark would be forced to spend his days surrounded by people with voices in their heads and a pill regimen.

My dad wouldn't allow me to go to the trial, even if I was feeling better. I had been healing better over the past few days, and now found walking with crutches a better fit for me.

It was definitely exercising all my upper body strength, that was for sure. At least my healing came with a sense of freedom in not needing help to get in the shower.

Yeah, that was mortifying.

My dad had filled me in on all the details of the trial today. He didn't go either but heard everything he needed to know by a court officer who he happened to play little league with.

They all pled guilty. Sharon's sentence was apparently the worst since she was the only one with a murder charge tacked on to her already growing list of charges. I heard through Kim that Anna's parents were there at her trial.

My heart broke for them. They were the only parents out of the four of us who didn't get to celebrate in the discovery of us. Their daughter did not survive the horrors we did, simply because of the selfishness, and evil that one person exhibited. Sharon was sentenced to life imprisonment, with no possibility of parole.

Paul was sentenced to twenty-five years, and George got four years.

While I knew her only just a short time, I would hold Anna's memory forever in my heart. I have been talking with Kim and Tara a lot more frequently lately, especially since my dad came home with a new phone for me the other day. I still have no clue what that family did with my damn phone, but Paul admitted at the trial that they had broken my car down into parts and destroyed it.

Now I needed a new car.

The phone company was able to attach my old number to this new phone, and I spent my days texting my new friends about all that was going on in our lives since we had been released. It had been less than a week, but life was changing drastically- and in a good way!

Tara and Johnny had been spending every waking moment together. He had spent all his time at her side throughout her recovery process. Tara's doctor had actually discovered that she had a broken rib that had tried to heal but had been broken again. *Probably from all the kicking.*

She was still healing, and would be for another four to five weeks, but was doing exceptionally well. She had been doing a lot of staying in recently, and Johnny had been chauffeuring her homework to and from school. Tara was already extremely bright, and so self-teaching and learning came natural to her. Last I talked to her, they had a "makeshift" date that would be taking place in a few days.

The plan was to have a picnic in her backyard, since she wasn't being permitted to actually leave the home. Her mom was much too worried, and I understood it.

Kim was also doing well. Her injuries were the only ones out of all three of us that allowed her to get right back to school, which was something that she had continuously expressed that she wanted. Kim hated that she had pieces of her life taken away, even for a short time. While school wasn't anyone's favorite place to go, she confessed to me that it felt good to settle back into her life with that familiar sense of control.

Kim was the one I had confided in about my feelings for Mark.
That didn't go over so well.

I knew Kim would be more understanding than Tara, but that was needless to say she wasn't very understanding to begin with. In her eyes, he had taken her, as well as three other girls. Mark in her eyes was just as complicit as his family members and he didn't deserve a redemption simply because he undid the damage that he originally caused.

That was a few days ago, and according to our most recent phone conversation, Kim seemed to be turning around. I called her right after Mark's trial and filled her in.

He took accountability for his actions, even against his legal advice.

Mark was trying to change.

I wondered if it was for me, because of me, or because Mark wanted to rid himself of all that his family had instilled in him for so long.

I knew deep down he wasn't a monster, not like them.

I didn't hate Mark. I couldn't. I will admit that I had grown to have some sort of feelings for him but couldn't decipher what they meant.

Mark and I would never be together.

People didn't understand, including my dad.

After the altercation between my grandfather and Mark, I doubt we would be getting gramps' stamp of approval anytime soon either.

So that was the realization I had come to. While I admired the man that Mark was stepping up to try and be, and acknowledged the way I felt towards him, there was nothing I could do about it.

So, I tried to move on.

I wanted to wear my necklace he gifted me every day as a symbol of what I went through. While Mark and Johnny ultimately led the escape, I had fought tooth and nail mentally and physically in the Iron Room. As much as I hated to admit it, it was now a piece of me and would always be. It was an extremely frightening, and tough time in my life that I couldn't forget... even if I wanted to more than anything.

The girls and I had plans to go to Anna's memorial service today. My dad was against it, but when I reminded him that the family responsible for everything was either locked up or deceased, he obliged.

Sharon revealed where Anna's body was buried, and the court ruled custody over her body to Anna's parents. They were grateful that they could at least bury their daughter in a place that meant so much to them. We had one small little cemetery in town, that was comprised of dozens upon dozens of family crypts. Generations of families had grown up in this town, and when another generation passed, they were buried in their family crypt.

Anna's family had a small crypt that started with her grandfather, and I know her parents wanted her to be buried there.

I hadn't seen or spoken to them at all. I was cooped up at home, and I didn't know what to say really. I had to think of something to say, as they asked my father to pass along the message that they wanted Tara, Kim, and I to speak at the memorial. *And I had zero idea of what to say.*

The only way in which I personally knew Anna felt like a topic that shouldn't be brought up at her memorial service, but it was inevitable.

I spent the better half of the morning dutifully writing a speech that I thought would honor her in a beautiful way.

I squeezed the necklace and finished getting dressed.

When I was ready, I called for my dad to help me with the stairs. I was good on the crutches, but all it took was one bad swing of the stick and I was coming down those stairs like a sack of shit.

He ran upstairs obviously thinking that I had fallen. When he saw I was fine, and just waiting for an escort down the stairs, he visibly relaxed.

"You look beautiful darling." He smiled as he admired my silky floor length blue dress.

"You know mom got this for me…"

"I remember. She also thought you looked beautiful. I know that she is looking down on you, and she is so proud. You have turned out to be quite the strong woman."

"Alright, don't make me cry. I am actually wearing makeup." I laughed.

My dad laughed with me and helped me to the couch so I could wait for my friends. Kim, Tara and I were all hitching a ride together. I was riding in the passenger of course, as my ankle was still not up to par.

Thanks again for that one, Sharon.

I heard a now familiar beep-beep, and I rushed out to the car, nearly knocking over a sprinkler head with my crutch. My dad bolted to the open door and called after me.

"I would have helped you... you know!"

"No need! See you later!" I waved my crutch around in the air. He hated it when I did that.

"Be careful. I love you."

"Love you." I smiled at my dad and allowed Tara to help me slip into the passenger seat. She saved me from the shame of having someone buckle me, and simply closed the door and climbed into the back seat behind me.

Kim looked at me.

"Ready?"

"No, but let's go."

This day was hard for all of us, but Tara to no surprise was taking it the hardest. Like I had mentioned earlier, none of us were close friends before all of this happened. But this room had a way of making you feel connected, and no one spent more time together in there than Tara and Anna. They were the first ones.

I did my best to comfort her in the only way I knew how- making people laugh.

I don't even know if I could count how many "Yo mama" jokes I had cracked in the last ten minutes alone.

Tara was getting annoyed, but that was a better emotion than grief.

We pulled up to the service, and people were already there surrounding the podium and the crypt.

Anna had already been buried, and this was simply her parent's way of sending her off.

When Anna's mom's eyes locked on ours, she motioned for us to hurry over.

"Hi honey. Thank you all for coming." One by one, she encased in a grizzly bear like hug. It felt good to be comforted by a maternal touch. That was something I really missed about my mother.

"Hi everyone, we are going to start with a few words by Anna's friends." She stepped aside and allowed me to go first.

Don't blow this, kid.

"Hi guys. I wanted to start by saying that while I didn't know Anna long, she left a mark on me that will remain there forever. She was a kind soul who deserved a lot more years than she was granted. To know her was to love her, and she was the absolute life of the party- without a doubt. She was the kind of person that people gravitated towards because she encompasses this beautiful, light, and euphoric energy. Anna and I are similar in the situation we found ourselves in. Anna brought me comfort just in her presence alone, and for that… I will forever be grateful."

I left the podium and allowed Tara and Kim to speak as well.

Kim's was short because she didn't know Anna at all… but she provided a very sweet and generalized sendoff that made her mother cry.

Tara's brought the entire crowd to tears. She didn't hold anything back and elaborated on how much comfort Anna brought to her while they were trapped in the Iron Room. She said that Anna always told her to never lose hope, and that she started to falter that when Anna died. She added that the spark, or burning desire in her to want to fight, didn't come out again until I pushed her to it. Tara said that she sees a lot of Anna in me, and that it makes her feel forever connected to her.

I found myself wiping the tears away with my dress. The speech was beautiful, and the sentiment behind it was even more wonderful.

The service continued on with amazing speeches and tributes to Anna for the next two hours, and then the ceremony wrapped up, turning into a banquet.

The banquet was moved from the cemetery to city hall, and the mood had drastically shifted. Tears were gone, and people were finding themselves in an upbeat and positive mood as they enjoyed good food while their hips swayed to the "Ladies of the 80's" station.

Anna would have really loved this.

I wondered why even at a time like now, where we were honoring the memory of a young girl who lost her life too soon... I found my mind drifting back to Mark.

He had probably already been checked in at the psychiatric facility and was beginning the first day to what would be a two-year sentence.

I found myself curious if he could have visitors but reminded myself once again that Mark was a thing of the past.

It couldn't and it wouldn't happen.

Ever.

My ankle started to throb from all the activity I had gotten today, and I asked Kim to give me a ride back home. Tara wanted to stay, and I saw her having a heart to heart with Anna's mom.

I made sure to say my goodbyes to everyone before I made Kim get me the hell out of there.

My mind found itself in the now all too familiar fog that it had been in since we were saved.

Amy was dead. Her parents were in prison. Mark was spending time at a psychiatric facility.

Now I was desperately trying to find my footing in a world without four of the people I used to consider family, and I was so lost that I was clinging on to every single good memory I held of them. I was struggling beyond belief, and no one understood.

For my dad, it was simple. They took and hurt girls, including his daughter. The years of friendship and comradery went right out the window when he discovered that. My dad always sees the world in black and white, while I lived in glorious shades of grey which can sometimes blur the lines beyond repair.

Kim helped me inside my house, and my dad helped me up the stairs into my room. I needed a nap, as the outing had completely worn me out. He helped me up the door, and then let me go in by myself.

"Need anything hon... just shout."

"Thanks dad." I closed the door and turned to my bed.

Imagine my surprise to find another jewelry box sitting there.

38

Mark

Sneaking into Katie's house was beyond risky... I knew that. I also knew that I needed to show her that I cared for her, more than anything.

I was willing to go to lengths I've never dreamed of, just to make her happy.

I knew she would love the bracelet, as it perfectly matched the necklace that I bought for her. Not only was it a sweet gift that was a symbol of my affection, but it was a demonstration of my wellbeing.

I knew soon enough word of my escape would reach her father's ears. It wasn't easy, believe me. I wanted to pay for my crimes, but not in a psychiatric facility. I wasn't crazy, but rather someone who had done some cruel and unfair things.

I refused to spend my time in a place like that. They were transferring me from the courthouse to a van, when a fight broke out inside with other "criminally insane" prisoners. Not only did it freak me out, but it provided a great escape window to get away before the officers knew I was gone.

I made it all the way to Katie's house without a single sighting of an officer. I knew I had a limited window to drop the bracelet, which I had hidden on the side of her house.

I had bought Katie three pieces of jewelry, which I had originally planned to give her slowly but surely as we were building out relationship. A woman as beautiful as Katie deserved beautiful things to match.

I didn't want any of my nosy family members to find them and thought the best place would be Katie's house. At the time it did seem weird, but now it seemed to work to my advantage. I waited for the Sheriff to leave, which took all of about five minutes.

I climbed up the trellis, which was extremely hard in cuffs, and laid it carefully on her bed along with a well written note.

I had barely rounded the house when I spotted a police cruiser driving by. I needed to get away from here.

They were looking for me.

The first place they would look for me would be my house, so I couldn't go there. I knew I would need to keep a low profile for a little while. I knew my dad had a garage full of tools and I could someone maneuver these damn cuffs off me.

I decided that traveling through all the forestry in Prairie was a good idea. I couldn't risk being spotted on the road. I desperately wanted a change of clothes and out of these handcuffs. They weren't very comfortable, go figure.

They're not supposed to be.

I hightailed it away from Katie's house, knowing that Sheriff Johnson would be there any minute. I cut through the back patch of trees and found my way to the usual forestry that covered the grounds of this town. I stayed far enough away from the road to where I wasn't easily spotted, but also close enough that I could readily see what was going on with the main roads.

I walked as far as my feet would take me, and stupidly enough found my way back to the patch of greenery directly behind my house.

I did a quick survey of the area and didn't see any officers in sight. I knew better than to walk out and expose myself, so I waited.

If there was an officer or detective there, they would show themselves sooner or later. I had no recollection of the time, but I waited for close to twenty minutes before I took the first step towards my home.

This is a bad idea.

Pushing the concerns aside, I continued on.

The house came into perfect view, and I was hit with a wave of emotions ranging from nostalgia, to fear, to hostility, then to rage. This was the home I grew up in and carried so many beautiful memories for such a long time, and it was a sad day now that they were replaced by nothing but horror stories.

I mentally shook my head at myself for ever being a part of this operation. I was going through a rough patch desperately trying to find my "sense of self", and I mistakenly took my family's agendas and mindsets on as my own- warping me into a person I didn't recognize.

I never wanted to hurt those girls, but day after day of my sister and my mother in my ears telling me how much they deserved it, and that we were helping our family in the process really got to me and wore me down tremendously over time. *I screwed up so badly. I'm so sorry Anna.*

One of them died here, and I could never forget that. I could sit there and name a million reasons why it wasn't my fault... my mom pulled the trigger, Anna tried to escape again... but the truth is I knew that I was the factor that ultimately created these awful dynamics.

I placed all my bets on the home being locked up but was surprised when I checked the back handle and it was open.

I was on a time crunch, so I sprinted up the stairs to my room. I pushed down on the handle and leaned against the door, opening it.

My room looked like a hurricane hit it. I guess that was the way they left scenes once they checked every square inch for evidence. I suppose in a way, it made it easier to pack a bag when everything was on the floor in front of you and you were handcuffed.

I bent down on my floor and easily found the duffle bag I used for everything. I grabbed pants, shirts, sweaters, socks, underwear, and a few pairs of shoes to which I haphazardly threw into the duffle bag.

I stood up and went rifling around my bathroom to find the essentials: a toothbrush, toothpaste, my hairbrush, face wash, deodorant, and lotion. I didn't ever plan to step foot in this house again.

There were too many bad memories attached to this place.

I threw those into my bag as well and did a once over of the room to make sure I had everything I needed. I would be destined to live a life on the run, or on the run until I found a town far enough away from here where nobody knew my name or all the messed-up things I did.

I wanted a fresh start.

I wanted it more than anything with Katie, but a part of me realized that she didn't deserve all the baggage that came with me. I knew her dad needed her more than I did and wanted to give in to my selfless inhibitions for the first time ever.

I wanted her to have a chance at a normal life, one that sadly would be without me. It was better for her after all. I would find somewhere to shack up for the night and would give Katie her final piece of jewelry before leaving her and this town forever.

I needed to get out of the house before they did show up. I held the bag in my hand and went down to my dad's tool shed. He had a power saw perched on the edge of the table and I dropped the bag. Switching on the power button, the blades started to whir loudly. Very carefully, I inched my hands spaced as far apart as the cuffs would allow and let out a big whoosh when it sliced through the center of them.

I was still handcuffed, but now had free range to at least use my hands. I would figure something out later.

I turned it off and started to head upstairs before remembering my dad's safe he kept hidden under the stairs. I knew there wasn't much in there, but all four of us knew the code in case something should ever happen. It was still closed, hidden beneath a loose floorboard. I knew the police would have cleaned this out... had they found it.

I typed in the familiar four-digit code- 0113. My mother's birthday. I breathed a loud sigh of relief when I realized that the money was untouched. Stacks and stacks of hundreds filled up the small safe. It had to be at least fifty thousand.

I stuffed the money into my duffle bag as quickly as I possibly could. I slammed the safe shut, replaced the floorboard, and headed up stairs. I didn't even look before I was sprinting towards the forestry which would be sure to hide me well.

The funny thing about this whole situation was that a week ago, I would have had no idea of where to go in the forest patch. It had been behind my home for years, but it wasn't until the first time I tried to help Katie escape that I actually was forced to attempt to navigate my way around it.
Katie.

I couldn't stop thinking about her, especially as I raced past the spot that I had us hide in that night. I was comforted in knowing that I would be able to see her one last time before I left Prairie and her forever.

I knew it was risky... trying to break back into the home of not only the girl I kidnapped, but the home of the Sheriff of this town.

It was insane, but worth it.

The last jewelry gift was a pair of sparkling diamond earrings.

I knew she would love it.

I reached the familiar edge of forestry and trekked across the road to the new patch. This one would take a little bit longer to get through especially since I wasn't too familiar with where this one led. I would follow my usual routine of trying to stay far enough out of sight, but close enough to observe everything else.

I was beginning to get hungry, and even more thirsty. I knew I had to get a lot farther than this before I was able to stop.

I had to be out of Prairie, and out of the next two towns at least if I wanted any chance of being unrecognized.

I had no idea of how many hours had passed since I began my journey but had yet to hear any police sirens. I had seen a small number of cars drive past, but none were police cars or seemed to be looking for anybody, just driving.

I knew I was halfway through the next town when I saw the familiar field that I had almost lost my life in… all thanks to Katie's gun toting grandfather with a taste for vengeance.

I made sure to take the long way around the field, as walking through the middle of it would leave me far too exposed, even though it was beginning to get fully dark outside.

I tried to keep a clear head as I mudded through the dirt, pushed past the trees, and navigated around large bushes. However, I continuously failed on that as my mind was an endless replay of the last week's events start to finish.

The moment where I realized that Katie could be someone that potentially could ruin my family and everything we built, the rash decision to stick the needle in her neck, wrecking her car and hiding the parts, especially the moment where I realized that I didn't belong in this family because I wasn't cut from the same cloth that they seemingly all were.
I wasn't a monster like them.

I tried so incredibly hard to fit in with my sister, my mother, and especially my father given that I always looked up to him.

Even growing up I did always feel like the odd man out, and when all of this started, I had tried to change myself and the way I did things to finally feel accepted by my family. Towards the end, especially after Katie and my first escape attempt failed miserably, that's when I think everything clicked. I would never fall in this line that they created for Amy and myself.
I wish I could say sorry to the other girls.

Maybe I could. I would leave a message with Katie so that she could pass it on to Kim and Tara.

I was able to see the hospital in the distance, so I knew I was getting further and further away.

Just then I heard police sirens coming and I ducked down, covering myself in the brush. My eyes peered out, trying to ascertain where they were headed.

The sirens were coming from the opposite directions driving towards Prairie.

I waited a few moments, desperate to see if there were any more police cars, but after a minute of dreadful silence, I concluded that there was no one else coming.

I stood up and wiped the leaves and branches off me. I continued on my walk, getting exhausted. I wanted to find a place where I could stay for the night and would see Katie tomorrow before leaving her and this town behind me.

Most people would have run the other way with no intention of ever looking back. But I knew the truth. Katie cared for me, and I didn't want to just fall off the face of the Earth with no explanation for her

I wanted to give her my reasoning for everything I did, as well as why I was choosing to leave everything behind. I knew her dad had told her about my escape by now, and I didn't want her to get the wrong idea about me.

I would set the record straight tomorrow.

It was well into the night now, and I really wished I had packed a flashlight.

I found myself stumbling over rocks, and branches which seemed to be haphazardly thrown across the path.

Finally, a small diner came into view, and not recognizing any other business or shops around me, I figured I was far enough away that I could stop.

I headed across the street and into the well-lit twenty-four-hour diner. I was greeted by an older waitress named Mary who gestured to an open booth and handed me a menu. The place way nearly deserted besides one lone coffee drinker at the counter.

"What can I get you to drink sweetheart?" She smiled at me.

"A place to live would be nice… just kidding um a coffee would be great." I joked.

"Coming right up." She turned and walked to the counter grabbing a fresh mug and poured coffee in, grabbing a cup of creamers on her way back.

"Thanks." I replied as she set the coffee and creamers on the table.

"No problem. And were you serious about needing a place to live?"

"Yes actually. I'm new to town and trying to set myself up. What town is this by the way?"

"We're in Gatlin. But, there's a new apartment up for rent in my complex if you want it."

"That would be awesome. Could you get me an address?"

"Sure thing." She pulled out her pad and scrawled on it, ripped it off and handed it to me.

"Anything to eat?" She gestured to the open menu in my hands.

"Yeah, can I get a turkey burger with fries? Thanks." She smiled, and grabbed the menu heading off to the counter.

Now that housing was taken care of, I could eat, relax, and focus on my next task.

Seeing Katie one last time.

39

Katie

The jewelry box on my bed started to make a lot more sense once my dad informed me of Mark's escape.

My dad seemed furious that Mark was able to skip out on his punishment, as he so poetically put it.

When he told me, I could tell that he was awaiting the same reaction as his, so I feigned disgust with Mark's actions.

Secretly, I thought it was hilarious. I mean Mark never truly belonged in a mental facility as it was. Sure, he had made some questionable decisions but had gone through the ringer in order to right those wrongs, including getting shot by his own mother.

Mark had nobody. His sister was dead, his mother and father were in prison, and now after the escape he would never be able to show his face in this town again. I knew deep down that it was probably for the best. Mark and I had no future together, we couldn't. My father hated him. My grandpa apparently hated him. This town... they would never forgive him.

I had the jewelry stashed in my underwear drawer, knowing that was a place that my father would never look. He would rapid fire questions if he saw me wearing any of the pieces, so for now, I would just keep it as my little secret.

The fact that Mark took the time to leave me a gift, even after he escaped and would be searched for made me feel warm and fuzzy on the inside. My feelings were fleeting, as I knew it did my heart no good to want for something I couldn't have.

I was still shocked with myself at how quickly the feelings for Mark turned from platonic to hatred and now love.

Did I love Mark?

No, it wasn't possible. I simply cared for him in a way that I would something I admired.

Despite what I had earlier believed, the only way that any of the girls taken would have been freed is if someone from the family had a change of heart. The locks, the location, no one else would have suspected. If you did seem to figure out the charade they had going on, that meant you were too close, and you were dealt with… just like Kim and myself.

I tried to push…no, shove, the thoughts out of my mind. I took Mark's last jewelry gift as a goodbye to me. I knew he wouldn't risk ever stepping foot in this town again, and I had to be okay with accepting that. In order to avoid mulling over the situation further, I decided that keeping busy would be the best course.

I used my new phone my dad got me to text Kim. I would've texted Tara, but she has been so busy with Johnny lately.

Katie: Hey Kim, are you free today?

Kim replied almost instantly. I could see that boredom was getting the best of both of us.

Kim: Anything for you. What did you have in mind?

Katie: Movies?

Kim: That sounds good, but for the love of God, no horror movies!

I found myself laughing because I agreed with her. We had basically been starring in our own horror movie, that the thought of watching one was incredibly off-putting.

Katie: I heard there's a new romantic comedy.

Kim: Then count me in. 5? We can eat dinner then the movie?

I checked the time. It was three. That gave me two hours.

Katie: Pick me up then.

I tossed my phone on my bed and headed downstairs to fill my dad in on my afternoon plans. I knew he would approve simply because my dad had liked that I was immersing myself in busy work lately. We were two of the same people and he had chosen to move on the same way. I had barely seen my dad lately because he was over his head in a ton of new police work. He had clocked more hours at the station than anyone else lately.

I'm worried about him.

"Hey dad. Kim and I have plans tonight."

"Yeah? What are you guys doing?" My dad was sitting in his armchair, sandwich in hand.

"Dinner, and then we're watching a movie. Is that okay?"

"Of course. Is she picking you up?"

"She is." I smiled and took a bite of his sandwich. He yanked it back jokingly.

"Okay. I'm sorry about you having no car. I'm working on getting you a new one, I promise."

"Dad, that is the least of my worries. Car or no car, I'm just happy to be home." I smiled and turned to go shower.

I was still using crutches but could now get up the stairs on my own, which felt pretty damn good. I always loved having independence and needing to be dependent on others to get around was really dragging my mood.

I turned on the hot water, and stepped in. It let the water cascade down my avoid, narrowly avoiding my ankle which was wrapped.

I poured the rose smelling shampoo into my hair and created a lather, letting the water rinse the soap away. I let the conditioner sit as I washed my entire body, stopping at a few inches over that ankle. I used a dry washcloth to pat the area around there dry to ensure no drips of water leaked into the wrap.

Compared to when I originally had my surgery, I was doing a lot better. It was still a long healing process but being able to mostly do things for myself again helped.

I rinsed the conditioner out and shut off the water.

Stepping out, I grabbed a towel to wrap around my body, and propped my ankle up on top of the toilet. I dried the entire leg, and the rest of my body before heading to my room.

I wanted something cute but warm, since it had been particularly cold out lately. I settled on a pair of jeans complete with bootie heels, a blouse, and a cashmere cardigan. The cardigan was a birthday gift from Amy last year, as I would have never splurged on a clothing item like that. Some people would have thrown it out, but it was cashmere, and I wasn't that petty.

Even though she did try to kill me.

I checked my phone. 4:12. I headed into the bathroom and began blow drying my hair. It took about ten minutes as I recently did a big hair chop. I wanted to create a fresh start, and nothing screamed that more than a haircut.

I plugged in my curler and started on my makeup. I just did a little mascara and lipstick. By the time I finished, the curler was hot enough and I swiftly curled my hair. I unplugged it, grabbed my phone and purse, and grabbed my crutches as I hobbled down the stairs.

I might have benefit from asking my dad for help, but I would never get better if I didn't try and do some of it on my own. I couldn't rely on my dad all the time.

"Wow. Honey, you look great." My dad beamed, still in the same armchair.

Oh, boy.

"Thanks. It has been a long time since I got dressed up for the hell of it."

He knew exactly what I was referring to. We used to go out with my mom all the time, and we would go all out. After she died, dad and I became homebodies and wouldn't bother with fixing ourselves up.

I knew it was nice for him to see me doing it again, and honestly, it felt nice to break out of that shell I was in for so long.

I walked in the kitchen and grabbed a coke while I waited for Kim to arrive. It was fifteen minutes until 5, and I knew she was an early bird so it shouldn't be too much longer.

My dad and I became engrossed in a reality show that came on the tv, that I didn't hear my phone go off. Kim responded by honking several times, to which I jumped up nearly dropping my can of soda.

I set it on the table, hooked my purse on my shoulders, stuck my phone in my pocket, and grabbed the crutches.

"Walk me to the door?"

"I would love nothing more." My dad smiled as he stood up from his chair and headed to me.

My dad swung the door open and watched me walk to Kim's door. I opened it myself, swung the crutches in the back and used the door as leverage into the car. I pulled the door shut, and my dad waved to me.

"Have fun!"

Oh, we would.

Kim drove off, as I stole a final glance at my dad in the doorway.

"Where are we going for dinner?"

"Le Meilleur. It's a new French bistro a town away."

I love French food!

"That sounds amazing. How have you been?"

Kim launched into a ten-minute breakdown of her life recently. She was settling back into school, had made a few new friends, and had a small crush on this guy in her history class, named Brian.

"Does he feel the same way?"

"Hmm, I think so. Or it at least seemed that way when he asked me out this Friday."

I started squealing with excitement for my friend. Everyone was finding a new center and happiness surrounding our captivity and it made my heart soar with adoration and excitement. Weirdly enough, Kim seemed happier now than when I had seen her around school prior to the capture. The whole thing had taken a lot out of each one of us, and it made us realize more than anything just how much we wanted to live.

We arrived at the restaurant, and our car was immediately valeted.

Fancy fancy.

The hostess inside greeted us warmly and had us follow her to a booth in the back. The ambience of the restaurant was warm and infectious. They had beautifully soft music cascading throughout the dining room, and the servers were all smiles.

"Hi, what can I get you girls to drink tonight?"

"Water." Kim and I both said at the same time, and then we burst out into a fit of laughter.

"Sure thing." The waiter smiler, and then ducked away.

He returned within a minute of two glasses of ice-cold water, garnished with a lemon wedge on each.

"Do you need some more time to look at the menu, or are you ladies ready?"

"I'm ready. I'll have the Ratatouille."

"And for you?" He said gesturing towards Kim.

"The Coq au vin please." She smiled and handed her menu back to him, and he turned to take mine before heading towards the kitchen. Just then, another server walked past, putting a basket of cut pieces of baguette and butter on the table.

My favorite.

The meal was served no later than twenty minutes later, and Kim and I practically devoured the entire plate. We opted for dessert later as well, and then split the check when it came.

We had about thirty minutes until the movie started, and we liked to watch the previews, so we started our twenty-minute drive back to Prairie right away.

The car ride was filled with smooth jazz, and laughter spurring from both of us. Our bellies were full, but so were our hearts at the warm friendship we had. We got along so well, and the conversation was never forced or awkward. We just clicked, and I did owe thanks to the Puntzer family for that one, although I didn't thank them for much else.

Kim snagged a sweet spot at the front of the theatre and we walked up to the ticket booth to purchase our tickets for the 7:00 showing.

We walked right past the snack counter, both of us too full to even think of eating again. I was always the movie goer decked out with snacks and drinks, but today I opted out... for my stomach's sake.

The trailers started, and just as I assumed, they were well worth it. They always gave me a good idea of what I was interested in seeing, and what I wasn't.

Finally, the movie began to start.

By the end of the film, both Kim and I were in tears. It shouldn't come as a surprise to either of us, given that the girl does end up with the guy every time, but the storyline was so beautifully written as well as executed by the up and coming actors.

"That was amazing." Kim turned to me as the credits started rolling.

"Right? I felt like I was a part of their story." I wiped a stray tear away.

We were the biggest babies.

We grabbed our purses and headed out of the theatre narrowly avoiding a couple who was smashing their faces together near the end of one of the aisles.

The walk to the car was chilly, as it was now dark outside. The cashmere was a good idea earlier, but now I found myself wanting something warmer.

Kim unlocked the door, and I did my usual crutch toss routine and crawled in. The foot was getting easier to walk on, but it was still hard.

The drive to my house was short, and the car was loud with Kim and I talking vibrantly about the movie. We loved it.

Sure enough, my dad was waiting at the door once I sent him an "On our way" text five minutes ago. He was big on my safety lately, and it was a miracle he let me out of his sight at all.

I waved goodbye to Kim as I hobbled up the cobblestone path to my door.

Once inside, I raved about the movie to my dad, who seemed less than enthusiastic about going to see a tear-jerker film. Nevertheless, he listened until 10:00 when he decided to turn in for the night.

I walked up the stairs deciding that the railing was easier to maneuver then the crutches. I walked into my room tossing all my stuff on the bed and turning on the lights.

I shut the door and nearly collapsed at the sight of Mark leaning on my windowsill.
"Mark… what are you doing here?"
"I wanted to bring you something." He cascaded toward me, palm open, holding a third jewelry box.
"You didn't have to." I grabbed it, opening it and being in awe over the gorgeous pair of earrings he brought for me.

I closed the box and tossed it on the bed. Mark took my hands in his, grabbed the side of my face and pulled me in for a kiss.

Every inhibition I had fought telling me that he was wrong for me, began to slip away one by one.

We broke the kiss, and Mark hooked his leg over the side of the window. He leaned his head in, extended his hand to me, and spoke.
"Come with me Katie."

I shocked myself when my hand reached out and joined his.

Made in United States
Troutdale, OR
04/25/2024

19433299R00192